THE BIRTHRIGHT

THE BIRTHRIGHT

by

LORALEE EVANS

BONNEVILLE BOOKS ™
Springville, Utah

ISBN: 1-55517-756-5
e.1

Published by Bonneville Books
Imprint of Cedar Fort Inc.
www.cedarfort.com

Distributed by:

Cover design by Nicole Cunningham
Cover design © 2004 by Lyle Mortimer

Printed in the United States of America
10 9 8 7 6 5 4 3 2 1
Printed on acid-free paper

Library of Congress Cataloging-in-Publication Data

Evans, Loralee, 1972-
  The birthright / by Loralee Evans.
    p. cm.
ISBN 1-55517-756-5 (pbk. : alk. paper)
1. Lamanites (Mormon Church)--Fiction. 2. Mormon women--Fiction. I. Title.

PS3605.V3685B57 2004
813'.6--dc22

2004000912

Dedication

To my family

CHAPTER 1
24TH YEAR OF JUDGES

The household of Aaron had risen with the rest of the tiny walled town of Morianton to its daily tasks. Small and square, the dwelling sat near the center of the village, one of several identical houses lining a dirt street that had been packed down hard by many years of human and animal traffic. Its walls were matted over with thatch. Its roof of tightly woven palm fronds slanted steeply upward to ward off frequent heavy rains. From its front door, which emptied into the street, the plaza was visible, with a cistern, a clear, glassy pool of water, at its center.

The packed earth was moist and steaming now, for a rain had passed in the night, leaving the air thick and warm with a heavy mist that glowed silvery in the predawn light, lending strange beauty to the unnatural silence that hung suspended above the earth as if the world held its breath, waiting for the first glimpses of sunlight to appear over the forest-lined horizon. A slight stirring in the doorway seemed amplified in the silence, and the young girl who brushed aside the hanging curtain and appeared on the stoop shivered as she gazed around her. Her frail throat, showing above a homespun tunic, shuddered at the freshness of the early morning that had surged forward to embrace her as she stepped outdoors.

Loose shreds of mist, like floating veils, stole through the air, catching on the faded shadows of neighboring roofs. The mist was decomposing into drops of dew that shone on the rough thatch of houses and leaves of sparse grass growing along the edge of the road. Then dripping, it gathered into small pools, filling the stream that ran down the center of the street, spilling away from the cistern at the center of the plaza. The girl sighed, hitched the clay jar she was carrying higher on her hip, and started along the vacant street toward the plaza. Her bare feet soaked up the damp, and pearly drops settled on the thick, dark locks of her unbound hair. She stopped at the edge of the stone cistern and dropped to her knees, gazing down into the depths of the glittering dark water that cast up a mottled, shifting reflection of her face and the gray sky above her. Her honey-brown skin seemed touched with warmth in spite of the cool air, framing large liquid-blue eyes that gazed somberly back up at her. She was barely aware of the task she was performing, unconscious of the cold water as her hands, well accustomed to their work, pushed her jar down into the pool and let the water pour down its clay mouth in a cold, clear stream, filling the jar's rotund belly, and weighing it down so that she had to heave as she lifted it back out again. Her mind was far away, remembering all that she had heard the night before as she cooked and served supper in the house of the town's chief judge. If only her father and mother were still alive, they would know what to do. Her father would have put a stop to it completely before it had gotten this far, but she was just a girl, barely thirteen. There was nothing she could do.

She set the pitcher beside her on the edge of the pool, careful not to let the gurgling, sloshing water spill out, and glanced about her. The mist was lifting, and the air was growing warm; she knew the sun was only moments from rising. Beyond the walls of the town, the forest was beginning to stir to life; wild gleeful noises of birds and monkeys filled the air as the mist slowly faded and the sky warmed. Another chattering of cheerful voices, closer and more human, told her that the other daughters of the town were coming with their own jars to fill. She yawned, trying to force a smile onto her face as she brushed a hand across her heavy eyelids, leaving an undetected smudge of dirt on her cheek.

The group of chattering, giggling girls appeared around the edge of a building, their faces shining and bright, each one balancing a pitcher on her head, shoulder or hip.

"Oh, Miriam!" the first of the group cried and waved merrily at the sight of her. "Again the first to the well! You are always the earliest to wake. Even sooner than our fathers, I think."

The cheerful group swarmed around her, their faces gleaming as they greeted her, chattering as they spilled out along the edge of the pool, each to bend down and fill her own pitcher.

"I could not sleep well," Miriam muttered soberly, turning away from their cheerful talk.

"Miriam, dear," one of the girls giggled, noting her somber face, "I am afraid that since your mother died, you have become too much of a mother yourself to your younger brother. Why do you not smile more?"

Miriam paused and turned back. "Last night I heard judge Morianton telling some of the other town elders that our neighbor, the town of Lehi, is encroaching on our farming land, and that we must take it back by force."

"Well," another girl huffed, "that is nothing new. My father says that Morianton says they have been taking our farming land bit by bit for several months now. My father has wondered for some time if it would not be justified for some of the men to arm themselves and force the people of Lehi to give the land back."

"But that would be wrong!" Miriam protested. "Why could our towns not take our case before the chief judge of all the land to determine where our borders truly lie?"

The same girl began, "But my father says—"

"All we know is what our fathers say!" Miriam groaned. "Do we know anything more? Do we know whether Morianton is truly justified in claiming that they are taking our land?"

The group quieted and each girlish face turned large eyes to gaze silently at her.

"Miriam, I fear you think too much," one of them murmured, placing a gentle hand on her arm. "Let us leave the thinking to Morianton and to our fathers, and trust them to determine what is best."

"But what if they are wrong?" Miriam pleaded softly, feeling the tears beginning to rise in her eyes. "Should we follow them blindly, like foolish sheep?"

The girls glanced helplessly at each other, and back at Miriam, none of them volunteering an answer to her question. With a sigh,

missing her parents all the more bitterly, she turned away and silently made her way back to her own house.

Brushing through the curtained doorway, she wearily set down
the pitcher and glanced through the shadowed interior to the corner where a small pallet lay, cradling a little bundle that was her
four-year-old brother, breathing quietly beneath a light blanket.

She moved to him quietly, and bent down to ruffle his dark hair
with her fingers and study his sleeping face, still so much like a baby,
before she rose again. She turned to the center of the room where
a tripod arched over the fire crackling in a scooped-out hollow. A
clay pot hung from it, filled with corn gruel that bubbled and
steamed. She dipped a wooden ladle into the bubbling mass and
sipped it, the sweet gritty warmth slipping down her throat and
warming her stomach as she swallowed. She sighed, and closed her
eyes briefly, remembering when she had the luxury of a few more
minutes of sleep, listening drowsily to the sound of her mother slapping corn cakes to fry on the griddle and the delicious smell of
them as she slowly woke.

A pounding at the lintel of the door shook her rudely from her
thoughts, and seemed to vibrate in the very beams of the house.

"Servant girl!" a deep voice shouted roughly, pouring over her
like a drenching shower of cold water. "Are you not awake yet?
Come to the door. I must speak to you. Now."

Shivering with a sudden dread, she rose to her feet and reluctantly made her way to the door where she brushed aside the curtain and glanced up into Morianton's swarthy, scowling face.

"Peace be with you, sir," she stammered. "Your wife does not
expect me at your home until mid morning."

Morianton sneered, folding his arms, large and sinuous, across
his chest, and as he glanced past her at the shadowed interior of the
house, she could see the distaste spread across his face.

"You knew that the town of Lehi lays claim to land which is
rightfully ours, do you not?" he demanded, glaring back into her
large eyes.

"I know that you claim it is ours," she stammered, her mouth
dry.

His lips curled back in a silent snarl, and at his side, his hand twitched, as if he wanted to strike her. She flinched, drawing a step back. He smiled unkindly. "During the night I took the town elders, and many of our best, most trusted fighting men down to the town of Lehi. We have endured their lies for too long—claiming that part of our land is theirs—"

"You were armed?" she gasped.

He snarled again, angry that she had cut off his words. "Yes, we were armed," he snapped, "but the town was deserted."

She was unable to hold back her sigh of relief. "Perhaps an angel warned them of your coming," she murmured.

Morianton's lips again drew angrily back from his teeth. His hand again twitched at his side. "Or perhaps the tormented ghost of Aaron your father warned them," he snapped, and sneered when he saw the pain flash across her face. "He always opposed me when I tried to warn our people of the Lehites' greed. Stupid old man. He was always too concerned about others to worry about his own kin. What did it get him? A pauper's death and burial, followed only a month later by your mother Sarah, leaving you and your brother orphans again. She could never be without him, could she? Like a dog at his side she was."

"Because my father loved my mother. And she loved him in return," Miriam whispered. She grasped the lintel of the door, stilling the fierce trembling that had seized her limbs. Her eyes darted to Morianton's hand where it twitched at his side, and thought of the bruises she had often seen on his small, timid wife's face. "My father was a good man."

"And wise, too," Morianton smirked. "So wise, even, that he gave up his birthright to go preach foolish nonsense to the Lamanites for fourteen long years, and nearly died doing it. Then when he finally came back and married, he wisely picked a woman who could not give him children of his own. So he had to take you castoffs in to raise."

Miriam grit her teeth together and bit back an angry retort. Morianton often spoke like this to her when he knew no one else could hear him. She finally managed to grate, "What do you want of me?"

"The Lehites must have fled to the camp of Moroni's army, west of here. He will doubtless take their side, and bring his armies upon us to destroy us. We must flee to the lands northward beyond Bountiful. You must help my wife gather our belongings together, weakling that she is," he chuckled softly to himself.

"You may go if you wish," Miriam murmured, her voice barely audible, "but I and my brother will stay here."

Morianton glared darkly. "All who live within the walls of this town will do as I say, and follow me. I will not be opposed by an orphaned girl-child."

Dread grew heavy in her belly, but again she heard herself speak. "I will help your wife if she needs me, but my brother and I will not go."

Morianton threw his head back and laughed. "You may not be his true daughter, but Aaron's blood is thick in your veins. You are as stubborn and foolish as he was, and that will do you no good now." His eyes fixed on hers fiercely. "He is not here to help you. You will go where I go, and you will do as I say."

She gulped, and gazed up at his hard, cold eyes as he towered above her like a dark, threatening cloud. Where her courage came from, she could not tell, but still she managed to murmur, "We will not."

She knew he had a violent nature, but still the blow of his fisted hand, which came without warning, was an instant shock to her. Stars exploded before her eyes and she staggered backward, the left side of her face strangely numb, warm sticky wetness seeping from one nostril. She did not see Morianton coming in after her, or the second blow that struck across her other cheek and sent her stumbling to her knees. A fierce hand gripped her hair and jerked her head back, forcing her to look up into his eyes. A sneer began to cross his face, but instantly it mutated into a grimace of pain and he released Miriam's hair, staggering backward as he howled in agony.

Scrambling up, she saw the source of his pain; her brother, still clothed in his skimpy sleeping shift, had clamped his teeth firmly onto Morianton's forearm, his tiny brown arms wrapped firmly around the man's.

Morianton glared with hatred at the boy as he raised his free hand, balling it into a fist to strike the child. Miriam whirled away, seized the bubbling pot from the fire, and slung its weight at Morianton's head.

It connected with his skull with a sickening clank, spilling hot porridge down his face and the front of his tunic. A moment passed as he wavered, an expression of surprise frozen on his face. And then, slowly, his eyes rolled up into his head and he toppled heavily to the earthen floor.

Open mouthed, Miriam gaped wide-eyed at his crumpled, unconscious form for several seconds before she shook herself and glanced at her little brother, who still hung tenaciously onto the man's limp arm. "Little Jacob, come," she hissed, grasping his small bony shoulder and pulling him away. "Dress yourself, quickly, and put on your sandals. We must leave right away."

"But you said we would not be going with them. I heard you." The boy scowled up at her, lifting a hand to brush a lock of straight black hair out of his eyes.

In spite of the fear that gripped her, she smiled down into his large blue eyes, the trait they both shared, and nodded her head. "We are not going with Morianton. We will leave, and travel west through the forest to find the camp of Chief Captain Moroni, where the people of Lehi have gone. We cannot stay, now that we have done this to Morianton." She pointed at the silent figure, then wiped a hand beneath her bleeding nose.

The boy nodded obediently, and scampered away to his corner where his pallet lay. Miriam glanced back again at Morianton, and shuddered. He lay as if he were dead, though his chest rose and fell with each breath. She sighed brokenly, then turned swiftly away to find her own sandals.

 basically basically

Night in the forest came quickly. The undergrowth was thick and grew damp as the night wore on, and Miriam's tunic quickly became soaked. She had been full of confidence at the beginning, that they would find the army's camp. But as they day wore on and grew hotter, her confidence began to wane. They traveled through the thickest part of the jungle, and with the canopy overhead, it was impossible for her to determine the exact position of the sun, or even if they were traveling toward their destination. She knew only that the army's camp was somewhere west of the town. And then night had fallen, and her little brother, collapsing with weariness, begged her to stop so that he could sleep. Instead, she hoisted him to her back, and allowed him to sleep against her shoulder as she continued on for the both of them, knowing only that she must not stop. Darkness closed around them, and the sound of night creatures filled the air.

Hitched onto her back, little Jacob slept, oblivious to the anxiety his sister felt. All around was silence. Where the trees became sparse, she could see the sky spread out above her like a black opal speckled with shafts of starlight. It seemed to Miriam that she could almost hear them singing as they hung in their infinite orbits far above her in the great openness, and she let the music of them fill her heart with comfort as the long night wound its path.

A brief memory stirred in her heart of a similar night, years before, when she as a child had been in her brother's position, and someone else had been in hers, carrying her away from danger as she slept . . . The memories of her childhood before her parents had taken her in were faded, the faces and images distorted. The clearest image was one of a young man barely older than a boy with brown hair and hazel eyes. She smiled as she let her memories carry her back.

CHAPTER 2
20TH YEAR OF JUDGES

*F*iltered light touched nine-year-old Miriam's honey-brown skin and she felt a flash of warm sunlight as she crept down a narrow path carved through the thickest part of the forest, following silently behind her young companion. She walked primly, with uncertainty in her steps, her borrowed bow clutched in the sweating palm of her hand. In front of her, her friend crouched along, his narrow brown shoulders bent, his bow clasped in his hand, an arrow nocked to the string in an attitude that the older men took when they hunted large game and needed to walk silently. His eyes darted about fiercely, as if he expected a ferocious beast to leap out at them, hissing, its claws bared, ready to do battle. Something brushed against her thin shoulder. She gasped and shuddered, drawing back, uncertain if it was a vine or something livid and breathing, with fierce fangs, waiting to drop down upon her. Her companion turned and smiled at her, his teeth white against his dark skin as he reached out with his bow and brushed the vine away so that she could pass beneath it.

He was a boy, not many months older than Miriam. His name was Thobor, the son of Amran, and he had been her best friend for as long as she could remember. Like Miriam, he had a sampling of Nephite blood in him, for his mother's father had been a dissenter from the Nephites, yet the boy did not appear Nephite at all. His hair was black and straight as wire, his eyes were dark, and his skin as brown as any other Lamanite. It was easy, however, to see the infusion of Nephite blood in Miriam. The angular Semitic features her ancestors had brought with them from across the sea were strongly visible on her face.

"I do not see how I ever thought this would be so glorious," she grumbled, rubbing her shoulder where the queasy sensation of the vine that had brushed against her still lingered. "Why did I ever persuade you to take me with you to hunt, Thobor?"

"Because you are different from other girls." He grinned, puffing out his little brown chest as much as he could. "You are brave. Like me. Besides, Grandmother Ishna would never have let you come with me if she thought something would happen to you."

In spite of the unease that still remained in her stomach, she could not help but agree with her friend. Grandmother Ishna, though not her grandmother by blood, had raised her from the time she had been a small baby. Her mother, Ishna had explained, had died in childbirth, and her aunt Isabel had brought her to Ishna to raise. Ishna was the only mother she had ever known, and she loved the old woman deeply, but many other villagers were puzzled by her, and sometimes frightened, for she seemed to possess strange gifts; seeing that which could not be seen, and foretelling things that had not yet occurred.

From her earliest memories, Miriam had learned that she could take Ishna at her word, and had come to trust the old woman's advice without question. Learning to do so had saved her from difficulty and danger on more than one occasion. As she recalled Ishna's farewell that morning, all she remembered was the smile and the kiss on the head, with the instruction to return before dusk.

"I suppose we will not come to any harm, as long as we return before night comes," Miriam said.

Thobor grinned again, his dark eyes twinkling through shocks of black hair hanging over his forehead. "Good, for now we are near the river. Perhaps we might find a possum or a rabbit drinking there."

He put his finger to his lips, indicating silence, and in the stillness Miriam could hear the gurgling of the river, not far from the trail, but hidden by thick forest growth.

His eyes gleaming with anticipation, he signaled her to crouch down, and together they scrambled noiselessly through the undergrowth to the edge of the river that scurried and bubbled over submerged rocks.

At her shoulder, Thobor gave a silent jerk, and pointed excitedly at the opposite bank. Following his pointed finger with her gaze, she saw a fat buck rabbit busily nibbling on a crop of tender green plants growing at the water's edge. Its tiny mouth munched rapidly as it ate, its large ears, laced with delicate pink veins, were perked up, and its eyes were large and brown, ever scanning its surroundings for predators. Its fur was soft and gray, and Miriam fancied for a moment, taking the rabbit up in her arms, and snuggling her face into its soft furry body.

"Quick, shoot it, Miriam!" Thobor whispered, noticing her hesitation. "My mother can make us rabbit stew tonight! You know how you love the stew my mother makes!"

With a sigh, Miriam drew a long, slender arrow from the quiver across her back and nocked it to her bow's string. Slowly, she drew the string back to her cheek, returning in her mind to the images of lessons she had persuaded Thobor to give her, seeing again her arrows peppering the side of the old dead tree she had used for practice.

The rabbit's head perked up and it stopped chewing, as if it sensed danger.

"Quickly!" Thobor hissed.

Quelling a squeak of protest in her throat, she finally released the string. It sang as it snapped back, and a moment later, the arrow plowed into the earth beside the rabbit, sending up a spray of moist black earth onto its fur.

The rabbit bolted and fled up the bank, its white cottontail flared, its chubby haunches surging rapidly as it pushed its way into the undergrowth and disappeared.

A breath of air burst from her lungs as she sat heavily on the ground, her head hanging as a sense of relief rushed over her.

"Almost, Miriam," Thobor said, the disappointment weighing heavily in his voice. "Perhaps next time." He rose to his feet and sloshed noisily across the river to retrieve the arrow buried in the bank. "Let us return home now. We promised Grandmother we would be back before dark."

Without a word, Miriam rose and followed him back to the trail, still trembling with relief that she had not hit the rabbit.

"Do not worry," Thobor assured her, resting his hand on her shoulder. "Next time you will hit it, I am sure."

Miriam sighed and did not respond as Thobor dropped his hand from her shoulder and took her hand in his.

Neither spoke as they made their way through the forest. The journey back was long, and the light around them faded to dusk which darkened gradually until the trees thinned and parted, and they found themselves once again on the wide village street lined with low-roofed dwellings of thatch and mud packed tightly together. People moved along the dusty street, to and from the market, scurrying to finish their duties before darkness claimed the sky. The sun was beyond the horizon, but there was still enough light to go by. The children's eyes moved up and down the lines of people, some walking slowly, others quickly, still others bowed down under heavy packs across their backs.

"You there!" A man's voice mixed with anxiety and anger startled the two children, and they glanced up to see Thobor's father, a towering, muscular man with long, glistening black hair, striding toward them with a scowl on his face. "Where have you children been?" he demanded, grasping each by an arm, and pulling them quickly into a narrow space between two houses, out of the view of the street traffic.

Thobor and Miriam cast each other a glance of confusion, and looked back up at his father who glowered down at them, his brawny arms resting on his hips as he waited for an answer.

"Please, sir," Miriam squeaked, "Thobor took me to hunt with him. I persuaded him to. It is my fault we caught nothing."

Thobor muttered timidly, "Father, you gave your permission this morning."

Amran drew in a deep breath and released it slowly, the anger ebbing from his face.

"Then you have been gone from the village all day? You have spoken to no one until now?" he demanded, glaring at his son.

Thobor shook his head.

Amran huffed, and glanced back at Miriam. "You will return home. Your grandmother asked me to send you there if I found you."

Miriam nodded, and started out toward the crowded street, but gasped as Thobor's father snatched her arm and pulled her back.

"Not that way!" he hissed, pushing her toward the trees where a narrow path wound a long route around the outer edge of the village. "Take the long way back."

"But, why?" she asked.

"I will find Ishna and tell her that you have returned. She will wait there for you," he spouted impatiently. "Now go."

"Goodbye, Miriam," Thobor muttered, glancing back as his father grasped his arm, and melted into the crowd traveling away from the town market.

Miriam lifted her hand in farewell though her friend had already disappeared, then turned back onto the forest path.

ᔥ

"Grandmother!" she called, rushing through the curtained doorway when she at last reached her destination. The plain little hut had been her home for as long as she could remember, and her heart warmed as she took in the room and its sparse, familiar furnishings. There was a fire burning, yet it was a small one, and the room was darker than the twilit night outside. She began toward the fire. "Gra—"

"Silence!" Ishna hissed, appearing from the shadows, fear written on her wrinkled face. "Come to the fire." As Miriam wordlessly obeyed her, Ishna slipped a beaded leather thong over her head. Miriam folded her legs beneath her and lifted the necklace curiously. Blue and silver beads patterned the leather thong on which they had been strung.

"It is a gift, from Isabel," Ishna murmured as she added some dark cocoa powder to a small pot and placed it on the heated rocks surrounding the fire.

"I have not seen Aunt Isabel for years," Miriam murmured, tugging the loose collar of her tunic so that the beads slid beneath the cloth.

"Yes, I know." The old woman rose, brushing past Miriam with her thin, dark skirt. "But she returned today. Briefly." Ishna's voice seemed laced with tension.

"Is that why you have searched for me? Thobor's father said you had."

"I knew I could trust him to find you," Ishna sighed. "He is a good man, and I knew he would help you, though he would have been well rewarded if he had not."

Miriam's eyes grew wide and Ishna answered her unspoken question. "There is a man who searches for you in the village. He asks everyone he can where to find you. He wishes to offer you up as sacrifice to the gods."

Miriam gaped, her limbs growing cold. "But why?"

"I do not know. Perhaps it is because he wants the praise of Amalickiah." Ishna poured a large mug of steaming brown liquid for the child, and one for herself. The girl gulped down her drink without tasting it, and watched the old woman creep to the far wall where she gathered up a blanketed bundle. Cooing softly, she returned, her features softened, and she smiled across the fire. "Isabel came after you left. She told me all I have told you and rushed away after she left this little one." Ishna indicated the bundle in her arms that stirred slightly and sighed beneath its blanket. Miriam's brows raised slightly at the small infant stranger that slept peacefully within Ishna's embrace. "You must take him and start north—"

"You mean to send me to the *Nephites*?" Miriam retorted with disgust, returning her glance to Ishna. "I hate them. Thobor's father says that they are the children of thieves and liars, that they have no honor, and are no better than animals."

Ishna sighed. "I trust and respect Thobor's father, but in that case, he is mistaken, for most Nephites are good and honorable. The man who searches for you though, has no honor, and if you stay among the Lamanites, there is no city or village where he cannot find you."

Miriam bit her lip and lowered her eyes.

"You must start tonight." Ishna came to her, gripped her hand, and pulled her gently to her feet as she set the sleeping infant in her arms. "You will need this for your journey." Miriam felt the thong of a water bag slip over her head, and suddenly a great weight settled in her stomach.

"But," she began weakly, "can you not come with me?"

"My mission here is not yet finished," Ishna explained, smiling sadly. She brushed aside the door, and gently pushed Miriam toward the jungle, only paces from the door of the hut, where the trees now glowed in the moonlight, and the soft rhythmic noises of insects rose into the air.

"But I do not want to go alone!" she moaned, turning back and grasping Ishna's arm, tears filling her eyes.

Tears were in Ishna's eyes as well, but she pulled Miriam's hand off of her arm, and again nudged her toward the thick of the trees. "Go. You will not be alone. God will be with you."

Out of the corner of her eye, Miriam could see torchlight, and could hear men's voices coming toward her along the village path, but she paid them no heed as she turned away and stumbled into the dark of the jungle. The undergrowth closed in around her. She pushed her way through, fighting her tears, until she stumbled onto a dry streambed, and began following it slowly into the night.

Behind her, the men with the lights reached Ishna's house, and without pause, brushed aside the door covering and walked in. "Old woman," the leader barked rudely, stepping into the light of the glowing fire and glaring down at Ishna where she sat before her fire. "Where is the girl child with blue eyes who lives here?"

"She has gone," Ishna muttered, soberly eyeing the man. The weak light of Ishna's fire danced off of him. He was not Lamanite. His skin, stretched over an expanse of muscle, was pale, and his eyes were clear, the color of the sky. His hair was yellow, and he would have been handsome but for a harsh, red mark scarred into the middle of his forehead.

The man scowled at Ishna's answer. His pale face twisted like a snarling dog to expose his fine, white teeth. "Where is she?"

"She has gone into the north wilderness to seek out the Nephites," Ishna returned.

The dissenter cursed and tightened his fists in frustration. "You will pay for this, old woman," he hissed. "She was mine."

Ishna met his hateful gaze calmly as the dissenter growled to his men, "Burn the house."

"She will have nowhere to live," one hesitantly observed, his eyes darting to Ishna.

At this, the dissenter turned and struck the speaker in the side of his face, causing him to stumble to one knee. "Bind her, leave her to burn. She has let my child forsake her birthright."

The Lamanite he had struck straightened slowly, brushing blood from the side of his mouth. "I will not murder an old woman," he breathed with furious calm.

The dissenter took a step back, a smirk of disbelief settling on his face. "Yet you are willing to help me carry the child to King Amalickiah to be offered up to the gods."

"The child would be immortalized with the gods. Yet this old woman would die needlessly."

The dissenter looked from the speaker to the other men. Each man's expression showed that he agreed, and the dissenter released a deep breath. They were many, and he was one.

"Very well," he growled. "The old woman lives."

"You are very generous, Lord Ahiah," several men mumbled, bowing their heads slightly.

The dissenter cast Ishna a glance filled with venom. Striding away from her, he flung aside the door curtain and he and his men disappeared into the night.

Unaware of her narrow escape, Miriam followed the streambed northward as hour followed hour and the stars wheeled overhead. The weight of the child in her arms dragged at her, at last becoming unendurable. She glanced about her, but she was alone, deep within the jungle, perhaps already within the borders of the Nephite lands. She set her little charge down on a cool bed of moss beside the empty stream. A soft coo interrupted her troubled thoughts, and she glanced with weary eyes at the tiny baby to see a pair of large curious eyes watching her, above a wide, toothless smile.

෮

The sun did not reach her through the canopy above, but the steam and heat of the jungle troubled her mercilessly as Miriam tramped northward along the dry stream bed. The sun was nearing its high point, and Miriam, who had been walking since the sun had first lightened the sky, could feel the weight of the baby as if it had doubled since morning. A low ache pulsed in the small of her back, and in her shoulders where the baby's weight hung. Her hair was matted to her head, and she could feel sweat running down her arms and legs as she moved. She longed to rest, to find a cool bed of moss, and sleep. Yet she did not dare, for fear that the man who had sought her in the village still pursued her. She remained in the hidden riverbed; her thoughts riveted on the motion of her feet, each in turn carrying her unwilling body and the baby farther north. Often the calls of birds would echo from the shadows of the jungle, but with her eyes on the path at her feet, she did not hear the life of the world around her.

With her head down, her eyes half-closed, she did not see the glowing yellow eyes watching her from the branches of a tree, or a flurry of spotted yellow fur, and the flicker of a tail. Nor did she hear the faint creak of a branch as the shadowed figure leaped silently to the ground.

The jaguar's muscles quivered with excitement. Its tail twitched, and saliva dripped from its jaws as it padded softly, patiently behind her.

CHAPTER 3

*N*ot far away, but out of her hearing, leaves rustled under the soft, leather-clad feet of a young man who moved swiftly and quietly through the undergrowth as he had been trained, for the Lamanites were again planning for war. They had become restless under the reign of their new king, Amalickiah,[1] who, like the dissenter Amlici fifteen years before, had wanted to change the free Nephite government back into a kingship for his own benefit. The government had been a democracy for twenty years, and as with Amlici, the voice of the people had stood against Amalickiah. He fled when he learned that the people did not support him, and like Amlici, had joined with the Lamanites. From information the young soldier had garnered from the spies whose messages he carried, he had learned that Amalickiah, through intrigue, had murdered the Lamanite king, and had taken the queen for his wife, thus making himself the king of the Lamanites.

The soldier's tired body was damp with sweat, and his dark hair stuck to his forehead like honey, but his light brown eyes were alive with fire. Beneath his tunic and a thick, protective vest of quilted cotton, his legs and body were as lean and muscled as a wild cat's, and his well-trained muscles took new energy to themselves with each step. He moved cautiously, but with confidence as his feet flew silently over the ground.

As he came to the edge of a long-dried-out streambed, he smiled. This was the last landmark he needed to find. He turned northward, following the faint shadow of a trail along the edge of the stream. Running silently along the bank, he could see dark jungle to his left, and to his right, he occasionally glimpsed bare patches through the trees and could smell the distant tang of the salty breezes off the sea, and knew he had passed the city of Moroni. Though he was now within the Nephite borders, he knew he must remain cautious, for Lamanites were not all that he should fear within the jungle.

Suddenly, his wary eyes caught something unusual that stopped him in his tracks. He checked his breath, turning to peer at the bright color that caught his eye. Down in the river bottom in the strange green light of the jungle crouched a jaguar, its spotted yellow hair matted with dried blood from a previous meal. Its tail twitched silently, its yellow eyes stared intently at its prey. There was a slight bend in the stream, and from the profuse growth of vegetation, he could not see where the cat's focus was directed.

As he crept around one last bush to view both turns of the stream, the blood froze in his veins. Stumbling along the streambed, bent over with exhaustion, was the form of a tiny Lamanite girl. Her long dark hair cascaded nearly to her waist. A bundle she carried on her back moved, and his eyes widened in alarm as a baby's curious head appeared. His eyes shot back to the jaguar, curling itself up to pounce.

In desperation, the young man glanced around. Why would two Lamanite children be alone, so far north? Aside from the child's labored breath, there was only silence.

His jaw tightened, for he knew he had no other choice. He unsheathed his knife.

The muscles in her shoulder and back burned, and Miriam knew that at last she must rest. So she stumbled to a halt, and lifted the baby's weight from her shoulders. She drew his squirming brown body from the sling, and set him, gurgling cheerfully, on a cool bed of moss on the overhanging bank and turned to uncork her water bag. In the movement, her eye saw a shadow behind her. Jerking in that direction, she gasped when she saw the jaguar. Its yellow eyes were locked with hers, its ears were laid back, and its long fangs were bared.

What followed seemed to happen slowly as if time had been distorted. As the jaguar leaped into the air at her, its claws stretching toward her face, a figure vaulted over her head and caught the jaguar in mid-flight. The two crashed to the ground, writhing furiously.

As she gathered her senses about her, Miriam realized that the second figure was a young man. He wore thick, quilted armor over a light colored tunic that hung to his knees, and had fair, lightly tanned skin. She knew that he was a Nephite, but she could not help admiring the way he fought the beast. He was a strong match. Miriam turned her head away as the young man raised a short knife and brought it down. She heard the jaguar shriek once, and then there was nothing but the wind stirring in the trees. She opened her eyes and turned back to see the young man who stood brushing his knife off on the grass at the bank as his chest heaved heavily. The jaguar lay silent at his feet on the soft brown earth. Fumbling, she turned back, took up the baby in her arms, and began to scramble down the streambed. The Nephite turned and called something she could not understand. Then after a pause, he cried, "Wait!"

She stopped abruptly, and turned, her eyes glaring with mistrust. The young man sheathed his knife, and stepped forward. He seemed young, and did not yet have the first growth of hair on his face that defined the beginning of a Nephite male's manhood. But he was old enough for her to feel like a small child. He was at least a cubit taller than she was, with short, brown hair, and strange, light eyes. Not a color like her own blue eyes, but a soft hazel, like new leather, flecked with bits of green and gold, edged with a ring of darker brown.

"Why did you do such a thing? You could have died," she asked bluntly, forcing herself to ignore the captivating color of his eyes.

"It meant—to eat you." He struggled with her language, and glanced around nervously. "Why have you come to our lands, little girl? Where are the others of your family?"

"We have no kindred," she scoffed with a haughty lift of her chin.

He studied her face closely, noticing her brilliant blue eyes for the first time, and the fair tone of her skin. "Why then, are you here?"

"We have come," she seethed, "to join the Nephites."

He stared at her a long moment, as if he wondered whether he understood her words, then spoke slowly. "Will you let me help you?"

Her heart pounded as he studied her, his bright eyes gazing into her own as if he could read the secrets in her heart. Four claw marks had shredded the cotton armor at his shoulder, and one deep gash had cut into the unprotected flesh at his collarbone. He mopped at the blood seeping from the wound. "The wilderness is dangerous for such a little girl."

She glanced away and scowled. "We have no need of your help." She tipped her nose in the air, turned and continued tramping ahead of him.

He smiled after the obstinate child, and started after her. In three easy strides, he had reached her. "Little girl, did you know that if you continue this way—"

She abruptly cut him off. "I am almost ten years old, Nephite! I am not a little girl!"

He threw his hands up in mock defeat as the girl stalked away, but followed closely behind.

Miriam stared intently at the ground before her, and had no view of her surroundings, nor could she see anything above the bank. As the foliage around her suddenly began to thin and she broke abruptly into a clearing, she did not notice nor slow her pace.

Miriam stopped however, when one curious voice spoke out. She looked up and gasped sharply. Under a clear, dusky sky, she saw that the meadow, nearly a hundred paces across, was filled with several pale, light-skinned men dressed like the one she had just met.

The man closest to her repeated his question, this time speaking her language. "Who are you?" he asked. He seemed older than the others did, and she guessed he was their leader.

He did not seem to be unkind, but Miriam knew he was a Nephite, and suddenly the Lamanite teachings of the thieving, hateful Nephites returned, and her heart hammered with fear. "I, I, uh," she stuttered as she crushed the protesting baby against her, and shrank against the bank opposite him. The other men had begun to gather on both sides of the bank, peering at her curiously, as expressions of sympathy mingled with distrust etched their faces. She glanced around desperately, wishing she had not left the young man, when he suddenly broke out of the jungle. He grinned, noticing her look of discomfort and began speaking to the older man in the mottled, distorted language of which she could only understand a few scattered words.

"Captain Teancum, sir," he gasped, saluting the older man. The hand with which he saluted his commander was bright with blood from the wound the jaguar had given him. The scratch had struck bone, and would leave a lasting scar. "A jaguar attacked her. I killed it. She says she is fleeing to our lands."

His commander frowned. "What is your name, child?" He knelt on the bank.

"Miriam," she whimpered.

"Miriam, will you come with us? It will be safer for you."

Miriam bit her quivering lower lip. "Yes, sir." She kept her eyes lowered.

The captain nodded and stood, turning to the young soldier who had climbed up out of the streambed and stood high above Miriam now. "Someone will come to clean your wound, and bandage it. Rest now, for a moment."

"Thank you, sir," he said, lowering himself to the grass.

Miriam did not move from where she stood, her head bowed, her arms wrapped tightly around the baby. Then she began to cry softly. Her shoulders shook gently.

"Miriam?" He spoke her name gently, and she sniffled, looking up to see him offering a hand to help her. She gazed at his large, callused hand a long time before slipping her small brown hand into it, and allowing him to lift her up onto the bank. She sat beside him, bent her head over the baby, and continued to cry.

"Grandmother said they meant to kill me as a sacrifice," she whimpered softly so no one else could hear. "That is why I fled."

He squeezed her hand. "No one will hurt you now. I will see to it."

"I am called Miriam." She raised her head to look at him. "I am from the land of Siron."

"It is an unusual name for a Lamanite."

"I am half Nephite by birth," she offered. "Do I look more like a Nephite or a Lamanite?"

"You look very much like a Nephite, and your baby brother as well, with your blue eyes."

"I have never seen a true Nephite," she admitted thoughtfully. "At least not until today."

"What do you think of us?" He smiled.

"Your skin is much lighter. Your eyes as well. They are light brown, like doe skin, but they have so many other colors," she observed, for she had already noticed how the shade of his eyes seemed to change with his expressions, and the play of light against his face. "Are the women fair skinned like you? With light hair and eyes, like you?"

"Yes. Some even have hair the color of gold, and eyes as blue as yours." His eyes looked sad for a moment, and he glanced away, lost for a moment in his own thoughts, but then he rallied, grinned, and turned back to study her features carefully. "You would become one of the most lovely among them when you are grown, I think."

"Is your wife beautiful?"

He swallowed a laugh. "I have no wife. I almost chose one, but—"

"Was she one of the ugly ones?"

"So many questions," he laughed, a hint of discomfort in his voice as he wiped another hand across his slowly oozing wound. "There are many kinds of ugliness, not all of them outward—,"

"Jacob." A voice startled Miriam, and she looked up. A young soldier, near the age of her new friend, stepped down into the streambed carrying a roll of white cloth.

"Helam!" Her new friend greeted the other boy cheerfully, and the two began speaking in the language of the Nephites. The other boy brushed healing liquid across the gash, and then pressed a cloth carefully against his shoulder to arrest the bleeding. Her new friend winced, but did not speak as the other young man worked.

At last, the wound was bound, and Jacob scrambled to his feet as the other young man stood and walked away. Miriam rose to her feet as well, fatigue showing on her face. Jacob wiped his bloody hand on his tunic, as he offered her his other.

"Will you come?"

Miriam nodded, and slipped her small hand into his.

಄

Night filled the sky, a skein of smooth black silk draped across the vast expanse above them, woven with threads of starlight, and Miriam yawned, trudging tiredly behind her new friend. "Where are you from, Jacob?" she murmured as she stumbled sleepily against his arm, resting her face gratefully against the warmth of his leathery skin.

"Zarahemla," he whispered, his voice barely audible.

"I lived in a village north of Siron. My best friend, Thobor, lives there," Miriam yawned, fighting the heaviness in her eyelids. "I miss him and Grandmother."

"I miss my parents."

"They are in Zarahemla?"

"My father died before I was born, in battle with the Lamanites. My mother died some months later, having me." In the darkness and the silence, his voice sounded faint, and lonely.

"Then like us, you have no family," she murmured. He released her hand to slip his arm around her shoulder, and she rested her head again against his arm, willing herself to stay awake, but at last she lost the battle.

Then her eyes snapped open as the sun peeked over the horizon to her right. They had emerged from the shadow of the jungle, and were coming into a clearing. The sudden beam of light that washed over her had roused her where she slept, hoisted to Jacob's broad back. She lifted her head from his warm shoulder. The baby was cradled in his arm.

Jacob chuckled, turning his face. His warm cheek touched hers. "Did you sleep well?"

She tried to speak, but her words were drowned by a yawn.

"Good," he chuckled, straightening his back as he allowed her to slide to the ground. A moan of protest escaped her lips.

"Do not worry, little Miriam," he laughed, wrapping his strong hand firmly around hers. "Our journey is almost ended."

She grumbled again and opened her mouth to ask him where they were, when they broke through the last of the jungle and began to cross a cornfield toward a sturdy, walled town. There was a straight, high-banked ditch that ran from the edge of the jungle to the great stone walls of the city. The soldiers walked along the edge of it so as not to crush the young corn leaves pushing their way out of the rich, dark earth. There was a small cluster of men who looked up like a herd of alarmed deer as the group emerged from the trees, but returned to their work when they saw that the soldiers were Nephites.

One man opened a floodgate in the ditch ahead of her, and Miriam's eyes grew wide with curiosity as water rushed from the gate into the deep furrows beside the young corn plants. The man raised his eyebrows in quiet curiosity as Miriam nimbly leaped over the water, holding tightly to Jacob's hand.

As she passed the man, she raised her eyes to his, and his face softened with a smile. He was a fatherly man, short and stocky, with his dark hair fading to gray, then white near his ears, like the thin, cold clouds that rode high in the sky on clear days. His eyes were kind, like Ishna's.

From the outside, the city of Morianton[2] appeared frighteningly inhospitable. All around the wall was a trench as deep as a man's height, and wider than a man could jump. Between the trench and the wall, were great spiked barricades, tree trunks sharpened to deadly points, leaning out over the trenches. The only area along the wall without the barricades was the narrow gate. None of the Lamanite cities needed such protection.

The gates slowly creaked open, and they walked through onto the broad, packed road leading toward the center of the town. Smoke rose lazily from the roofs of thatch houses lining the street. There were a few men and women out, intermixing in groups of two or three as they began their daily chores. A small number of light-haired, fair-skinned children were chasing each other in a corner between two houses, their bright laughter ringing out clearly in the morning air. Their chatter cut short suddenly when they stopped to gape wide eyed at Miriam as she walked primly beside Jacob, holding tightly to his hand. She glared back at them, but they merely turned and continued with their play.

A small stream flowing through the center of the town emptied into a stone cistern, forming a clear, glassy pool of water. Several young girls with long unbound hair, all of different hues, knelt at the edge, filling water jars, but when they saw the soldiers coming, they giggled shyly and scattered like a flock of brightly colored birds. The tense silence of the soldiers lifted as they reached the edge of the pool, and they set their heavy packs down with soft grunts of relief, some dropping to their knees to scoop up mouthfuls of the clear water.

Miriam thumped heavily down onto a step beside the pool of water, thirsty, but too tired to rise to take a drink.

Jacob set the baby in her arms, and she took it without protest as Jacob knelt down to scoop handfuls of water eagerly into his mouth.

She shook her head and looked down at the baby still sleeping in her arms. If only she was young enough to sleep all day as he did. She sighed and stared at the ground, pushing small stones about with her toes. While she sat, she heard a new voice, and lifted her face to see a man approaching the leader of the soldiers and talking softly with him. She straightened, recognizing him to be the same man she had seen in the field. The captain nodded in her direction and the man turned and trotted toward her.

"I am called Aaron," the man boomed in her dialect, towering above her, his back to the bright morning sun. "You are Miriam?"

Miriam gaped, her mouth ajar, unable to speak as she stared up at the man, unable to see his pale features, as the sunlight streamed around him.

Jacob rose from the water's edge, and in spite of his youth, stood head and shoulders above the older man. "She has come from the land of Siron to join the Nephites."

"What is to become of her?" the man asked, glancing up at the younger man.

Jacob shrugged. "In truth, sir, we are not certain."

Aaron shook his head with concern. "The child needs rest, and a bath, and good food. And that baby needs a woman's attention." He indicated to the baby in her arms, and then turned to a woman standing in a nearby doorway, looking on. "Sarah!" he called, beckoning to her.

The woman was as old as her husband, but much thinner, and carried herself gracefully.

As she drew closer, she warmed Miriam with her smile. Jacob stepped back with hesitant reluctance, but Miriam did not notice this as she scrambled to her feet. This woman reminded her so much of Ishna that she found herself biting back sudden tears. Aaron laughed heartily as his wife gathered up the baby, and let Miriam bury her face against her skirt, hiding her tears. He spoke a few words to his wife, and then reassured Jacob, "We will care for them."

Jacob's face was a study of protective concern before he nodded in consent, and gazed after them with wistful, worried eyes as Sarah put an arm around the shivering girl's shoulders, and led her toward the wood and thatch house she had come from.

03

The sun was sinking low in the west when Aaron came again through the door, his shoulders sagging with weariness. He smiled tiredly at his wife who was bent over a pot of bubbling porridge, and at Miriam who sat beside her, then glanced at the baby sitting in a corner, chewing on a wheeled, clay toy.

Aaron breathed deeply of the aroma of cooking porridge as Sarah rose to greet him. She spoke words Miriam could not understand as she kissed her husband, and nodded to the steaming pot of corn porridge bubbling over the fire in the center of the room. Sarah stepped to the baby and scooped him up in her arms as Aaron brought a pitcher of milk from a corner. Sarah smiled her thanks as Aaron poured some of the milk into a dish, then set a clean cloth into the milk. The baby squirmed in Sarah's arms, and reached fat hands out toward the dish of milk, his dark face bright and eager. He had been bathed as Miriam had, his thick dark hair straightened, and he wore a cloth diaper.

Sarah and Aaron sat cross-legged before the bubbling porridge, and Sarah handed the baby to Aaron who set him on his knee, bouncing him. At the movement, the baby's face glowed, and he chuckled, flailing his fat fists through the air.

"Where are all your children?" Miriam asked as Sarah ladled bubbling yellow mush into bowls.

Aaron's smile faded and he lifted his eyes from the giggling baby to look at her. "We have never had any."

"You—," Miriam hesitated, glancing to Sarah and back again at Aaron, "you are sad you have no children?"

Aaron shook his head, and reached out, grasping Sarah's hand. He lifted his eyes to his wife's who smiled at him, though she did not understand his words. "We have always wanted children, but we have each other, and that is enough."

"Oh." Miriam lowered her eyes to the corn mush Sarah had slipped in front of her. Sarah filled her own bowl last, and at a nod to Aaron, folded her hands and lowered her head. Without thinking, Miriam did the same. She did not understand the words Aaron spoke, but sensed their meaning, for she had heard Ishna speak similar prayers countless times. And when Aaron finished, Miriam instinctively spoke her amen along with Sarah, then dipped her spoon into her food without sensing the stunned silence of Aaron and Sarah.

"Miriam,"

She looked sharply up to see Aaron's warming smile.

"Did you pray with us?"

She stiffened, frightened. In Siron, to be found praying to any other gods meant punishment.

"Where did you learn to pray?" he continued, without waiting for a response.

"Grandmother Ishna taught me," she gulped, but his expression was not threatening, so she continued. "She raised me from a baby, and taught me how to pray to the god of the Nephites."

Aaron's eyes grew wide and round. "Ishna? The friend of Abish? We never knew what became of her. She was baptized, but her husband did not believe, and took her away to the land of Siron," he whispered. He turned to his wife and spoke quickly, and Miriam watched as Sarah's expression grew to match her husband's. Aaron turned back to Miriam. "Is she well? And faithful?"

"Yes. She has always been. She says God is mindful of her."

"What other teachings has she given you?" he stammered eagerly.

"Not many, but we prayed together. It helped us feel safe."

Aaron studied the child intently, and Miriam hesitated. "You are—Christians?" she breathed at last, her heart giving a wild thud.

Aaron chuckled heartily. "Yes." As he lifted his eyes to his wife's, and spoke Miriam's words, a smile grew across Sarah's face.

⋘

It was evening, and a light rain was beginning to fall as Aaron and Sarah spoke in hushed tones, mindful of the children sleeping in the other room, when soft footsteps approached, and a young man's quiet voice murmured, "Peace be with this house."

Curious, Aaron moved toward the door, and brushed aside the curtain. Sarah came to look over his shoulder.

Outside the door in the bluish-gray shadows of the clouded sky, stood the young man who had brought the girl to them that morning. He stood respectfully, an apologetic smile on his face.

"Forgive me," he began politely, squinting in the light that streamed from behind them, "but my captain and the other men are preparing to leave, and I hoped that I might say farewell to the child. I do not know when I will see her again."

"Of course," Sarah spoke quickly, trading a glance with Aaron who nodded and pulled the curtain back, allowing Jacob to come in. She led Jacob to another doorway and slowly parted the linen curtain, beckoning Jacob into the dark room where Miriam slept.

Reverently, Jacob stepped softly into the shadow, and lowered himself to one knee beside the little girl snuggled under a warm cloak. Her dark, wavy hair had been washed and combed until it shone, and spilled across her feather pillow, glistening like obsidian glass. Her face was serene in childish sleep. He took one of her little hands in his, and her eyes fluttered halfway open. Wordlessly, she looked up at him.

"It is time that I leave, Miriam," he explained quietly.

"When will I see you again?" she murmured.

"I am not sure. Someday, I hope." He smiled, releasing her hand, and touching her cheek.

Miriam sat up slowly, her sleeping cloak slipping down to her waist. "I will never forget your kindness," she yawned, rubbing her eyes, and smiling sleepily up at him.

Jacob's gaze took in the sweet expression on the child's face, rested a moment on the beads around her neck as they peeked from beneath her new sleeping gown, and then again on her large, luminous blue eyes.

"I will never forget you," Jacob said as he pulled back and brushed a hand across his eyes. He rose and turned away but stopped as he felt Aaron's callused hand on his shoulder.

"Do not worry. We will care well for them," he offered as the younger man turned back.

Jacob nodded, swallowing a hard lump in his throat. "I am glad, sir," he gulped. "Thank you." He turned quickly away and marched out into the rain and the lowering darkness to join his companions.

CHAPTER 4

24TH YEAR OF JUDGES

*M*iriam stepped gingerly over a jutting tree root that crossed her path, grateful for the faint gray light at her back. For four glorious years she'd had her own secure family, a father and mother who loved her, and taught her well; it had been like a dream that could never end. And then it did, first with Aaron's death, then with Sarah's, only a month later. It should not have been unexpected, she sighed to herself, for her parents were old, and beyond the age when most people die. But in her childish heart, she had thought of them as deathless, almost immortal, and their passing had come as a painful blow to her. She had not known how she could endure, or stand for anything she believed in without her father there. Still, she had stood up to Morianton, and was here, she smiled to herself, hitching her brother higher on her back in spite of arms that had long since lost all their feeling. So, somehow, something in her father must have become part of her.

The light behind her grew warmer against her back, and began to creep slowly up into the eastern sky, and brighten to a light blue, edged with a veil of gold, hiding the distant sparks of stars.

While her numb legs tramped beneath her through the early morning mists, she began glimpsing torchlight through the trees. There was a clearing, a great open space in the trees, with countless tents scattered across it. She caught sight of the Title of Liberty, set at the top of a long slender standard, and she staggered to a halt, her heart thumping in her chest. The camp! She had found it! Forcing her legs to begin again, she stumbled eagerly on, hoping she had enough strength to carry her the last short distance.

As she rounded the trunk of a fat tree at the edge of the camp, she saw a sentry standing alone in the chilly light of the morning, his powerfully broad shoulders wrapped beneath his crimson cloak against the early morning chill. She could see only half of his face, and noted the strong, sharply-honed angles, the day-old growth of scruff on his jaw and above his upper lip, the tight line of his mouth and the concentrated set of his one visible eye. His short hair was dark brown, and though it was bound back with a leather band, a few stray sections still hung down over his forehead.

She tried to quicken her pace, but almost stumbled. She clenched her jaw in renewed determination, and willed energy into her weakened legs as she stumbled toward the lone soldier.

The sentry had begun to grow bored from his long watch, and he leaned against his spear, listening to the sounds of the rising morning as it came creeping across the ash-colored sky in streaks of pink fire. All around him was silence, and a loud crackle of twigs behind him brought him fully to his senses in an instant. He spun around, glaring at the gray darkness of the trees, his stance widening as the javelin in his hands lowered. He pointed it at the shadows and demanded boldly, "Who goes there?"

"Forgive me, sir," said the exhausted girl as she stepped from the shadows, "I did not mean to alarm you. My brother and I have come from the city Morianton. We have news that Captain Moroni must hear."

He squinted at her, recognizing something familiar as he straightened, lifting the spear, and planting it, point up, in the ground. She was a girl of thirteen, perhaps fourteen years, with dark hair, and skin of a color like dark honey. Her eyes were large and blue, like two clear pools of water, accentuating the youthful beauty of her face in spite of a massive bruise along one cheek, and a streak of dried blood on the other. Her hair was long and glossy and hung unbound down her back. She wore no adornments but for a strip of leather patterned with small beads, almost Lamanitish, in its appearance.

"Sir," she spouted impatiently, grabbing his arm with shaking fingers that were almost as thin as twigs. "We are from the city of Morianton. We have news that Captain Moroni must hear. We must see him, now."

"Oh." He shook himself, chagrined, realizing he had been staring at her, studying her smooth, pleading features, his own frozen. "Of course." He glanced at the boy hitched onto his sister's back, and reached out for him as the girl more than willingly surrendered the small boy's weight into the soldier's sturdy arms. Little Jacob shifted against the soldier's shoulder and sighed, but did not awaken.

"The Captain's tent is this way." He pointed with his head and offered her his hand. But the exhausting night had taken its toll, and she stumbled, dropping the hand he extended. He caught her around the waist before she fell.

As his strong arm raised her up, her eye caught a strange scar crossing his collarbone. A shiver drove through her, not unpleasant, but she forgot it quickly as she managed to gather her own weight under herself.

The young man half guided, half carried her through the city of tents to one set in the middle of the camp. It was larger than the others, and two soldiers guarded the door.

"Helam," her guide said, informally addressing one of the men, "this young woman wishes to see Captain Moroni."

The sandy haired man her guide had spoken to, and the other guard looked at her curiously, and at the sleeping boy resting against the sentry's shoulder.

The man looked at her guide questioningly as the other guard queried, "For what purpose?"

"I am from the city of Morianton," Miriam stammered. "Morianton believes the Lehites have come here. His plan is to flee to the lands northward. I have come to tell Captain Moroni this."

The man whose name was Helam studied her closely, his eyes, showing a touch of sympathy as they took in the bruises on her face. He traded a glance with his companion who nodded, and lifted the tent flap, waving her and her guide inside.

A single oil lamp lit the inside of the tent, and Miriam could see two captains standing over a table, studying a map spread before them.

"Sirs," one of the guards spoke. The two men looked up. As their eyes turned to her, Miriam blinked at the face of the older officer whose dark hair was laced with gray. He seemed vaguely familiar.

Upon seeing Miriam, the other captain straightened in alarm. He was much younger than his fellow captain; no gray showed yet in his sand colored hair, but his eyes showed a wisdom beyond their years, and were kind and discerning, like her father's had been.

"Who did this to you?" he asked with concern as her guide's fingers clasped her arm, lest she fall.

"Are you Captain Moroni?" she blurted without answering his question, then without waiting for an answer, stammered on, "I am Miriam, daughter of Aaron of the city Morianton." At this, the sentry's grip on her arm tightened softly, and then relaxed, but she took no notice. "The man, Morianton, knows that the Lehites whom he tried to wage a battle against, have fled here. He fears that you will come to avenge them, and so his plan is to lead all the city to the lands northward beyond Bountiful. I told him I would not go, and he beat me,³ but my brother and I escaped."

Moroni stared at her, anger and admiration competing to show themselves on his face.

The older officer made a low sound in his throat. "Morianton is a coward, if he only beats women," he growled. Fire smoldered in his voice. "He must be taught a lesson."

"You will get the chance to show him what it is to fight an equal, Teancum," the younger one promised as he brought a wooden stool forward for Miriam to sit on.

The sentry released her arm and she sank gratefully on the stool, her head sagging wearily.

"When did he plan to depart from the city Morianton with his people?" Moroni questioned, kneeling before her so as to be at her eye level.

"Yesterday, I think." A tired sigh escaped her lips. "I am one of his servants, and he demanded that we prepare his belongings to depart to the north immediately. I do not know any more."

He touched her shoulder gently. "Thank you. What you have told us is more than enough."

"Sir, the people of Lehi are at the southern end of camp," the sentry said. "Should I take her there?"

"Yes, lieutenant, that would be wise." Moroni nodded. "She has earned a long rest."

He offered her a hand, and with his help, Miriam was somehow able to rise, and stumble toward her guide who grasped her arm and led her back into the open air.

Jacob smiled at the girl who leaned tiredly against him and studied her face, recognizing at last, the familiar features he remembered, made only more endearing by the added grace the years had brought to her. She had changed. The day he had left her in Morianton, she had been a child. Now she was almost a woman.

"Miriam?" He latched his arm around her waist to support her weight, marveling at how light her body still was.

"Yes?" she mumbled as her head lolled against his shoulder.

He chuckled. "I am taking you and your brother to the Lehites' camp. They will take good care of you."

CHAPTER 5

*M*iriam woke with a start, not sure how long she had slept. The walls of the tent she lay within glowed with the red light of evening as they billowed in the light breeze outside, and the breathless laughter of children at play carried easily through the fluttering canvas. She lifted her head to find herself alone, a padded pallet beneath her, and a warm cloak draped over her. On the other side of the tent lay a smaller pallet, a cloak crumpled beside it, showing that a child had been sleeping there, but had since risen.

She touched the bruise on her cheek gingerly, and winced with the pain that it brought, then rose slowly to her feet, wincing again at the stiffness of her muscles.

Footsteps crunching over the sandy ground signaled a man's approach, and stopped before her door. A hushed voice hesitantly whispered, "Miriam, are you awake?"

Miriam stooped out the tent's low door, squinting in the fierce red light of the evening, at the circle of tents where a group of children chased among them while their parents sat in tent doors and looked on. The sun slowly sank beneath the horizon, and the sky was a great, smoldering ember behind the man who stood before her, etched in flames. His features were faded and indistinct with the sun at his back.

She let the door fall shut behind her as she moved so that the sun was no longer behind him, and his countenance became clear.

"Peace be with you, Miriam," the young man said, towering over her, a congenial smile on his face, his hands clasped behind his back.

"Peace be with you, sir," she returned, not knowing why she should suddenly be out of breath.

Before her stood the young man she had met when she had come into the camp that morning. From the insignia on his shoulder, she could see that he was a lieutenant. He wore a cloth tunic, and a chest covering made of thick, quilted cotton. Leather boots were strapped to his shins, and he wore a short metal sword at his side. He did not have the red cloak he had been wearing earlier, which made it easier for her to note his muscled shoulders, and his broad chest. His sharply angled face gave him a pleasingly handsome, bold countenance, one that smiled easily in spite of the hardened undertones of his features. His dark brown hair was bound back, with a few rebellious strands brushing against his forehead. Dark brows hung over honest hazel eyes which seemed to stare deep into her soul, and she gulped as she looked into them. His nose was straight and almost slender. His mouth curved upward, parting slightly as he smiled, and she could see the gleam of his white, even teeth.

She heard herself gulp again, and out of shyness, she finally broke her gaze.

"I am Jacob, son of Ezekiel of Zarahemla." His deep voice had a smooth, almost caressing quality to it. "We met before. Do you remember?"

"Yes. We met this morning. You helped my brother and me." She managed to look up into his golden brown eyes, streaks of green and gold catching the light that hit his face at an angle. "I am most grateful." She dropped her eyes.

He chuckled softly, then changing his dialect, asked, "Surely there is more that you remember."

Her head jerked up. "Why are you speaking the tongue of the Lamanites? How did you know I would understand?"

"Little Miriam, surely you have not forgotten me." He grinned, and her eyes, almost without her bidding, fastened on the scar that crossed his collarbone.

The memory struck her with the force of lightning. "Jacob?" she gasped.

He laughed, and the sound of it danced through her soul. "Yes. Do you not remember me?"

"I do—now. But you have—," she bit her lip as she studied him, hoping the blush that was returning to her cheeks was not visible, "changed," she finished.

"And so have you." The hands that had been behind his back came forward. He came toward her and caught her hands in his. "But all the things I admired most about you have stayed the same." His hands carried rough calluses, yet they were soft and warm as they encircled hers. "It must have taken great courage to flee to us from Morianton." He grinned sheepishly. "But then I knew already how brave you are."

"I did not feel brave." Her voice trembled, and she dared to look up.

"But you were." His smile faded slightly, and his hands tightened gently. "Especially coming so far alone, with your brother." Jacob's eyes grew soft, and his voice lowered. "I spoke to him, and he told me of your parents' deaths. It must have been difficult for you."

She acknowledged him with a sigh. "But since their passing, we have managed to take care of each other."

"Jacob!" a childish voice cried, and she turned to see her brother rush out of the crowd of children and fling himself into Jacob's arms. He squealed with delight as the older Jacob tossed him up into the air, catching him again as he came down.

Miriam blinked, feeling strangely envious that her brother could have formed such a bond with Jacob so quickly. Yet at the same time, she was relieved as well, with her brother between them.

"Jacob, come back and play!" a boy called from the group of children. One of the boys had a small rubber ball, and the children were dividing into kickball teams.

Barely glancing at his sister, little Jacob raced back to join his new friends.

"He's growing into a good, sturdy boy," Jacob murmured as they both watched his retreating back.

"He has always been strong. Even from the time he was a baby," Miriam returned, watching her brother's bright eyes as the children brought their game under way. "That is why I asked my father to name him after you," she gulped and stuttered. "You saved us, after all."

Miriam studied the earth below her feet with an intensity she had not given it before. She felt a strange awkwardness between them that she had not felt as a child. It was laced with a thread of discomfort, yet not without a spark of excitement as well.

Miriam glanced slowly up, and waited until Jacob's eyes rose to meet hers. They were the same golden-brown hazel that she remembered, but now, gazing into them, her heart flopped like a freshly caught fish.

"I am honored that you would choose to name him after me." His voice was gentle, and his mouth curved into a soft smile. She found herself returning his smile, but her throat could not form words to answer him.

"Make way, there!" A harsh, masculine voice cut through the air like a knife, and Miriam glanced toward the source of the voice, flinching as a horse shouldered its way through the group of children, throwing their game into chaos as they ran shrieking to hide in their mothers' skirts. Little Jacob came racing toward her, his eyes large and frightened, as he dove behind her. She could feel him trembling as he clung to her skirt, and peered out from behind her at the horse.

It was a powerful chested, gray horse, with a long mane, flowing evenly down one side of its neck as it stepped smoothly into the center of the circled tents. Miriam gaped at the dark eyed, sober creature as it snorted, and pawed at the earth, tossing its head. Horses were rare creatures here in the Nephite lands; she had never seen them here before, though she remembered as a child seeing them occasionally in the southern lands of the Lamanites. Even then, common people walked where they had to travel, and only the rich owned horses. The horse's rider was a young, fierce-faced man, wearing a sleeveless tunic, his bulging shoulders and arms exposed. A double bladed, metal sword was sheathed across his back, its hilt within easy reach of his right hand, as if to threaten any who dared to challenge him. His long hair hung to his shoulders, framing a chiseled face, handsome in spite of the hardness Miriam could see in his eyes. He eyed the people clustered at their tents with obvious distaste, before he spoke with rancor. "This is a military camp. Where are the soldiers?"

"These people are refugees from the city of Lehi, who have journeyed here for protection from those who would harm them," Jacob spoke, stepping forward and planting himself directly in front of the man's horse, as if responding to an unspoken challenge. "Why are you here?"

The man glared stonily at Jacob and did not speak, but indicated to a group approaching from behind him. Jacob glanced at them, and Miriam followed his gaze, missing the sudden expression of astonishment that seized his features as he watched the two riders approach. One was a man of middle years, though his girth suggested greater age. His fine clothes, tailored for one who could afford such luxuries, did not disguise his round, swollen body that sat astride his horse like a fat, rotund barrel. His chin, which rose above the silken collar of his tunic, lay down his neck in folds of extra flesh. His jowls hung pink and damp with sweat, against his jaw, and Miriam could see that the journey he had made had taken its toll on him, as he drew a white handkerchief from a pouch at his side, and mopped his round shining head, covered over with a thin skiff of graying hair. His eyes were dark and beady, and they glanced with disgust at the group of people surrounding him. The woman who rode beside him on a smaller, well groomed mare, was slender and willowy, a stark contrast to the corpulent man she rode beside. She was young and light skinned, with fair shining hair that rolled in golden waves down her back. Even the silky whiteness of her gown seemed to repel the dust that covered the garments of the men she rode with. It was of a soft material that flowed like wind around her, and flattered the soft curves of her slender figure. Her skin was smooth and flawless like cream, and her face was light-boned and delicate. Her eyes, deep blue and piercing, were fixed on Jacob.

"Pachus." Jacob spoke low and evenly, his eyes narrowed and distrusting.

"Jacob, my friend!" the large man boomed, spreading his arms as if in a benevolent gesture of welcome. "You are the very man my daughter Lylith and I have journeyed so far to see."

Jacob's eyes darted from the man to the young woman, and lingered for a long moment, before they traveled slowly back to the man again.

Jacob shifted his stance, and licked his lips. "Why have you come to see me, Pachus?"

"I have a matter of which I must speak with you," the large man boomed, his voice mirthful and generous. "One that would be of great benefit to you."

"And to you as well, Pachus? For I know you do not do anything unless it will somehow benefit you."

The man's face remained frozen in a smile, but Miriam detected a minute tick at the corner of his mouth.

Jacob glanced for an instant in Miriam's direction, then lowered his eyes to the ground, and drew in a deep breath that swelled his chest, then released it. He spoke again, the timbre of his voice returning to a dutiful tone. "I will take you to the tent of our chief captain to announce your arrival. Surely there is space to spare a campsite for you."

"You are a good boy." Pachus grinned, and nodded at the younger man who dismounted, and followed Jacob as he turned and led the group away. The young woman, still mounted like her father, glanced backward, and nodded wordlessly at a girl who came riding behind them. The girl, dressed in the plain, roughly spun garments of a servant, returned the nod, and patted the weary neck of the horse she rode. Unlike the other horses, it was tired and old, its coat the same dirty gray as the hair on the round man's head. Its neck hung dejectedly, but at the girl's gentle pat, the horse flicked its tail and started after the group that followed Jacob slowly. The girl was near Miriam's age, with long black hair and a brown sheen to her skin that suggested that she too, had Lamanite blood in her. As she passed the tent where Miriam and her brother stood, she glanced over once at them. Her large brown eyes shone with a friendly twinkle before she passed them and disappeared between the tents.

☃

Weariness sunk to the center of Miriam's bones as the sun dipped below the distant horizon. Beyond the jungle, far in the distance, rose towering mountains, jagged and circular, like giant pyramids. It was a view that had become familiar to her over the last few days. Grayish pink evening mist swept up from the darkening forest where the distant peaks rose out of the green tangle of jungle, crowned with billowing clouds.

Miriam studied the vast red sunset, burning above the cool green of the jungle as she ladled stew of beans and corn into a wooden bowl, and handed it to her brother who sat staring numbly into the fire where the pot of stew rested on heated rocks, and simmered slowly.

She smiled, observing his weary expression before she crouched beside him, and spoke. "You played hard with your new friends today. I can see why you are so sleepy."

At her words, little Jacob straightened, and drew in a deep breath, forcing his narrowed eyes wider. "I am not sleepy," he claimed.

She grinned, and rose slowly. "Oh. Well, tomorrow, we will begin our journey with the others to the city of Lehi, where we will live from now on. Perhaps laying down to rest may give you more energy for the trip."

"Yes, perhaps it would." Little Jacob pushed aside his bowl of stew, and rose to stumble sleepily inside the tent. A moment later he emerged, dragging his pallet. He unrolled it before the fire, and crawled into his own cocoon-like ground cloth, curling up cozy and sleepy, his eyelids already sagging.

"Are you not hungry?" she murmured, lowering herself to one knee while running a hand through the thick strands of his black wiry hair.

He glanced up drowsily. "No," he whispered, "just a little thirsty."

"Then I will bring you a drink of water." Miriam smiled, then rose as her brother nodded.

She drew a small gourd from a light pack of utensils that some of the Lehite women had given her, then turned toward the trees beyond the edge of the tents where she could hear the inviting gurgle of the stream where she and other women had drawn their water for the evening meal. She gripped the cool handle of the gourd as she drifted into the shadows, where gentle breezes swirled playfully around her, and the burble of the brook grew louder.

"You're a good mother to your little brother," Jacob's voice spoke suddenly from the shadows.

Miriam caught a gasp in her throat, seeing him now as her eyes adjusted to the dim light beneath the thick canopy. He knelt beside the gurgling stream as it tumbled merrily over rocks on its course toward the river as he dipped his water bag into the flow. It bellied, swelling full in the bubbling current, then he lifted it, frigid and dripping, and tied it to his belt.

Miriam knelt beside Jacob, her movements demure though her face felt hot. "Thank you. I try to be, since our own mother is gone." She dipped the gourd into the clear water, and lifted it to her lips. The cool taste was lost on her, her senses aware only of Jacob's eyes as they studied her.

Her thirst satisfied, she dipped the gourd again into the water, and without thinking, offered it to Jacob.

"She taught you well. Both your parents did, I can tell." Jacob's hand brushed hers as he took the gourd, nodded his thanks, and drank.

She started at the touch of his hand, and drew in a deep breath, her eyes focused on a fixed point on the ground. "I try to remember what they taught me. It is hard sometimes, alone."

"Someday you will marry. Then you will not be alone."

"I am in no hurry to find a husband," she huffed, covering her shyness with sudden gruffness. "And when I do marry, it will be for love, not because I am weak, and need a man to take care of me."

"It should not be any other way," Jacob agreed evenly. "I am sorry if that is what I implied." He held the empty gourd out to her, and she drew it slowly from his hands, clasping it tightly to herself.

"My parents have not left me entirely alone, I suppose," Miriam sighed. "Sometimes I can feel their spirits near. That brings me comfort."

"You are a Christian?"

Miriam glanced up, his question startling her. "Yes, of course. Are there many in Zarahemla who are not?"

"Quite a few," Jacob returned with a shrug. "My parents were before they died, but I was raised in an orphanage, with no religion of any kind. I do not belong to any church. I am unsure what I believe in, but sometimes I, too, feel as if my parents are near."

Miriam busied herself with dipping the gourd once again into the chilled water. The revelation that Jacob did not share her faith bothered her, though she could not tell why.

She searched for words to speak in the place of her pause, but realized she did not know what to say. She ran her tongue over her lips, and turned her eyes from Jacob to the water, sparkling and gurgling over the stones beneath it.

Jacob's eyes must have caught the flash of blue in the same moment she did, for as she leaned forward, curious, wondering if her eyes had tricked her, his hand shot downward into the water, caught the stone, and lifted it dripping into the air.

Miriam's breath of admiration was not lost on Jacob, and he smiled as he surrendered the blue stone into her hand. It was polished to a reflective smoothness, almost perfectly round but for one end of it that tapered to a point, giving it the distinctive shape of a rain drop.

"It's beautiful," she murmured, glancing up at him with a smile, forgetting for a moment her previous awkwardness.

"Like the color of your eyes," he returned, smiling back at her.

Suddenly nonplussed, she glanced away again. "Or Lylith's eyes, that young woman who came into camp a few days ago with her father."

If she had turned her face back to his, she would have seen him frown softly, and lower his eyes to the stone in her hand. "No, only yours," he said softly.

She gulped, and looked down at the winking, shining stone, in the center of her palm, still wet from stream water. In the flashing blue of the stone, she saw the young woman again, mounted regally on her horse, her deep blue eyes fixed on Jacob, and his own eyes on her.

"If you wish, I will make it into a necklace for you." His offer interrupted her thought, which she shook away gladly, turning her eyes from the stone in her hand. Without looking back, she held the stone out toward Jacob, and felt his warm fingers touch her palm as he took it.

She pursed her lips, her jaw tight as she rose to her feet. She did not look back as she started through the trees toward camp while the light slowly faded in the sky.

CHAPTER 6

$\mathcal{M}$iriam lay awake in the dark, staring up at the canvas ceiling that hung limp and unmoving in the heavy night air that had settled over the camp. Outside, the cooking fires were dying slowly, casting weird and mottled shapes against the walls of her tent. Beside her, her brother slept, snuggled warmly in his blanket, a smile of contentment curling his lips, even in sleep.

With a soft groan, she sat up and rubbed her sleepless eyes, wishing she did not have such thoughts scampering so mercilessly through her brain. Again and again she saw the face of the woman on the horse, her long flowing hair, and hopelessly beautiful features gazing with undisguised hunger at Jacob, who returned her gaze steadily, without wavering.

What did it matter, anyway? she demanded of herself. Why should such thoughts torment her and keep her from sleep?

With a sudden burst of angry energy, she scrambled to her feet, and quickly slipped her sandals on, swatting aside the tent door in almost the same motion. The camp was silent, and aside from the flickering of the fires, nothing moved among the tents. The trees were not far beyond the edge of the camp, and she made her way silently toward them and the sound of the burbling brook, drawn there by the image in her mind of Jacob near the stream. Beneath the trees, as she entered, there was almost no light but the firelight that still flickered weakly against her back. She picked her way carefully and silently among the trees, following the laughing splash of the brook that occasionally caught a glimmer of firelight, and guided her way along its edge.

At last she stopped where a fat tree jutted out over the stream. She curled up on the ground beside it, her back against the sturdy bark, her legs pulled up close, listening in the silence to the gurgle of the water, breathing the heavy night air in and out of her lungs, willing herself to let go of her troubling thoughts.

What a fool I am to feel this way, she sighed to herself, letting her head rest against the firm bark. She frowned hard. *And why does having Lylith here bother me at all?* she finished, clenching her teeth in confused frustration.

As she sat hugging her knees in the quiet, she heard a soft flurry above her, and jerked up. Two shadows, belonging to a man and a woman, stood out against the faint light behind them. They were too far away for her to hear their words, but she could hear the resonance of their hushed voices, and Miriam's heart sank into her stomach when she recognized the familiar timbre of Jacob's voice, and Lylith's lighter tones. Miriam's first instinct was to drop her eyes, but she forced herself to sit upright, and watch them.

ಐ

The darkness of the forest surrounded him, embracing him in its heady earthy scents as Jacob paced slowly along the edge of camp, his eyes staring out into the shadowy depths of the forest. The homely light of fires was at his back, and he could still hear some few snatches of speech as the refugees from Lehi settled down for the night. They would be departing tomorrow, at first light, to return to their city, and his thoughts unwittingly moved to Miriam, and how she and her brother would be going with them. Against the blackness of the jungle, he saw her face again in his mind, when he had spoken to her at the edge of the stream. She had seemed shy, almost sad, and he wished he had known why. She was still a child in many ways, and his heart ached for her, sensing only a hint of the burden she bore in being forced to raise herself, as well as her brother, alone. Her eyes, still large with the curiosity of childhood, were also filled with womanly pain and wisdom. Her shoulders, still so small and narrow, carried weight many grown women did not have to bear. And yet she endured so well, at least as far as he could see, unless there was some hidden pain she bore in silence that he was not aware of. Instinctively, he longed to reach out to her, to discover all of her hidden secrets, and somehow take her burdens on himself, enduring them for her. A breath of heavy night air swelled his chest, and he shook his head. There was no way he could do anything for her. He was no longer close enough to her to gain her trust. She would be gone the next day, and he would likely never see her again. The thought filled him with a strange emptiness, and sense of loss, though he knew there was no reason it should. They had become friends once, when they were young, but now, he barely knew her.

A crackle of twigs startled him from his reverie, and he turned, hoping to see Miriam there, sober faced and timid, her large, sweet eyes gazing up at him shyly. But instead, he saw the willowy outline of Lylith approaching, her form etched against the firelight behind her.

"Jacob," she murmured huskily, and in that one word, a sea of memories crashed over him. Memories he had thought he had forgotten threatened to drown him with their suffocating clarity.

"Lylith, you should not be here," he stammered, weakened by her familiar scent, by the press of her cool, sweet hair against his cheek as she came forward and embraced him. His own arms went around her. He had held her like this before, long ago when they were barely more than children. In the sweet blissful days when he had once wanted her more than the air he breathed.

"I know," she sighed against his neck, her breath warm, "but I could not help it. It has been four years since I have seen you. I have been waiting for you to come to me these last few days, but you haven't and I could not wait another moment." She pulled back and gazed pleadingly up at him, her eyes large and plaintive.

Longing swelled up in him, and he wanted to believe she had changed. Surely someone as beautiful as she had become could no longer contain the heart she once had. Surely the softness he saw in her eyes now would not change to hard, haughty stares when she saw beggars at the edge of the market, or gaunt little children who had wandered from the poor parts of town, begging for bread. Gazing down into her gentle eyes now, he wanted to believe it more than anything. She was soft and yielding in his arms, even more than he remembered, for the added years had only given her more beauty. Her hair was soft against his arm, her eyes that danced with the firelight were large and pleading, and her mouth was parted slightly, her lips full and eager.

He gulped, and stepped back, letting her slip from his arms. "Lylith—," he stammered, closing his eyes, and shaking his head to clear it.

"What is it, Jacob?" He felt her approach, and again draw close to him, her small hands, white and uncalloused by work, rested against his chest.

"Lylith, I want to show you something." He took her hand, and led her toward the gurgling stream, nearly to the same spot where he and Miriam had found the blue stone together.

"I was at this stream not long ago," he stuttered slowly, glancing down at the water that flashed against the dim light. Even in the darkness, he could see the stones at the bottom. "I found a stone."

"There are many stones here," Lylith whispered back, her voice suppressing laughter.

"It was a blue stone. Like . . . blue eyes."

Lylith sighed and grasped his hands, pulling him away from the stream. "Jacob, please. Forget this nonsense about blue stones, and look at me."

He sighed, his eyes down, but slowly lifted them as she bid him. She smiled again and drew close, her hands resting against his chest before they slipped up and around his neck, pulling his face down closer to hers.

"Please," he pleaded, taking her hands, and pushing her gently away. "This is not right. I have to think."

"What is there to think about?" she laughed softly, and came close to him again. She grasped his wrists, and pulled him back to face her. He opened his eyes, and his heart grew heavy, seeing that much of the softness was already gone, replaced by a look of impatience. "I am here. What more do you need?"

Jacob's jaw knotted in frustration. "Lylith, please. You should not have left Zarahemla. You should not have come here. Long ago, I told you I could not marry you, because you were not the one for me. Do you not remember that?"

Lylith's voice was like a soothing caress. "Do you say that because you were not born into my class? I do not care. Neither does my father. He wants for me whatever I want." Lylith sighed, "My father is a lower judge. He wants to prove to the common people that he is not above them by giving his daughter to a man who is not of his class. I told him I wanted you, and that pleased him." Lylith smiled, running her small white hand across his chest. "But I do not care why my father wants you for a son-in-law. I only care why I want you as my husband." Her sweet fragrance was making his head spin. He pulled away, but she moved closer.

"Jacob?" she murmured.

He glanced at her, hoping against his better judgement to see gentleness in her eyes, and understanding. Instead, she leaned into him, and rising up onto her toes, kissed him boldly on the mouth. Startled, it took his bumbling hands a few seconds to grab her shoulders and push her back.

"Do not do that, Lylith," he choked. "It is not right. I cannot—"

"Jacob," she protested, "it is you I want. I wanted you from the moment I saw you five years ago at the garrison in Zarahemla when you were a new recruit. I still remember the way you looked when I first saw you. I was fourteen, I remember, and you were barely fifteen. But you looked so much older in your uniform. I did not see any of the other soldiers, only you."

"Would you have noticed me at all, before I joined the army?" Jacob ground out, unable to look at her. "I had no parents, no prospects, or family. No birthright worth mentioning. As I came to know you, I learned that you hate people like me, Lylith! You would never have given me a second glance, except that I was pleasing for you to look at."

"And am I not pleasing in your eyes, Jacob?" she snapped. "Do you not remember the way you felt about me? I almost convinced you to take me as your wife. I knew you wanted to. I tried to tell you, Jacob, my father would have approved." She thrust her bottom lip out into a pout. "But you said no. You acted like a Christian. You pushed me away just as you do now. Are you not a real man? Do you not find me beautiful at all?"

"You are beautiful, and I am just a man, with all the feelings men have," Jacob moaned, turning away from her. "But I do not love you. And you do not love me."

"I do love you, Jacob," she answered, stepping toward him, her presence like a heat at his back. "Anything you ask of me, I would give you."

Jacob gulped, his throat dry. "Lylith, I will not take what is not mine. And I will not—,"

"I am yours, Jacob. My father has already given his consent. That is all you need," Lylith murmured, her voice gentle once again as she came behind him, and circled her slender arms around his waist. "What more is there?"

Jacob turned to face her, pushing her arms back. "You are not the one for me, Lylith," he groaned, his voice mournful.

Lylith suddenly gave a short, derisive laugh, cutting Jacob to his heart. "What has blinded you to me, Jacob? That Lamanite girl?"

Jacob's heart wrenched. "What do you mean?"

"You know what I mean." Her lovely eyes narrowed, and her mouth drew up in a sneer. "The first day I was here, I saw you look at her. She was standing before one of those ragged tents with a mangy little boy beside her."

"Miriam is hardly more than a child. You cannot blame her because I do not love you."

"But she is already very beautiful, even under that dirt," Lylith stabbed back. "Do you truly wish for me to think you have not noticed?"

Jacob looked away, and did not answer.

"Tell me you do not love her," she demanded. "Tell me you have never thought of taking her to wife."

The strength was gone from him, and it took all his will to remain on his feet. "Miriam is her father's daughter. She is truly a princess, just as her father, Aaron, was the son of a king."

"You speak foolishness, Jacob," Lylith scoffed. "She is a dirty commoner."

He lifted his eyes and studied her face. Lylith was still beautiful in spite of the mocking sneer that had seized her features. He had once thought he loved her more than anyone, and that he could never live if he could not have her.

"Leave me," he ordered at last, the words seeming to drain him of his remaining strength. He turned away, staggering against the trunk of a tree.

"I should have known that you would seek after your own kind, Jacob," she hissed at his back. "Now that you have found yourself a woman, do not think I will not find a man who is truly worthy of me."

"I hope you will find a husband, Lylith. And I hope he is a good man who will treat you well. I want you to be happy."

He leaned against the tree, grasping a branch for support as her footsteps moved away and finally disappeared.

Nothing stirred while Miriam watched Jacob and Lylith against the backdrop of firelight. They stood so close together that their shadows had blended into one. Miriam bit her lip as she watched them, unable to take her eyes away. It did not come as a surprise, yet the disappointment was bitter in her mouth when Lylith leaned close, and pressed her lips against Jacob's.

That was all she could endure, and she scrambled up, running blindly back toward camp, crushing twigs and dead brush beneath her feet. She did not heed the branches that caught her hair and scratched her face as she ran, as if fleeing could rid her of the image that had seared itself on her brain. Once she tripped over a root and fell, tearing her dress and skinning a knee against a sharp rock. Heedless of the trickle of blood that ran down her shin, she scrambled up and ran on, not stopping until she had burst through the door of her own tent, her lungs burning. Little Jacob was still asleep where she had left him.

Biting back a sob, she flung herself onto her own pallet again, though she knew sleep would never come to her now.

❧

The firelight flickering off her tent wall was not what kept Esther awake, and she rolled over with a sigh of frustration and clamped an arm over her head in an effort to shut out the low voices of Pachus and his guard, where they sat around the fire. She knew by their muffled, guttural laughter, the base stories and jokes they were trading, and she shuddered, wishing there was more between her and them than the wall of a tent. It had been less than a month since she had begun working in Pachus's household as his daughter's servant, and though she desperately needed the money she earned from him, she was beginning to regret her choice. Pachus's eyes seemed to burn into her wherever she went, and though Lylith was unkind to her, she dreaded being without her, for fear of what Pachus might say or do.

The sudden cessation of their voices brought her head up, and then she heard soft footsteps drawing close.

"Father. Nusair." Lylith's voice was hard and angry, almost a bark.

"Frowning does not become you, Lylith," drawled the man called Nusair, as he and Pachus scrambled clumsily to their feet.

Yawning, Esther rose from her pallet, and parted the tent door enough to see Lylith and the men standing at the fire. Lylith's usually lovely face was etched with frustration and anger.

"Did the man you came to see refuse your charms, Lylith?" Nusair chuckled. He folded his arms across his broad chest and sneered at her. His long sandy hair hung almost to his shoulders, framing his stark, handsome face.

Lylith sniffed, and looked away.

"Hah," he snorted. "You could do better than him, anyway."

She glanced back at him, studying his features, etched in dancing firelight. "Do you think so?"

The man said nothing, but grinned and glanced at Pachus who stared stupidly at his daughter, his face red and swollen from drinking too much.

"What is it, daughter?" Pachus mumbled at last, his voice heavy with drink. "Speak up now."

"I went to speak to him," Lylith sniffed, anger heating her voice. "He sent me away, father!"

Pachus blinked, his glance void of any emotion, but Nusair sneered. "The man is obviously a fool for refusing such a woman as your daughter, Pachus. Her beauty and breeding are beyond compare, and any man who would not want her would have to be blind. He is not worthy to be your son-in-law."

Esther sighed inwardly as Nusair glanced at Lylith, awaiting her reaction to his words. He grinned as her eyes turned to him, filled with insipid, foolish gratitude.

"Lylith," Esther murmured, stepping from her tent into the fire-light. "Come to bed. You are distressed, and sleep will help to calm you."

"No one asked you to speak, Lamanite," Nusair barked sudden-ly, his grin flaring into a glare as he turned toward her. "If Lylith does not want to sleep, she is not required to."

"Nor are you required to, girl," Pachus laughed, his numb stare growing into a pinched expression. His eyes were narrowed into slits, as if they were serpents' eyes. "Come out and join us." A hand darted out and, before Esther could protest, grasped her wrist in a steely grip, and pulled her out into the firelight.

Caught off guard, Esther stumbled, and crashed into Pachus's chest before she regained her balance, and pushed herself back, fighting the hold Pachus had on her.

"I think she likes you, Pachus," Nusair laughed.

Esther's eyes shot to Lylith's. "Lylith!" she pleaded desperately, but the other girl sneered and shrugged, enjoying her discomfort as much as the men were.

Turning back to Pachus, she forced her voice to stay even, hid-ing the fear that beat fast in her throat, and hissed, "Release me, Pachus."

"You live in my house. I pay your wages," Pachus snapped back, his eyes filled with scorn and malice. "You have no right to make any demands of me, Lamanite!"

"I no longer work in your house, Pachus," she snapped, and at last jerked herself out of his arms.

"What are you are saying?" he demanded.

"You are a wicked man, Pachus. I would rather starve than work in your household another day," she answered.

"Then go ahead. Starve," Lylith spat, driving herself between Esther and her father. "For that is what will happen to you now."

"We shall see," Esther returned evenly.

Lylith's eyes narrowed, and she lifted a hand, striking Esther's face with a sharp crack.

Esther's eyes remained level in spite of the sting that burned her cheek, and though her lip trembled, she said nothing as she turned and without preamble, walked sedately into the darkness.

"May peace be with this family." A soft, unobtrusive, feminine voice caused Miriam to lift her head from the roll of scriptures she was reading in her lap before the light of the single lamp she had lit, unable to sleep.

Sighing, rubbing the aching spot on her temple that had begun to throb gently, she parted the curtain, and looked out into the darkness. "Yes, may I help—," she stopped short. "You! Are you not the servant of—,"

"May I come in?" the dark haired girl interrupted, her hands wringing nervously.

"Of course," Miriam sighed, and beckoned her inside.

"Forgive me if I woke you. Yours was the only lamp I could see," the girl began. She looked to be near Miriam's age. Her skin and eyes were dark, and her hair glistened black in the wane lamplight. She struck Miriam as very comely, though she lacked the haughty beauty of her mistress. "I am Esther. I am seeking shelter, at least for just this night." She paused, and her large dark eyes glanced around the spacious tent, which could easily occupy an entire family, though it contained only two people. "I apologize for my unwarranted intrusion. I will understand if it is inconvenient for you."

"No, not at all." Miriam shook her head, surprised, yet pleased by the girl's unfeigned politeness and quiet dignity. "If it is not too bold to ask, what—"

"Lylith's father dismissed me when I would not, uh . . . " Esther blurted a bit too suddenly.

Miriam smiled, and shook her head, indicating that Esther owed her no explanation. "You are welcome to join us, Esther. There is only myself and my younger brother. Please, use my mat, and blanket if you wish."

"Thank you." The girl smiled her gratitude, and her smile heightened her soft prettiness. "But I am used to sleeping on the ground."

"Then at least use my blanket. It is a warm night. I do not need it."

"Miriam. Miriam, I must speak to you. Are you awake?" The whispered voice outside shot in at her like a barbed arrow.

The voice had been Jacob's, and she groaned as she turned to the door and parted the curtain. She saw his silhouette against the night, and glanced away, uncertain if she could contain the confusing emotions that resurfaced when she saw him.

"Miriam, is something wrong?" Jacob murmured, putting a hand on her arm, his voice suddenly gentle.

Miriam studied his eyes, soft in the firelight, and could only see again, the image of him with Lylith in the forest. She opened her mouth, but she could not speak, finding her throat impossibly choked with emotion.

"Miriam, I have made the stone we found into a necklace for you." He held up a thin leather string. A tiny hole had been bored painstakingly through the narrow end of the stone, and a leather thong had been looped through, its ends hanging loosely over Jacob's hand. The drop-shaped stone dangled, glittering like a gem, even in the darkness.

She pulled away from him, as if his touch caused her physical pain. "It is late, Jacob and I am tired. And surely there is another you would rather give that to."

"Miriam," Jacob's voice was startled, pleading, but she ignored it as she ducked her head and disappeared back into the tent.

"Miriam, please," he called from beyond the door. "What do you mean—,"

"Good night, Jacob," she interrupted. "Do you not have your duties tonight? Should you not be at your post, instead of seeking out the company of young women who would rather be sleeping?"

Beyond the door there was no sound, then after a long moment, the crunching of feet moving away over the soft soil, faded into silence.

Esther stood in the semi darkness, her hands clasped tightly, her dark eyes large in the lamplight. "Who—?"

"Jacob," Miriam groaned darkly. She collapsed tiredly onto her pallet, tossing her blanket to Esther in the same motion.

Esther took a step toward her. "He seemed kind. Why—,"

"He is kind," Miriam echoed. "Unbelievably kind." She tucked her legs close into her chest, and buried her face against her knees. "And in love with someone else," she mumbled.

Sensing her wish to be left alone, Esther nodded understanding, retreated to the darkest corner of the tent, and said nothing more.

CHAPTER 7

25TH YEAR OF JUDGES

Silence hung heavy in the air as the young man waited, having made his request clear. Seated in the carved stone throne of the chief judge, Pahoran appraised the younger man, and let out a long breath. Pahoran was not an old man, but a hint of gray was already showing in his brown hair. Nephihah, his father, who had been the last chief judge, had died less than a year before, and Pahoran had been chosen to take his place. Now, as inexperienced as he was, Pahoran had the responsibility of handling this new radical group that seemed to have sprung from nowhere, made up mostly of members of higher classes. He sighed, remembering his childhood when King Mosiah, the last great Nephite king, had proposed that the Nephites choose their leaders, rather than letting chance dictate who the ruler was. In this way, as long as the majority of citizens was righteous, their leaders would be righteous as well. Though Pahoran had only been a child then, he understood, and grasped the new idea eagerly, thrilled that he could have a voice in his own destiny.

"Do you have your petition with the signatures, then?" Pahoran finally asked. He made no effort to hide the fatigue in his voice as he reached out an expectant hand. His eyes were locked with the younger man's in a silent, rigid battle.

"Certainly," the younger man smirked, stepping forward, and stiffly handing over the sheaf of paper. He stepped back, smiling confidently. "I think you will find it very adequate."

Pahoran broke the deadlock gaze to examine the names. Men's signatures lined every page—the stark, black strokes of ink bold and mocking.

"The lower judges voted this petition down five-to-one and you have brought it to me because my vote could overrule theirs," he said, returning the papers to the young man's hands.

"Yes, sir." The young man grinned, his eyes exposing his suppressed hostility.

"Tell me, if I were to make this change," Pahoran sighed, "would you desire to be king yourself? Or are you another man's political puppet?"

"No, sir. Of course not." Nusair smiled, with feigned humility. "You are a great leader already, and if you were to become king, you could achieve so much more than you can now. You would no longer have to deal with the inefficiency of lower judges, but could make laws or change them according to your own pleasure."

Pahoran smiled tiredly, and leaned forward. His eyes flashed from the young man before him, to the two guards standing at the door, their eyes focused on Nusair's back. "You do not have my vote," he said at last, his eyes boring into Nusair's. "As a free citizen of this nation, I will not relinquish my freedoms, and I will not sign away the freedom of my fellow citizens." He nodded wordlessly toward the door.

Nusair's eyes narrowed, and he shot Pahoran one last indignant glance as he pivoted around, and marched through the doors the guards pulled open for him, and was gone.

Pahoran sagged back against the cold stone of his throne, as weary as if he had been through a battle, and dropped his face into his hand. "I have not heard the last from him," he muttered to himself.

℣

"I see three of them," Helam whispered, the sweat forming rivulets down his mud-caked face.

"I see them, as well," Jacob answered back, wiping the heel of his hand across his eyes. He glanced at his friend, seeing the sand-colored hair plastered with sweat and mud against his scalp, at the sky-colored eyes that continued to blink in a futile attempt to keep the sweat out, and chuckled to himself before he turned back to gaze down the slope at the Lamanite camp below them.

The two Nephites lay flat against the surface of the sun-beaten ridge. Their faces, arms and legs were plastered with dark mud, and their foliage-covered clothes hid them from any stray glance that might wander up from the camp.

"Those Amalickiahites drive the Lamanites as if they are slaves," Helam added, a hint of frustration in his voice. "They must be preparing for something."

Helam referred to the feverish activity of the rest of the camp. In open clearings, copper-skinned warriors battled back and forth with wooden swords, and forests of practice arrows peppered wooden targets. Other figures scurried busily, doing other unnumbered tasks as frantically as an army of ants.

"Perhaps they kicked a hornet's nest by mistake." Jacob allowed a light chuckle to come to his throat as he scratched a lump of charcoal into a ragged book he pulled from beneath his armor. "But I doubt it. Let's go."

They turned away from the ridge, inching along the ground slowly. Their tired muscles moved rhythmically as they crawled into the steamy shadows of the jungle.

Rising to their feet, they pushed silently through the undergrowth until they reached a wild animal trail, and started northward at a swift trot. Reports of such activity were coming in from other scouts in the southern-most cities on the east coast, Moroni as well as Nephihah, and the reports were no different in the cities on the western coast. The Lamanites were clearly planning for conflict.

Jacob smiled to himself and wiped another hand across his brow. His forehead would be glistening with sweat, and his face red with exertion by now, as Helam's was, but they would push themselves hard, though they still had many hours left to go.

The sun was sinking with a reddish glow in the west, bringing the welcome veil of night, offering him better cover, as well as cooling night winds that helped to ease his discomfort some. He would be back to the borders of Moroni before sunrise at this pace. His lips, still tasting mud, smiled. His limbs ached, and his breathing was strained, but Jacob was content. Marches like this brought back good memories. He could almost feel the little girl's tiny, trusting hand in his, her sweet lilting voice questioning him on this thing or that. He laughed inside himself, contemplating the wonder of how time changed things. Miriam would be nearly fifteen now, and little Jacob would have started school and would be learning the law that all young Christian boys began at his age.

"Jacob," Helam's voice murmured in the quiet. "You're not thinking of that girl, Miriam, again, are you?"

Jacob grinned, and glanced back at Helam. "Why would you suspect that?"

Helam chuckled softly. "I know you too well, friend."

"I barely knew her," Jacob muttered, frustration in his voice.

"That is not keeping you from thinking of her constantly," Helam chortled. "I can understand why. That other girl, that Lylith you used to know when we were in Zarahemla all those years ago, wasn't nearly as pretty."

Jacob's expression grew thoughtful as Helam continued. "Perhaps Miriam is thinking of you as well. Write to her when we get back, or request leave, and go visit her! We can travel together for a while when I go to visit my wife and son in Gideon. Tell her how you feel about her, and ask her if she feels the same."

"But why should she want to have anything to do with me?" Jacob moaned. "She seemed so distant the night before she left to go to Lehi. And she did not speak to me at all the day she left."

"Then perhaps it would be wise to find out why."

Jacob heaved a sigh, and Helam clapped his shoulder again. "Take my advice, friend. At least write to her when we return."

Jacob grumbled, and nodded at last. Helam grinned, and the two continued on in companionable silence.

The shadowed world seemed to pass like a dream to him. But when the first golden glints of dawn kissed the sky, he shook himself back to the present and hurried faster. In the distance, the sunlight touched off the alabaster walls and the high, spiked barricades of the city set between jagged barbs of mountains.

"Hey, we're almost home!" Helam grinned, clapping Jacob on the back. "In only another hour we'll—,"

His words were cut off sharply by the hiss of a flying arrow, and a moment later, a muffled grunt of air burst from Helam's lungs, and he toppled forward, gasping.

"Helam!" Jacob cried, whirling back, and dropping to his knees beside his friend as a second arrow whizzed past his head.

He stared in horror at the arrow protruding from his friend's side, at the bright red blood already flecking Helam's mouth.

"Jacob, run," he grunted, his eyes bright and pleading. "Lamanite spies—you must—make it back with what we have learned."

"I won't leave you, friend," Jacob growled, stripping his own bow from his back, and kneeling protectively over Helam's body. He nocked an arrow, and drew the string back to his cheek, searching the dense growth around them, then whirled at a faint movement to his right, and released the string.

A deep grunt, and the heavy topple of a body told him he had hit his mark. His next arrow was drawn and nocked as a brown shadow whirred and faded from his vision.

There had been two, he guessed. He had gotten one, but the other had fled. Gritting his teeth in frustration, he relaxed the string, and returned the arrow to its quiver.

"Helam, I got one, but the other escaped," he murmured, moving back to look down at his friend. "I wish I had gotten them both. There is no way to know how much they saw of our—"

Helam lay prostrate on the trail, one arm resting across his chest, his head tilted to one side. His eyes were still open, his sandy hair damp with sweat and mud.

"Helam?" Jacob whispered, fitting two fingers to his friend's throat. The flesh was already beginning to grow cold.

"Helam, no," Jacob demanded, as if by ordering him, he could bring him to life again. But he did not move, or respond in any way to Jacob's words.

"No, Helam," Jacob repeated, but now his words were weak, pleading, half sobbing. "Please."

A gentle wind stirred Helam's sandy hair, brushing it silently across his forehead, and Jacob began to weep.

☙

The night was almost pitch black, and without the torch he carried with him, he would not have found his way. Pachus had never been in this part of the city with its narrow, twisting streets and black, shadowed alleys.

The houses, ancient and decrepit, crowded each other, dark and silent as crypts as they pressed over the narrow streets. Thick, tangible steam rose silently from open sewer ditches like tormented ghosts ascending from the Abyss. His heart pounded in his chest, and he panted desperately in the hot muggy air. He continued on, his determination and hunger for power outweighed his fear, forcing him to continue.

Finally, he stopped, eyeing the door of one of the dark houses. If he had not missed any of the turns, this would be the right place. He held his torch up close to the door, and noticed a secret mark etched into the wood. He laughed to himself, and turned his torch upside down, crushing it out in one of the fetid puddles at his feet.

He tapped softly, glancing around nervously as he did. He waited only a few seconds before he heard mumbling inside, followed by the slow creak of the door as it opened.

Light leaked weakly out into the narrow street as Nusair poked his head out, grinning as he recognized Pachus, and held the door wide, allowing Pachus to squeeze through.

The room he entered was small and cramped, the air filled with the smoke of a meager fire. Pachus followed Nusair to the fire, grunting with effort as he sat on the ground and folded his legs beneath him. "Why did he not take it?"

"The man is the chief judge." Nusair explained calmly, his grin unchanging as he stared at Pachus across the flames. "If he changes the law, he loses his position. He does not want to give up the people's power to vote. Otherwise, he loses power himself."

"What shall we do now?" Pachus scowled.

"We will do what we must," Nusair sneered as he picked up a crude obsidian knife, and studied it so that the light from the fire glinted off its shiny black blade.

Pachus frowned. "We must not kill him, not now. It would be too obvious."

"Very well," Nusair grunted. He lifted a sheaf of papers, and thrust it toward Pachus with a proud grin. "Perhaps these men will support you if you speak to them. You might recognize some of these names."

Pachus grunted almost cheerfully as he flipped through, and paused as he recognized several names. "I know those men."

"They are willing to help us form a rebellion against Pahoran. That is how we dethrone that pompous judge without taking a knife to his throat."

"Good. I am pleased with your work," Pachus grunted as he rose. "I will see you here the next time we meet." He turned and waddled to the door, opened it and faded like an apparition into the night.

෪

Beside the rain that drummed gently on the roof slats above, the barracks were silent and dark, and empty except for a single figure seated against the wall beside the door, reading intently from a scrap of fine, thin paper. His form was lean and powerful, but his young chiseled face showed fatigue.

Jacob's heart was empty and cold, and he felt alone, more than he ever had in his life, unworthy of everything he had ever wanted. His life was worth nothing anymore, except perhaps to die at the hands of the Lamanites. Perhaps death in battle would redeem him from whatever he had done to deserve this.

"Jacob?" The voice in the silence startled him, and Jacob jerked, looking up into his captain's face.

"Sir?" He asked, a harsh cutting edge to his voice.

"Our church has finished, and I have no other duties. May I join you?"

Jacob grunted with a nod, wishing he had not sounded so sharp. "I have no duties either, sir. You can come in if you wish."

Teancum entered, muffling the sound of the rain as he pulled the wooden door closed. He hung his wet cloak on a hook, and seated himself against the wall beside Jacob. He folded his legs under him, and dropped his eyes to his hands, studying them intently as Jacob continued to read. The captain was a lean, darkly tanned man, and had the eyes of one who had seen much, and understood much. Aside from the strands of silver beginning to pepper his dark hair, he looked no different than the younger men he commanded. His arms were those of one who was skilled in the use of a sword and shield, muscling his strong frame. They were only outmatched by his powerful legs that never seemed to tire, constantly able to out-train and out-work men much younger than him. He looked up as Jacob spoke to him, a kind interest in his dark, wise eyes, which carefully masked the abiding pain of his own personal loss, which he kept locked in his own heart.

"Sir, surely you can find something better on your Sabbath to do than sit on the cold floor with a mute for company."

"I cannot think of anything else I would rather do," Teancum smiled, not looking up.

Jacob fell silent again but suddenly looked up. "Sir, may I ask you a question? Of a personal nature?"

Teancum glanced up and nodded soberly.

"Sir," Jacob implored, glancing again at the paper in his hand, "your wife and children—,"

He paused as Teancum stiffened almost imperceptibly. But Teancum shook his head, and nodded for him to continue.

"Sir, where did they go, after they were killed in the Lamanite raid on your village?"

"I buried them on one of the hills outside our town."

"But sir," Jacob was quick to cut in. "Where did their souls go?"

"Oh." Teancum nodded, understanding now what Jacob was asking. "To the spirit world."

"I wish that is what I believed," Jacob groaned. "I was raised in an orphanage. I had no spiritual guidance as a child. My parents were members of your church before they died, but I was never taught the things they believed in. I was never baptized a Christian."

Teancum pursed his lips thoughtfully but did not speak.

Jacob lifted the paper slightly. "This letter. It—," He squinted hard at the floor. "It is from Helam's wife, thanking me for the letter I sent her." Without looking up, he thrust it toward his captain, who took it gingerly, glancing at him silently before he began to read.

"She is alone now, with a small child, and soon to give birth to another one. I do not know how she endures, why she would write a letter so—," The words froze in his throat, and he tightened his jaw, blinking fiercely.

"So hopeful?" Teancum finished quietly, glancing up from the letter.

Jacob nodded silently, and took back the proffered letter. "She is so certain that she will see him again, someday. I wish I had such surety."

Teancum smiled lightly and did not speak.

Jacob furrowed his brow. "Though I was never taught, I some-how always believed that there was some benevolent god ruling in the heavens. That there was a reason why my heart felt peace when I did not give in to worldly desires. I have never known it, though. Not as you do. Not as Helam's wife does."

Teancum drew in a deep breath. "For you to know and recog-nize the voice of the Spirit in your heart, though you were never taught what it was, is to be admired."

Jacob's shoulders sagged. "My parents were Christians before they died. I was never taught of Christ as they were, or baptized, but perhaps a part of them is alive in me."

"Those who love us, and whom we love, are never truly gone from us." Teancum clapped his hand on Jacob's shoulder. "Your par-ents left you the birthright of their righteous lives. And if they loved you as I loved my children, they would watch over you, no matter where they were."

Jacob dropped his eyes to the ground. The sharp, angular lines of his face grew even tighter as the sinews of his jaw rhythmically contracted and relaxed while he pondered Teancum's words. "I always believed that, but it brings me comfort to hear such words from someone else."

A grin flickered across his mouth as he glanced into Teancum's weathered face, and his kind, gray eyes. He had known Captain Teancum from the first days he had enlisted, and he had always imagined him to be the father he had never known.

Teancum's face returned the grin as he spoke. "You say you were never taught as your parents were, when you were young. But it is not too late to learn now. If you would allow me, I would be happy to teach you what I know of Christ."

Teancum saw the tears spring into Jacob's eyes, and lowered his face, pretending not to notice.

Jacob took a deep breath. "I would like you of all people, to teach me, Sir."

CHAPTER 8

*T*he sun had long since disappeared from the sky, leaving nothing but a trace of gray in the west. But one light in a window of the judgement hall continued to burn brightly, silhouetting a figure that leaned on the window frame, gazing thoughtfully out into the night.

Only a few days before, the news had come from spies in the south that the Lamanites had organized themselves and were marching forward with Amalickiah himself at their head. Half the city it seemed, had gathered in the plaza before the government building to protest the imminent war. They claimed it could be avoided if only there was a king to buffer relations with the Lamanites, and to open correspondence with them. They had made it apparent that they would refuse to contribute to the war effort if they were asked.

"I do not know what to do, Micha," Pahoran groaned, hearing the door open behind him, and seeing Micha, the captain of the guard, waiting respectfully for his attention. "I give my entire life for these people, and it seems as if suddenly half the city does not care any more. They are happy that the Lamanites are coming. That is something I cannot fathom."

"Do not forget the others who would do anything for their freedom, Sir. They support you, and so do I," Micha murmured in the quiet.

"But the people who want a king." Pahoran gestured with disgust at the darkness beyond the window. "They make it impossible for those of us who desire freedom to defend ourselves."

"Chief Captain Moroni[4] has thought on the same thing." Micha stepped closer. "So he sent you an epistle."

Pahoran glanced behind him into the shadow where the guard Micha stood, and noticed a younger, leaner figure standing erect beside the larger, brawnier man. He wore the uniform of a courier, and his chest rose and fell heavily.

"From Captain Moroni, sir." The young man held out a parchment, set with Moroni's seal.

Pahoran nodded and broke the seal, reading down the page. Out of the corner of his eye, he watched the young man who waited, tired, though he tightened his jaw and hid it well. Pahoran thought of his own son, his oldest, young Pahoran, who was nearly at the age to enlist, and a smile touched his mouth. If he had the power to keep it so, his son would have a free nation to defend.

"Wait, and I will send a response back with you."

The young man nodded as Pahoran moved to a desk near the wall where paper and writing tools were. He sat before it, and spread a sheet of paper before him, then dipped a quill into a clay well of ink.

He glanced up once at the young man who waited expectantly, then began. "I, Pahoran, who am the chief governor of this land, send this epistle unto chief captain Moroni." The scratching of his quill was the only sound in the quiet room. "I have read your epistle and delight in your desire to maintain the cause of liberty. If it were requisite to allow these kingmen[5] to rule over us as they wish and to ally themselves with the Lamanites, we would subject ourselves to them. But God does not command us to subject ourselves to our enemies, but that we should trust him, and he will deliver us. Therefore, come with all speed, and assist us that we might put an end to this contention that we may compel these dissenters to defend their country, or to be put to death. Fear not, my beloved brother, for God will deliver all those who stand fast in this liberty wherewith God hath made us free."

Pahoran drew a shaking breath, quickly reading over what he had written. "And now I close my epistle to my beloved brother, Moroni."

The room was silent as he rolled the letter, and closed it with the seal of the chief judge, then handed it to the courier.

"May God go with you, and be your strength," Pahoran said to the young man.

"Thank you, sir." He saluted, then rushed out the door, his footsteps fading in the empty hall.

As the echo of his footfalls disappeared, Pahoran turned back to the window.

"If they would not fight against us, we would leave them alone," Micha stated, sensing Pahoran's troubled feelings. "We must end the contention, or the Lamanites will overrun us."

Pahoran nodded. "But it is painful to punish those who ought to be our comrades."

Micha nodded and Pahoran glanced again out the window, but jerked his head back around as three sets of quiet feet echoed softly in the stillness as they came closer to his office. Micha peered out the door, his hand moving slowly to the hilt of his sword.

Pahoran watched, curious, as a smile appeared on Micha's face. Then three boys entered the room. Their eyes were wide as they glanced around in the dark, empty space.

"Abba," the first one, a tall, fourteen year old, began. "We came to see how you were."

"Boys?" Pahoran grinned, and moved across the room, catching two of them in a sturdy hug.

"Mother sent us," said nine-year-old Pacumeni, his blue eyes luminous in his golden face.

Pahoran stepped past his first two sons, and embraced his son Paanchi. The freckle-faced twelve-year-old endured it, then backed away, glancing about, dispassioned and bored.

Pahoran studied the boy, and shook his head sadly. "Tell your mother and sister and your other brothers that I will come soon. Tell your mother I love her."

"Yes, Abba." The oldest and youngest boys grinned and hugged him again. They trotted from the room, and Paanchi followed them, muttering under his breath.

"Perhaps it is time to join my family," Pahoran mused as his sons' quiet footsteps faded. "And you must be exhausted as well, friend."

Micha grinned wryly. "Never, sir."

Pahoran smiled, gathered up his satchel of papers, and started down the hall after the fading tapping, with Micha at his shoulder.

cs

"Sir, you wanted to see me?" Jacob stood stiffly, waiting for a response from his captain.

Teancum looked up from his map, and beckoned him inside. "Yes, come in."

Jacob nodded his consent, and closed the wooden door behind him.

"You know Moroni routed the kingmen," the captain said, his eyes down as he made small marks with a quill.

"Yes, sir." The battle had not lasted long. Men driven only by hunger for power were no match in the end for Moroni and his seasoned troops who fought for a better cause.

Teancum nodded slowly.

Jacob's shoulders drooped a little, but he quickly regained his composure, and straightened up again. "Is there anything else, sir?"

The captain looked up at him for a moment. "How has your life been since your baptism?"

Jacob's spirits returned, and he smiled. "You work me as hard as before, sir." Teancum gave a wry smile. "But I can feel a difference with the spirit in my life. And I feel more hopeful of the future, whatever it may bring."

Teancum's eyes crinkled. Gruffly, he brushed a hand over his face and muttered, "That will be all. You are dismissed."

Jacob smiled and nodded as he straightened himself, saluted, and shut the door behind him.

It was amazing now, how difficulties seemed so much smaller, he thought as he made his way outside. Even the coming of the Lamanites did not seem so overwhelming now. Yet the thought made him nervous, because in spite of his newly acquired faith, he was not immune to death. Death, he did not fear, but what he would not have if death claimed him too soon, did frighten him. For a moment, his thoughts strayed to Miriam, glad that she was safe in Lehi. He remembered her face, wondering how it had changed in a year, wondering if she would be glad to see him if they met again, and how she would receive him. He glanced thoughtfully at the ground as he stepped outside into the morning sunlight, but his daydream was cut short as the sharp cry of a conch shell echoed down from one of the watch towers.

Jacob tensed at the sudden alarm that shot through him, knowing what the signal meant. Disbelieving, he rushed to the wall, and scaled the ladder to the parapet. Sure enough, as he squinted hard, shading the morning sun from his eyes, he could see that they were there, out over the southern bluffs, brownish forms moving over hills, trickling through the jungle like a poisonous river. *Not now!* his mind pleaded. *Because of the contention with the kingmen, our forces aren't sufficient!* He released a disgusted breath, slid back down the ladder to the ground, and sprinted to the gate in time to see his squad clambering to their places on the wall. They were as startled as he was, but he saw with a touch of pride, that they were ready for battle. There was, however, the familiar look of fear that creased each face, and that Jacob felt searing his own heart.

"Lieutenant!" A shout addressed him from across the compound, and he turned. Teancum beckoned to him as he buckled his sword belt, rushing toward the gate at the same time, several soldiers flanking him. "Are your men at their stations?" The captain demanded, pulling to a stop as he rushed to the gate, glancing up and down the wall as masses of soldiers flocked past them.

"Yes, sir," Jacob returned.

Teancum nodded, tight-lipped, and looked around him at Jacob and the other officers who stood waiting, and spoke slowly. "At the pace that they are coming, the Lamanites will be to the city in less than an hour. You know Amalickiah has no mercy. He cares nothing for his own men, and will send them at our walls in uncountable numbers, and with our insufficient numbers, we are disadvantaged. But we have truth on our side. We fight for our freedom, and," Teancum's voice wavered, "our wives and children. May God be with us."

Jacob and the others nodded grimly, and each went his own way. Jacob scrambled up to the top of the wall. From this distance, it looked as if the very ground itself was moving toward him from the thick ranks of marching Lamanites. He had never been in such a battle as he could see was inevitable today. He tore his eyes away from the approaching armies, and glanced around him at the men along the wall, and out over the fortifications.

One of his men stood by, an arrow nocked on a bowstring, a quiet fear behind his eyes.

"All will be well, Kib," Jacob grated, his own hand gripping a bow tightly.

"Yes, sir." Kib's eyes did not agree with his words.

Jacob nodded, too involved in his own thoughts to hear what Kib had said, now that the wild shouts of the Lamanites had begun to reach his ears.

Several minutes passed, but they only seemed to be a few seconds to Jacob. Sooner than he wished, the swarming masses of dark bodies were close enough he could see individual faces. He had finished a prayer with his small squad, the first and most sincere prayer he had offered out loud in his entire life, and his eyes were wet. The unnatural howl that swirled up from the sea of Lamanites below him, however, dried his eyes.

There was, somewhere among the swirling mass, a huge tree trunk that floated along, on the current of brown bodies. It was cut to a wedge on one end. Jacob moved near the gate, his arrow ready on the string. He crouched low now behind the ridge of a parapet, and waited. They were no more than a hundred paces away, and it would not be much longer. Perhaps if he died today, he would see his parents once again. He closed his eyes and tried to picture them, wishing that he had a memory of them. Then his mind shifted again, and he pictured Miriam's face. She lived a mere day's journey away, yet in the space of a year, he had not seen her. In the sum of his life, he had known her not many days, yet he thought of her often, finding himself almost giddy as he studied her face in his mind. He smiled in spite of himself, remembering the deep blue of her eyes, and the curve of her mouth when she smiled. A strange tenderness stirred within him as he imagined the changes of her appearance now that she was a year older, and he thought on it for a long moment, wondering.

ଔ

"Ah, my poor back!" Esther's girlish voice mumbled in a tone of playful complaint. "Miriam, how is it that you seem so tireless?"

A girl in the bloom of young womanhood straightened her back from her work, and surveyed the speaker beside her. Miriam's dark hair was bound loosely, her braid glistening in a long rope down her back. A few short wisps of unruly hair, too wild to be pulled back from her face, caught in the warm wind that played across her skin as the sickle in her hand dropped limply to her side. Esther's hair was bound back as well, though shimmering black and smooth as silk within its braid. A damp sheen of sweat rested on her soft brown skin, but from Esther's smile, she seemed hardly to care.

"Esther, you say that only to make me feel better," Miriam teased in return, flashing her friend a small grin. "Ever since we came here to live in Lehi, you have worked far more than your own share, and you do it so tirelessly, I sometimes wonder if you only rest to keep the others of us from feeling ashamed of our own paltry weakness."

Esther snorted softly, and gently swatted Miriam's arm. "I do that only because I already owe you and all the people of this town so much." Her smile softened, and her warm brown eyes took on a deeper look as she added, "When my parents died, I never thought I could ever feel as if I belonged anywhere. But now with you, I have found a sister. And your little brother has become my own. I have family I did not have before, Miriam. such a thing I could never repay."

Miriam smiled at Esther's soft words and the warm look within the depths of her eyes. "Esther," she offered, with a shake of her head, "surely you know that the gift of your friendship leaves me indebted to *you*."

"Pah. Enough arguing. Let us agree that we are even then, shall we?" Esther scoffed with good humor, throwing up a hand, and shaking her head with an expression that made Miriam laugh.

"Very well," Miriam chuckled, squeezing Esther's hand as the other girl reached out and caught Miriam's hand within her own.

"Oh," Esther breathed, her expression suddenly changing as she lifted her hand to shield her eyes from the sun, and glanced over Miriam's shoulder to the far edge of the field. "I wonder what your brother wants?"

Miriam turned, glancing in the direction Esther gazed across the waving stalks of grain, to see the figure of her brother upon the edge of the field, gesturing excitedly. Furrowing her brow, she raised one hand, screening the sunlight from her eyes, and her brother's slight figure became clearer as he waved his hand about, clutching a small with object.

"Miriam, Esther!" his excited voice cried out to them across the wide field. "Look what I have! Come see!"

"He has a letter," Miriam breathed in wonder, then turned to Esther, her mouth curving into a smile.

"Should we find out who sent it?" Her friend smiled encouragingly.

"Of course!" Miriam chirped as she slipped the curved tool into the sash at her waist. Together, they darted across the field behind other harvesters who were bent over the flaxen grain, cutting the stalks cleanly from the ground with smooth, even stokes. The stubble glistened golden, stretching in a long carpet behind them.

"Who is that letter from, little Jacob?" Esther gasped as they reached the excited boy, their breath labored.

"From the city of Moroni, to our south." Young Jacob smiled, handing the scroll of paper to Miriam. "From Jacob."

"Jacob?" Miriam breathed, glancing down at the scroll in her hand, running her fingers almost reverently over the roughly beaten bark paper. "Why would he—?"

"Oh," Esther breathed thoughtfully, "this is the same Jacob from Moroni's camp, is he not?"

Miriam nodded. "The same one who found us when we were small, and brought us to our parents."

"He appears to be as thoughtful of you as you are of him. You speak of him and think about him constantly, Miriam. Perhaps he thinks of you just as often." Esther gave an affectionate tug to Miriam's braid. "Open it, and find out what it says."

Miriam laughed, feeling the warm blush that rose to her cheeks. "We barely knew him, really." Miriam unrolled the letter, and settled back on the sloped edge of the field to read, studiously ignoring Esther's eyes.

She barely heard Esther and little Jacob settling beside her as her eyes devoured the dark characters that covered the page, unable to still the rush of emotions that caused her heart to hammer within her.

"What does he say?" young Jacob asked at last, his arms wrapped around his knees, rocking back and forth with impatience.

"He was baptized." She lifted her eyes from the letter, her fingers gripping the edges of the paper to keep it from rolling in on itself. Then, when she realized that her eyes were swimming in tears, she dropped her face and studied the earth with hard intensity. "He thought he should write to me, and let me know. I am glad he did. I am so happy for him."

Esther laughed, "Of course you are. Now, you can marry him."

Miriam returned her friend's smile even as her heart wrenched. "Jacob would never have me. I am a child in his eyes. If he felt otherwise, he would come to see me. Besides, he has Lylith."

Esther rolled her eyes. "We have spoken of this before, Miriam. I knew Lylith. She is nothing compared to you. Perhaps you should write Jacob back and ask him what his true feelings are."

"I could not do that. I am nothing compared to her—,"

Esther smiled, and opened her mouth to speak, but as her eyes looked beyond Miriam's shoulder and focused there, she stopped and the smile dropped from her face. "What is that?" Her brown eyes widened.

Miriam turned her head to the southeast, shading her eyes from the glare of the late morning sun. In the distance, a black cloud billowed into the sky, tall and shapeless, like a sinister apparition.

Her heart caught in her throat as Miriam realized from the distance and direction that it came from near the city of Moroni.

"Judge Lehi must see this," Esther whispered, her voice strained as she scrambled to her feet.

Miriam turned and glanced toward the threshing floor where the men were, the town's chief judge somewhere among them. Esther was already hurrying toward the group, and young Jacob was scrambling behind.

"Wait," Miriam called weakly, hoping for a moment that if they said nothing, the smoke would disappear, like the memory of a bad dream. But when she glanced back, and saw that the billowing smoke had only increased, she reluctantly rose to her feet as well, and followed after them.

CHAPTER 9

"Haran, I must stay here, with you," a woman protested, struggling against her husband's grip as he bodily lifted her and set her in the wagon beside Esther, Miriam, and little Jacob who clung to Miriam's arm. "I cannot go to Morianton without you."

"You cannot stay here, Dinah," Haran objected, gently prying her fingers from the sleeve of his tunic.

"The city of Morianton is more fortified, and safer for you. The other women and children from Lehi will be there. You will not be alone."

"I will be alone without you, no matter how many people there are," Dinah wailed as the wagon lurched and began to move outside the city gate.

Haran gulped as she said this, and his eyes glistened with tears, too proud to fall. "I will be with you wherever you are, Dinah," he managed to call out, his voice catching roughly.

At his words, the woman broke into heart wrenching sobs, and would have leaped out of the wagon, but for Esther who gripped her shoulders tightly to hold her in her place.

"I love you, Dinah," Haran's sad voice echoed back as the gates boomed shut.

Dinah continued to sob hysterically as the wagon slowly trundled along the dirt road toward the city of Morianton, her head buried in her arms as Esther tried vainly to soothe her, stroking her hair and crooning softly as if Dinah were a child. The other women and children who sat about in the box of the wooden wagon gazed mournfully at Dinah.

Miriam sat by herself stroking her brother's quiet head, and nursing her own wounded feelings. Her heart felt bruised and broken, and the tightness of her throat choked her, but her tears had dried. She sat silently, her legs pulled into her chest, and her forehead resting against her knees as the words that Judge Lehi had said weeks before echoed in her ears as if he had spoken them only moments ago.

"It was swift." His voice had been emotionless and hollow. "They lost nearly half the men, and the city fell to the Lamanites. The survivors fled to Nephihah. For those of you with loved ones in Moroni, I pray that they escaped to Nephihah, but I cannot give you false hopes."

Miriam glanced up, her eyes searching the faces of those around her, each one lost in her own thoughts, each one drained of emotion. For a month now, they had lived each day with an unbearable pall of gloom hanging over them as each moment they expected an attack from the Lamanites. Fear for their husbands and fathers as well as for themselves hung heavily in their hearts.

Shaking herself, she drew enough strength into her limbs to straighten her back, and drape an arm around Esther's shoulder as Dinah's sobs finally began to subside.

"Is she any better?" Miriam asked sullenly.

"I hope," Esther sniffled. "She must be strong, as the rest of us must be, in order to last through this." Her voice was close to tears.

The jungle closed in overhead, submerging the creaking wagon into the depths of shadow, and the occupants shifted nervously, each one lifting her head, tuning her ears for any sound.

Miriam as well as everyone else was keenly aware of their exposure and helplessness if the Lamanites were to attack now. But the trip promised to be short, and each one kept it in her heart that the Lamanites would surely not attack today, after having waited for so long in the city of Moroni. Surely today would not be the day that they would come.

Dinah's sobbing had finally weakened to exhausted sniffles, and Esther's tightened frame relaxed and drooped against Miriam's shoulder. Miriam leaned her own head against Esther's brown hair, and closed her eyes, picturing Jacob's face in her mind.

She saw him again, his face shining in the morning sun as he had walked beside her when she was a child, before he had delivered her to her parents. The angled lines of his face sharply drew out light and shadow across his features. Her memory shifted, and his face appeared as it had been the night she had spoken to him at the edge of the stream. Light danced off of his features, bringing him in and out of focus, distorting his image, clouding her vision. Smoke filtered past the image in her mind, and she fought to bring his face into focus, but when it came clear to her, she cried out, and with a jerk, her eyes flew open.

"Miriam!" Esther gasped, her eyes filled with concern.

"Oh, forgive me," Miriam apologized, realizing she had been sleeping. "I had a bad dream."

They were closer now to Morianton; within a few minutes they would top the ridge that led down to the city, and she breathed out a sigh, wishing to forget the image of Jacob that would not leave her thoughts. Clouds of smoke had surrounded him, and when she had reached him, he had been crumpled on the ground, his eyes closed, his face pale with death.

A mild incline led up to the ridge over which they would be able to see the city of Morianton, and Miriam forced her thoughts back on the present. Soon they would be safe again within stone walls. Trees parted, and warm sunlight streamed around them as they crested the ridge.

From here, both cities were visible, and everyone turned to glance once more at the city of Lehi.

As their eyes focused on the distant city, a collective gasp of despair rose from every throat. Even through the haze of the evening, and across the distance, Miriam could see the tiny brown forms swarming up against the walls of her city. A moan of despair caught in her throat.

"No!" Dinah wailed with no warning, jerking herself from Esther's hold, and jumping out of the wagon. "Haran needs me!"

"No, come back!" Esther yelled as she clambered down, and ran after the woman.

"Go on," Miriam assured the driver, a boy of only twelve, as she hopped over the side, lifting little Jacob down to stand beside her. "We will bring her along."

The boy nodded, and clucked to the old, haggard horse, urging it forward down the road to the city.

Miriam watched the wagon disappear over the ridge, and then turned, jogging after Esther, holding tightly to her brother's hand.

Up ahead of her, she could hear Esther crying out in weak, breathless gasps for the frightened woman to stop. Farther ahead was Dinah, her dress clenched in her fists as she ran, blindly, mindlessly. Surely she would not last, Miriam assured herself. Surely she would tire soon, and Esther would catch up with her, and help her weakened, exhausted body back to the safety of city walls.

And then she saw her stumble and fall, almost in compliance with her thoughts, but Miriam quickly realized it was not from exhaustion.

"Dinah!" Esther shrieked, as she rushed to her side, and fell to her knees. Miriam broke into a run tugging little Jacob along after her, until she stumbled to a stop, falling to her knees beside Esther who held the woman in her arms, trembling and sobbing with disbelief.

Miriam stared with horror at the arrow protruding from the woman's chest. She trembled, noting the fletching and markings that showed it was clearly Lamanite made.

"They are here," she gasped solemnly, staring around her at the darkened shadows as a heavy feeling of dread filled her stomach.

Esther did not hear, bending with grief over the silent form, shaking her as if to waken her.

"Esther, we must get away." Miriam's voice was filled with urgency, but Esther did not hear.

"Dinah, wake up," she moaned as if she were a child, shaking the silent form.

"The old one is dead," growled a low voice from off the trail in the language of the Lamanites. The speaker, a burly man with a long scar on his cheek, was wielding a wooden cimeter, its edges set with blades of sharpened obsidian. As he stepped from the shadows he said, "But the two young ones and the boy we will take as our captives." He was dressed as a Lamanite and darkly tanned, but his hair was only a dark brown, not black, and his features were Nephite, as if his blood was a mix of both races.

At his voice, Esther gasped, and jerked her head up, finally realizing that they were not alone.

Four other men emerged from the darkness at the side of the road to stand beside their scar-faced leader.

"You are bad men!" Miriam shouted, leaping to her feet, unable, for the moment, to feel fear as anger boiled inside of her. "All of you! Shame on you! Why do you come to our lands to destroy our homes and make us your slaves when all we desire is to be left in peace?"

The men stopped, stunned. The scar-faced man glared heatedly.

"Go away!" she shouted, her hands balling into fists.

The man with the scar cursed at her under his breath, and began to step forward.

"Wait." The youngest of the men grabbed the man's arm, and pulled him back. "They are Lamanite-born. You can hear from their speech, and their skin is dark. Let them be."

"You are wicked men!" Miriam continued, her voice rising. She was barely aware of Esther and her brother, huddled at her feet, shivering with fear and grief.

All of them, but the scar-faced man, seemed to shrink and withdraw in shame.

"Go away," she repeated.

"No, you must come with us. You are our prisoners," the scar-faced man ordered.

"We will not. We will return to Morianton."

"We move on the city this very day," the scarred Lamanite answered, a sneer crossing his face.

Miriam stiffened, thinking of the others whom she had left only minutes before. "Then we will go to another city. We will not come with you."

"This young one is full of fire, Tuloth," the man with the scar chuckled, nudging the young man. "You have taken no woman to wife yet. You would do well to take her for yourself."

"No!" Miriam stamped her foot. If young Jacob's trembling hand had not been on her arm, she would have flung herself at the scarred man, her fists flailing.

"She is right," the young Lamanite agreed, clearly embarrassed. "I will have no wife who does not choose to be mine."

"I have heard enough talk," the scar-faced one grumbled. "We will take them with us."

"No," The young one insisted, again grabbing the scarred man's arm. Turning to Miriam, he grumbled, "You will do well to flee now. Far away."

Miriam nodded. She reached down, and gripped Esther's hand tightly, bringing her to her feet.

"Come," Miriam muttered under her breath. She tightened her hold on young Jacob's hand, then turned and fled with him and Esther into the darkening underbrush on the opposite side of the road.

CHAPTER 10

Jacob marched ahead of his broken little band, his strides steady and long, as if his strength and energy were continual and unfailing. In truth, they were all somewhere beyond exhaustion, but reality was a harsh teacher, and they kept on their northward course. With every heartbeat, the feeling was reinforced in him that they must press on, and trust that somehow they would survive. Night had long since closed over them, yet they walked on, a disheartened, yet brave little group, less than ten men, one woman and a boy.

The battle had been swift. The Lamanites had hardly been spotted before they attacked, carrying with them, it seemed, ten times the fury with which they had attacked the city Moroni. Nephihah had been fortified with barricades and bulwarks as the city of Moroni had been. Yet the Amalickiahites did not value the lives of their men, and sent wave upon wave at the walls of the city of Lehi, until they overcame the Nephites' defenses, and swept through the city like a hurricane through a stand of palm trees. Lehi could not stand long against such an onslaught.

If Jacob had the strength, he would have been sick with fear for Miriam, but he had only energy and thought for the tiny group in his charge. They had not stopped to rest since fleeing from the collapsing city, and they had not slept in the space of a whole day, from sunset to sunset, and he would not let them stop. Their time was precious. Thankfully, the boy Moronihah was a hardy youth, and had not complained, putting the soldiers, including Jacob, to shame. And his mother had given the men no need to slow down for her. Jacob wondered to himself with a tired smile, if he were to give her the lead, that perhaps she might push them faster than the rest of them were able.

The biting hunger pangs gnawed at his stomach, and he stamped his feet harder as he stepped, shaking his hunger away. He looked up at the obsidian sky above them, the stars peeking through chips in the blackness. He knew the stars, and a spark of comfort surfaced in his heart. They knew where to point, and without a map, Jacob needed their guidance now.

From what he judged, they would reach the city Omner in a few hours, perhaps before morning. Omner was due north of Nephihah, and in the collective opinion of the group, the most practical way to go. If the Lord saw fit to bless them, the Lamanites would give them a brief respite, and hold the cluster of the four southernmost cities before trying to move further north. Perhaps they would be able to mass their numbers, and hold off the Lamanites.

They had been marching in silence for hours, and when the boy's voice near his left shoulder broke through the darkness, Jacob started, grabbing instinctively at his sword before he recognized it as Moronihah's, and relaxed.

"You are very much like my father, sir," he whispered. "You do not fear anything."

Jacob shook his head. Fatigue was in his voice as he spoke. "I fear many things."

"Yet you saved us," Moronihah pointed out. "If not for you, my mother and I would be dead. I think that I want to be like you when I am a soldier."

Jacob laughed in spite of his failing energy. "You will be much better." He grinned. "You will lead armies as your father does."

Moronihah again opened his mouth when Jacob jerked to a halt, putting a hand in front of the boy to hold him back. The other soldiers halted as well, checking their breath, listening to the silence. He had heard something ahead of them, so soft and quiet that he was not sure if he had heard anything at all, but his instincts screamed that he had.

"Draw your swords," he whispered, as the rest of the group huddled tightly together. The faint rasp of blades sliding from their sheaths echoed in the stillness. Moronihah, although weaponless, struggled to see ahead in the darkness, but Jacob pushed the boy roughly behind him. "Stay with your mother," he hissed, as he stared into the blackness of the jungle. It was like trying to see through tar.

Soon he saw a movement through the trees, something that caught in the almost invisible light of the stars. It had been a brief flicker of a shadow, almost as if it had been a ghost.

"Sir, there," one of the soldiers whispered, pointing out another movement to the side.

Jacob's chest tightened with a feeling as black as the moonless night around them. Whoever they were, they were coming closer, and were as aware of Jacob's band as he was of them. A confrontation in the jungle would not be to their advantage, Jacob knew, with only eight men, and a woman and boy to protect. He held his sword, unflinching, as somewhere beyond the trees, he caught sight of the glimmer of torchlight. It bobbed along, above the floor of the jungle as if floating, transported by some otherworldly being. He watched it approach, his sword in his fist as he kept his other hand on Moronihah's shoulder, keeping the boy behind him.

He heard now, snatches of words in the Lamanite tongue. His heart thumped rapidly in his chest, and he clenched his jaw, ready to defend his little band until the life was torn from him.

Finally, the torch bobbed, bent, and was before him, clutched in the grip of a smiling man. His bronze face and weaponless arms shone in the torchlight, and his dark eyes reflected the flickering flame. His black hair was long, past his shoulders, and his plain cotton tunic reached to his knees. He wore only a short knife at his waist, and it was in its scabbard. He looked at Jacob, and Jacob looked back at him. Neither man moved for several seconds.

After a moment, the man finally blinked, and his wide smile grew even larger. "Please, have no fear, we are friends." He spoke the Nephites' language with only the trace of an accent as another figure stepped out of the shadows, a young, pale-skinned Nephite with uncertainty in his eyes, dressed in the same fashion as the torchbearer.

"Are you from Lehi or Morianton, sir?" the boy asked timidly.

Jacob's distrusting eyes slowly crinkled into a relieved smile, and he sheathed his sword as did the rest of his men. "Nephihah. We are headed to Omner."

"Omner, is it?" The man chuckled heartily. "You strayed a bit to the west, my friends. You are in the land of Jershon. The city is beyond these trees."

"Jershon?" Jacob's voice and those of several others chimed in surprise.

"Yes." He nodded, coming forward and extending his free hand. "My name is Laman. I have not taken the oath as the other Ammonites have done, and so I am here from Melek, training. My young friend, Amnor and I were patrolling the perimeter of the city."

"Of course." Jacob nodded, taking the large muscular hand, remembering the sacred oath of the original Ammonites never to shed human blood.

He retrieved his hand, but from the exhaustion of the march, stumbled slightly, and Laman caught his arm.

"We have not stopped since we fled the city," he apologized, regaining his balance.

"Well, then," Laman boomed, looking at the bedraggled group, his face wrinkled with concern. "We must take you where you can rest."

Jacob nodded gratefully, and stumbled after him as Laman and his younger companion led the way through the trees. Sure enough, not twenty paces farther, the trees abruptly ended, and above them, on a gentle hill, rose the sturdy wall of a Nephite built city. Jacob nearly cried in gratitude, gazing at the high wall silhouetted against the night sky. A surge of strength flowed to his legs as Laman led them toward the gate, bearing his torch before him.

◌

Toward the end of the night, the dream returned to Jacob. He could feel the darkness closing in around him like a net as he crawled through the smoke of the battle toward the side of his fallen comrade. The din of war and the screams of the dying surrounded him, but he was conscious only of the unnaturally still form of the fallen warrior. Reaching the soldier's side, he lifted the lifeless wrist, searching for a pulse. Feeling none, he glanced at the face turned halfway to him. The sight made him jerk and start back in horror. He heard himself cry out, and then his eyes snapped open.

His pulse was racing, and a cold sheen of sweat covered his body. He lay motionless, wondering for a moment where he was as he looked up at the gray wooden ceiling. He could feel a coarse blanket around him, and under that, a hard, wooden floor.

Exhaustion dragged at him, but he did not wish to go back to sleep. He pushed the thin blanket off, and sat up, shivering as the cool air brushed his bare chest. He could see now, his men, all seven of them, lined out along the floor, sleeping their weariness away. Across the room, behind a shuttered window, he glimpsed the faint hint of distant morning.

"Sir, are you not tired?" a voice behind him echoed in the room.

He turned to see a young man sitting near the door as if guarding them, and he recognized Amnor, Laman's companion from the previous night. "I feel rested."

"Well, you do look cold," Amnor shrugged, noting Jacob's shivers. "At least put this on." He tossed him a cotton tunic.

Jacob took it, and pulled it over his head as he stood up. He looked away out the window, the gray light seeping through the cracks.

"You had a bad dream, sir?" the young man asked quietly.

Jacob picked up his sword belt from the floor, and tightened it securely around his waist, and then rested his hands on his hips. He turned to face the younger man. "Why?"

Amnor ignored Jacob's defensiveness. "You cried out."

Jacob cleared his throat. "Where are the two who came with us? The boy and his mother?"

"They are sleeping at a house nearby," the young man responded, pointing with his thumb over his shoulder. "They are safe." As he said these words, he stood up, stretching cramped muscles, and it suddenly struck Jacob that he must have been watching over them all night.

Jacob turned his eyes again to the window. "It was her face, I saw," he breathed.

"Sir?" Amnor asked.

"In the dream," Jacob repeated, his back to the young man. "Miriam was dead."

"Oh." He heard Amnor gulp. "It was only a dream—,"

"I do not know that." Jacob shook his head before turning back to the young man. "Do you have anyone here from Lehi? Or any news at all? Do you know if it has been attacked yet?"

Amnor grimaced at the look of pain on Jacob's face. "Sir—," He paused. "There are four men—," He could not finish, and lowered his eyes.

"Tell me," Jacob begged, feeling his hands tightening involuntarily into fists.

"They escaped after the city was taken. They arrived only a few hours after you did. All of them had lost much blood," he continued, his face tightening as if in pain. "They reported that everything was destroyed."

Jacob's voice grew taut. "Where are these four men?"

"Here."

Jacob brushed past Amnor's shoulder to fling open the wooden door.

"Sir, wait!" Amnor rushed after him. But Jacob was already through the door, in an open room warmed by the heat of a crackling fire.

The man called Laman whom Jacob recognized was kneeling at the side of one of four men spread out on the floor, covered over with coarse blankets. Three of the four shivered in their sleep as if they were cold, though Jacob felt sweat instantly pricking his skin from the heat of the fire. The fourth one, the man Laman knelt over, did not move.

Jacob paused, watching as Laman's head drooped. Amnor joined Jacob, and Jacob heard him utter a soft moan. A short breath of air escaped Jacob's own lips at Laman's expression as he lifted his face to look at them.

"He has died," Laman said. Deep lines of fatigue were under his eyes. "He lost much blood. The others—their wounds are deep, but I think they will live."

"Can I speak to them?" Jacob asked, coming forward. "Someone I knew was in Lehi."

"Well, if he is not one of these three, he is dead, or a prisoner."

"I must speak to one of them," Jacob stuttered. "I must know."

"Can it not wait?" Laman begged.

"Sir?" a voice weak and tremorous called from behind Laman, and they both looked toward the source of the voice. One of the other soldiers' eyes were open. "I can speak. I may have an answer."

Glancing at Laman for his nod, Jacob hurried to the side of the pale young man who smiled tiredly up at him. He dropped to a knee at the soldier's side, surprised at how pale his face was. One arm was bound in a cloth.

"Sir," the soldier struggled up on his good elbow and saluted, his voice weak. "Forgive me—I lack the strength to stand."

Jacob returned the salute. "I would like to know of a young woman of about fourteen years."

"All the women and children went to Morianton," the soldier began softly.

"Do you know anything of the city Morianton, then?" Jacob forced his voice to stay calm.

The young man paused. "Before we made our escape, I heard talk from our Lamanite captors that others were to move on the city of Morianton that very day."

At his words, Jacob's head dropped against his chest, and he clenched his eyes shut at the clutching pressure that had seized his heart.

"Forgive me, sir," the soldier gasped, sorrow in his tired voice. "I wish I knew more."

"I thank you for telling me all that you know. Rest now." Jacob returned, lifting his face.

The soldier nodded, and sank back against his pillow.

Slowly, Jacob forced himself to stand, and turned to face the two men. Laman opened his mouth to speak, but he could find no words.

⋈

"*Most Venerable Chief Judge, Pahoran, greetings.*" The letter began formally, belying the emotional undertones it contained.

"*Your eminence has heard of how the Lamanites have taken Lehi. I will say that from the report of a few men who escaped the battle, that the judge, Lehi was killed, as were many of his men. The women and children were taken to the city Morianton before Lehi was attacked. But from the report that we have received, Morianton was under siege not many days before it also fell, and the inhabitants taken prisoner. My heart is sore, for I know there is nothing more I can do. I would that I had all power and strength to stop the Lamanites and the misery they bring, but I am no more than a man, and I can do only what one man can do. We have received the report that the city of Gid has also fallen to the Lamanites, and as of now, Mulek is under siege. If Mulek falls, Bountiful will be the last barricade between the Lamanites and the land northward. With your blessing, my men and I will go to join the troops mustering at Bountiful. Please pray for us that we will be successful in defending our lands and freedom.*

Your servant, Lieutenant Jacob, son of Ezekiel, 11th squad, 5th battalion of the city of Moroni."

Pahoran walked to the window and gazed up at the stormy sky. It was the season for storms along the east coast, and even here far from the coast, the sky was boiling furiously. Hard rain was beginning to pelt down from the sky as merciless as daggers. "How could anyone have stopped them?" Pahoran murmured to himself, leaning against the cold stone of the window. "They swept through like a tidal wave."

The room was silent as the intensity of the wind outside escalated. Finally, Pahoran closed the shutters to keep out the steadily growing wind. A sudden feeling of awkwardness and ineptitude seized him as he looked back at Micha, his ever present guard. "I wish I knew what to say, Micha, what to do."

But for the rain that was beginning to come down hard now, the room was quiet. Pahoran stood near the window, his hands behind his back, his head bowed thoughtfully.

"Micha," Pahoran finally said, clearing his throat, "your wife's brother was in Nephihah. I think it would be best for you to return to your house, and comfort her."

"I cannot," he spouted. "I have a duty to you."

Pahoran came to him, and placed a hand on his shoulder. "Go. Be with your family."

Micha released a long, haggard sigh. He looked at Pahoran, and smiled slightly for an instant, but then his smile dropped.

"Libnor will take my post." His voice deepened with reserved emotion as he turned away and stepped out the door. Pahoran gazed sadly at the heavy wooden door a long moment before he turned back to the window. The only noise was the merciless drumming of the rain battering at the window.

❧

Water squeezed up from the moist ground as they stepped, and large broken leaves bent, snapping beneath their feet as the group marched swiftly along the road, each man's drawn sword in his hand. Their eyes shifted, gazing suspiciously through the thick jungle foliage surrounding them.

Jacob led the way, his intense gaze fixed on the rough trail ahead of them as it twisted northward. They were well out of the areas taken by Lamanites, but Jacob knew he could not be careless.

The man beside him moved stealthily along, as silent as a wild-cat, and Jacob turned his head to flash Laman an encouraging grin. Laman returned the smile, his sword ready in his hand. Though he had lived among the Ammonites for the past several years, Laman had not taken the oath that the older generation of Ammonites had. He would not only add one more man to the group, but also much needed insight into the ways of Lamanites, their strengths and, most importantly, their weaknesses. He would be a valuable asset in Bountiful. In his earlier years, Laman had been a loyal bearer to the king of the Lamanites, but when the servants of Amalickiah had murdered the king, Amalickiah had lain the blame on Laman and his fellow servants. And to save themselves, they fled to the Nephites, joining themselves to the people of Ammon.

Remembering Laman's story, Jacob could not help thinking of Miriam, and he tightened his jaw to keep the tears from surfacing as the path broke through the trees, and the long alabaster wall came into view. Jacob drew to a halt. The stalwart wall shone like silver in the clear afternoon light, causing the men to blink in the sudden glare after passing from the shadows of the jungle. Directly in front of the company, over the western gate opening slowly in front of them, the Title of Liberty fluttered in a gentle breeze.

The wall they walked under as they came through the gate was thick and high; the heavy stones had been skillfully placed together without the use of mortar. The size of the city rivaled even Zarahemla. As the rest of the men passed through the gate, they found themselves at the head of a wide and open street, straight and long, which ended in what Jacob could barely see as the center of the city. The great temple at the center rose majestically in the afternoon light, tier upon ascending tier. He sucked in a slow breath, gazing at the distant building, unaware of the two men who made their way toward him through the crowd.

"Jacob," Laman elbowed him gently, and nodded toward the approaching soldiers.

Jacob jerked out of his lethargy, shook himself, and looked about him, noticing the captain with the sergeant at his shoulder, striding toward them. They looked war battered, and their uniforms bore the marks of battle, but a welcoming light shone in the older man's kind gray eyes.

"Jacob." Teancum clasped the arms of the startled young man. "I read the letter from Pahoran which said that you would come. I am glad to find you safe." He tried to smile.

"I've arranged for Sergeant Ahimaz to debrief the men, and for you and Laman to come with me." Teancum's face was drawn and tired. "We have a great deal of work ahead of us." He turned to Laman and reached his forearm toward him, which Laman clasped. "You're Laman?"

"I am." Laman nodded.

"Sir," Jacob blurted, "I thought you were dead."

Teancum turned to Jacob. "Lehi and Morianton were taken. Prisoners were taken, mostly women and children, but many were killed."

"Yes, I know," Jacob nodded, a heavy blackness in his stomach.

"I hate the bloody business of war. Especially when the innocent suffer." Teancum's chin trembled as he stood in front of Jacob, and his stalwart wall seemed nearly to crumble, but he tightened his jaw. "Come with me. We have much work to do."

CHAPTER 11

*T*he stinging drops of rain struck her face mercilessly and the wind threatened to throw the tiny group off its feet as the two young women stumbled up the slope of a hill through the downpour, dragging a small boy between them, and clinging to one another for support. Miriam's ebony hair hung down her back in wet waves, streaming rivulets of water. The ragged dress she wore was no protection against the battering wind, or the icy rain that was pouring, unrestrained, from the sky. Her feet were bare and raw. With each step, the impression her foot left in the spongy, mud-soaked earth would fill up with water, flooding away the faint hint of crimson left behind.

Esther's sandals were worn, and quickly falling apart, and young Jacob's sandals had been lost days before, but she no longer had the strength to carry him.

Miriam reflected as she stumbled along, for conversation was impossible in such a storm, how they had come to be here. They had thought their trials were over when they came into the land of Omner, hungry and exhausted unnumbered weeks before. They had topped the ridge looking down into the city, their hearts full of hope, only to see smoke curling up from the ruined buildings, the city as bleak and lifeless as a discarded snake skin. Dozens of tiny forms that had patrolled the walls were dark skinned, with nothing but animal hides tied around their lean waists. Disheartened, the two girls had returned to the cover of the forest, knowing they would fare better at the mercy of the wild beasts, than if they were to fall into the Lamanites' hands. They had continued to Gid, two days' journey to the north. Then to see Gid as they had Omner, they had no choice but to continue on to the city of Mulek. After several days of wandering, sleeping under the stars, they had found Mulek, scarred, and broken, in the Lamanites' hands.[7]

Miriam's heart was heavy. The Lamanites had been victorious, and if they were to try to go to Bountiful, they would surely find that the Lamanites had taken it, as well. But they had no choice. Because of the exposure and the strain of the journey, little Jacob had grown weak and had begun to show the first signs of the dreaded fever that was so prevalent in the land. The shivering had begun to wrack his little body, and Miriam knew that he could not last much longer without medicine and a physician's attention.

Another shudder shook the boy's body, and Miriam pulled him closer to her as the rain beat down on them, soaking through the thin cloth of her skirt to her skin. The soles of her feet burned, and she hesitated at each step, flinching as she anticipated the pain that shot up her legs.

Feeling the first faint chills and flushes in her own face, Miriam turned to look at her friend. Esther's face was flushed, her own intermittent shivers draining, though they had not grown as violent as the boy's had. But as she looked up to meet Miriam's gaze, she smiled weakly, and nodded wordless encouragement. She tried to speak, but her soft, weak words were ripped away by the screaming wind.

Miriam returned her smile, and gazed ahead through the rain, the grayish green of the jungle unending through the dark curtains of rain that hung from a black boiling sky. She let out a sigh, hearing the despair of her soul as the noise escaped on the wind.

But she gritted her teeth and continued, trudging slowly up the hill. She stopped at the top to rest, the breath burning in her lungs, as Esther paused beside her, fighting to stay upright.

"Miriam," Esther's voice cracked as she leaned close, "what do you think that is?"

Miriam lifted her face and focused her eyes on the distance where her friend's trembling hand pointed.

To the north, barely visible through the sheets of rain, a dark object, thin and tall, like a flag pole, thrust up into the jagged sky at

the crest of a small hill as if to defy the storm. Something, a shredded tatter of cloth, hung like a wet sack from the cross pole at the
top.

"Is it perhaps the Title of Liberty?" Esther's dry voice measured
a hint of hope in it, and Miriam took a deep breath, hitching her
whimpering brother higher in her trembling arms.

"It is difficult to see." She drew in a breath and stumbled down
the side of the hill.

She kept the object in her sight, her eager eyes focused on it.
Her heart lifted as the two of them struggled nearer to the small hill,
but as she stopped at the bottom, her hopes sank.

"There is nothing here," she whispered. "No one."

"There is a reason why the flag is here," Esther muttered, shivering.

Miriam shook her head, gazing up through the rain at the
ragged flag clinging to the standard in spite of the angry wind lash-
ing around it.

On the ample west face of the hill from which the flagpole rose,
the raging wind was not so fierce, and the earth was dry. She stumbled to this side, and lowered little Jacob to the ground. Esther collapsed gratefully beside him.

"There is no one here," Miriam coughed, as she crouched
down, her dry eyes feeling hot as she rubbed little Jacob's hands
between hers. "Nothing but the flag on the hilltop."

"But look behind you." Esther nodded beyond Miriam's shoulder. "Through the trees."

Miriam turned. Far ahead of her through the trees, there was a
bright light, a torch, blazing in spite of the drenching rain. Miriam
rose on her shaking legs to get a better look, rubbed a muddy hand
across her eyes and looked again.

"You go. Send someone back for us," Esther whimpered.

"I cannot leave you." Miriam turned back.

Esther shook her head. "We will be fine, if you hurry."

The pleading eyes of her friend begged to her through the dimming grayness of the stormy twilight, and Miriam finally nodded
reluctantly, and limped toward the trees. She glanced back once.
Esther had placed her arm around little Jacob's shoulders, and the

child had leaned into her, eager to share what little warmth they could. Her determination renewed, she turned forward, and stumbled away through the trees.

The flame grew steadily, peeking now and again through the trees that thinned as she neared the bottom of the hill and finally revealing a high wall, stretching off into the haze in both directions. A blazing torch was set on the top, mounted over a massive gate. There were easily more than a dozen Nephite guards before it, with hooded cloaks over their heads to keep the rain off. Each of them had a drawn sword in his hand.

Miriam trembled with cold, and rubbed her shoulders, wishing she had more than the rain soaked dress she wore.

The skirt slapped against her legs, sticky and clinging, but she pulled at it and stumbled with eager determination toward the gate, ignoring the painful numbness in her feet. She could almost feel the warm comfort of a roof over her head, and dry clothes again.

"Excuse me," she gasped, when she finally lurched to a halt beside the gate, the thick mud squeezing between her raw, bleeding toes.

"I am Miriam, of—," The soldiers, surprised, turned toward her, scowling. She backed up a step, confused. "—of Lehi. My friend and my brother and I escaped, but they are sick, they could not come farther."

Her pleading voice did not make any change in them.

"Please," Miriam begged, almost crying. "I need men to carry them down."

"I think we have heard enough lies," one of the soldiers spat, marching at her so suddenly that she scrambled to back away, slipped, and fell flat on her back. The mud soaked heavily into her dress, and her long, dripping hair. Instantly, there were three soldiers standing over her, each one's sword pointing at her neck. The cruel cold of the steel seeped into her feverish veins.

"She is one of those half-Nephites," growled one of the soldiers who wore a sergeant's insignia, glaring at her. "A dissenter's daughter. Whoever sent her thought we would think she was one of us, and go out to find these others she mentioned."

"No!" Miriam cried in shock. "I am a Nephite, from Lehi!"

"You were unwise, to think you could fool us," the sergeant drawled slowly.

"But I—," Miriam's protest stopped mid sentence, and she glanced at the speaker in surprise. A satisfied sneer was creeping over his war-scarred face, and she realized he had spoken in the Lamanite tongue. "I am a Nephite," she repeated. "And I am from Lehi. I speak the truth."

"Bind her. Let's take her inside," the sergeant growled. Miriam looked on in disbelief as hands, strong as iron bands, seized her arms, and lashed her wrists behind her back with a narrow length of rope.

The sergeant and another soldier gripped her arms, and shoved her roughly through the gate that opened a crack, and dragged her through the drenched mud of the draining streets. Her whimpering protests availed her nothing as her feet left prints of crimson behind her. She was hardly aware that buildings surrounded her. But one, in spite of her frustration and fear, caught her attention and held it. Its walls rose starkly up into the air as if to challenge the angry, boiling clouds that roiled above it. The structure was so massive that it could have been a little city on its own. The two soldiers pushed her toward it, and through two gate-like doors, then into a huge building, a hall overcrowded with soldiers, young and old, either sitting or standing against the walls. All of them looked as exhausted as she felt. The water and mud from her clothes dripped onto the sanded wood of the floor. Her bloody footprints followed her, but no one noticed.

"See this?" the sergeant mocked, jerking cruelly on her arm. "This is the work of your kind; all this suffering because of the Lamanite pigs who think it their right to conquer us, slaughter our women and children, and make slaves of us."

Miriam was too tired to struggle or argue any more, and hardly let out a sound as they shoved her to the floor at an empty spot along the wall. She could feel warm blood on her feet; bits of leaves and twigs clung to her mud-soaked hair. Esther and her brother were still in the storm. They could not survive alone with the storm growing fiercer, and the night colder as the minutes passed.

The ropes behind her back caused her arms to ache, and her wrists to lose all feeling. She had lost all of her strength even to cry. If she died here, no one would care. If only Jacob was here, he would take care of her. But he was dead. She turned to hide her face against the wall.

"Go and find an officer to interrogate her, and find out how many are out there, waiting for us."

"Yes, sergeant," the younger soldier said, and turned away, but Miriam heard the scrapping of his leather boots on the wooden floor as someone she could not see, blocked his path.

"What is this?" A startled voice caused her head to jerk. "Why is this woman bound?"

Who had said that? She had only a moment to wonder why the voice was familiar when two strong arms went around her shoulders, gently pulling her away from the wall, and up until she was sitting. A warm hand brushed the mud from her face while another hand supported her back. There was a faint metallic whisper of a blade being drawn. She jerked reflexively, but she soon felt the cool flat side of a knife slip between her wrists and cut the rope away.

Her weary wondering eyes flickered open, and a set of hazel eyes gazed into hers, as startled with recognition as she was. "Miriam?" Jacob's voice whispered.

"Why did you do that?" a far away voice demanded. "She is a Lamanite."

"She is my friend, Ahimaz." The blue eyes snapped, glancing up for a moment, a steely lightening glare flashing from them. "Keep silent."

"Miriam, what has happened to you?" Jacob's worried hazel eyes again looked back into hers, his voice filled with disbelief.

"Ja— Jacob?" Miriam gasped, not yet daring to believe. "Where did you come from?"

"Miriam, where did you come from?" he demanded gently. "How did this happen?"

"We escaped—little Jacob, a friend, and me. We have traveled in the wilderness many weeks. The guards refuse to go bring them into the city. "

Jacob's lips curled as he looked up into the faces of the soldiers who stood over them. "Don't fear, Miriam. I will find them."

"Jacob, hurry," Miriam begged, gripping his arm frantically. "They are alone, and sick with the fever, and the storm is growing worse."

She let out a shaky, exhausted breath, and collapsed back against Jacob's sturdy arm.

"Where are they?"

"On the west face of the hill outside the southern gate," Miriam gasped, trying to point, but barely able to lift her arm now.

"Sir—," Ahimaz's voice intruded, harsh and defensive.

"Ahimaz," Jacob barked, looking up into the face of Ahimaz whose expression was as stone. "Return to your post." Jacob's face tightened in anger, though he fought to control it.

Ahimaz scowled, and turned away. The younger soldier followed after him. Once their steps had faded, Jacob turned back to Miriam, his old, familiar grin returning.

"We will find them," he said, cradling her head against his warm shoulder.

She was too exhausted even to nod, but quiet grateful tears slipped from her eyes as he picked her gently up off the hard floor and rose to his feet.

She tried to open her mouth to speak, to thank him, but she had used the last of her strength. And with his shoulder cradling her head, her eyes, without her willing them, closed into fitful, wearied darkness.

ᑕᑐ

A sound, barely audible in the cool shaded room in which she lay, stirred her, and she opened her eyes, blinking in the light, softened by a thick curtain across the window behind her. A young woman stood over her, a smile on her face.

"It is good to see you awake, Miriam." She smiled as she tilted Miriam's head up with her arm, and placed a cold, much appreciated cup to her lips. The liquid slipped soothingly down Miriam's throat, and she gulped at it greedily. She caught the last drops before the cup moved from her mouth. The young woman's face again smiled down at her.

"Where—?" Miriam asked, struggling to her elbows, the words grinding painfully in her throat.

"You are in Bountiful," the young woman answered, pushing her gently down again.

Miriam struggled back up again. "My brother? And my friend, Esther? They are safe?"

"Esther is sleeping beyond this curtain." She indicated the curtain beside her bed. "Your brother is in a room not far away."

Miriam looked doubtfully at the curtain, and thrust out a hand, as if to pull it aside.

"No, Miriam," she scolded gently. "She is asleep."

"But she is sick. My brother, too."

"Miriam, do you not know how long it has been since you came here?" she inquired, reaching across the bed and pulling Miriam's rebellious hand back.

"Last night," Miriam put a hand to her head, struggling to remember. There had been a storm, she had met soldiers, but the memories of both were fuzzy.

"You have been in Bountiful for a week," she said quietly. "You caught the fever, and you were sick. But your fever has broken. And with the medicines, you have grown stronger."

"A week?" Miriam breathed. She pushed away the young woman's attempts to make her lie down again, and sat up in bed. "My brother—he must be frightened without me."

The girl tried to push her down again, but Miriam batted her hands away as she struggled out of bed, the floor icy against her bare feet. "I must find him." She scuttled across the frozen floor that seemed to buck and sway as she moved. The young woman tried to grasp her by the arms to guide her back to bed, but Miriam, even in her weakened condition, was stronger. She twisted out of the young woman's grip.

An uncommonly powerful wave surged then, and pitched her forward. Her arms flailed frantically as she fell headlong through the doorway.

But before she struck the floor, she found herself caught gently in a pair of strong arms.

"I must find my brother," she protested, fighting to get to her feet again.

"She is very strong for such a sick girl," she heard the young woman apologize. "I tried to make her go back to bed, but she would not listen."

"She's a very strong-willed girl," a man's voice echoed above her.

A moment later, she felt herself lifted in a pair of strong arms, and a memory surged back into her mind from where it had lain dormant. Jacob was here. He had found her, and had carried her here, as gently as if she had been a baby. But this time, Miriam felt giddy as Jacob held her, gazing at her with his penetrating hazel eyes. She blinked into them, noticing the flecks of gold and green set against light brown, the edge framed with a ring of darker, gentle brown.

"Jacob," she stammered. "Jacob." Her hands wrapped around his neck, felt the muscle in his shoulders ripple as he shifted her in his arms. "You are alive."

Jacob's mouth curled into a smile, his captivating eyes blinking slowly. "Miriam," he murmured. His low voice calmed her, and she grew still. "Little Jacob is fine."

"Oh," she sighed and let her head fall against his shoulder, growing limp as a great burden lifted from her.

Jacob carried her back to her bed, and lay her in it, as the young woman pulled the soft blankets back up around her.

She caught his hand and kept a tight hold as she looked into his eyes. "Is he safe?"

"He was very sick." He made no attempt to free his hand from hers. "And he is still weak from the fever, but he will recover."

She relaxed her head against her pillow and nodded, tears trickling from her eyes. She said nothing more, but clung to his hand, her eyes searching his, his presence dispelling the agony she had endured over the last months when she had been sure he was dead.

At last, after several long moments, he drew back, and released her hand, his own reluctance evident on his face. "I came to see you only for a moment," he explained, touching her face with a gentle hand. "I have many things to do. Captain Teancum has made me a lower captain, and has given me much responsibility."

She nodded, and clasped her empty hand to her blanket.

"I will come back soon," he promised as he brushed his fingers against her forehead, and smoothed away a lock of damp hair. Then he stepped back, and turned toward the doorway. Miriam followed him with her eyes until he was gone.

CHAPTER 12

*T*he thunk of an arrow slamming into the bark of a tree made Jacob jerk reflexively. The men with him, tired from their long night watch, their nerves worn, tensed at the unexpected noise and grumbled. They glared at the young woman whose back was to them as they moved on along the narrow road. Jacob, though he was tired, stopped to admire her aim. Her arrows were clustered in the one spot on a rotting tree where she had marked a crude red circle.

She wore a simple brown dress, loose, with a wide sash tied about her slender waist. Her long hair was plaited, hanging down her back in a dark, glittering rope. Her feet were small in her little sandals, almost delicate, but by the rigid stance of her small frame, he could see that she was anything but delicate. Jacob turned off the road, the growth crackling under his feet as he made his way to her.

"Good morning, Jacob," Miriam said without looking over her shoulder as she released the string. Her arrow hit the old, dead tree with a thwap, and the trunk shuddered.

"Good morning, Miriam." He touched her shoulder and she turned toward him, a smile curving her soft lips.

"How does it look?" she asked him, pointing at the target with the bow.

"Very good." He grinned. "Where did you learn this?"

"A friend taught me," she answered. "When I was little."

"When you lived in Siron?" he asked.

Miriam turned, her enthralling blue eyes meeting his. "He used to take me hunting."

Jacob cleared his throat. "He taught you well."

"Thank you." Miriam smiled. "But I never hit anything unless I shoot at trees. I think it is easier to shoot at a target that does not move." She shrugged. "I am glad I am not a man."

"It is difficult, is it not?" he asked quietly.

She furrowed her brow, questioning him with her eyes.

"The Lamanites were once your people. You have friends among them," Jacob explained. "If you were a boy, you would become a soldier. You would have to fight your own people, perhaps even your old friends."

She dropped her eyes, releasing a shaking sigh. "Sometimes it frightens me how much you understand when I say nothing." She lowered her face, and started toward the target to pull her arrows from its surface.

Jacob followed her with his eyes. It had been a hard night for him, but watching her move as she walked away, his weariness disappeared. Something compelled him to her side, and he darted forward, the grass crackling under his feet as he hurried to her.

"Let me help, Miriam." He smiled, and she lifted startled eyes as he wrenched the last of her arrows from the rotting tree trunk.

"Thank you, Jacob." The handful of arrows rasped brittle and wooden as she drew them from his hands into her own, and turned away from him.

He studied her down-turned head, the glistening rope of her hair, and the soft profile of her face. The trees fell away and the massive gate loomed before them, but Jacob barely noticed as the shadow of the gate passed over their heads.

"I am sorry I kept you," she murmured in the quiet of the early morning. "You must be exhausted from your night watch."

He drew in a deep breath. "I would like to walk home with you at least, if I have your permission?"

Miriam drew in a breath, and a smile touched her lips. "Of course."

He returned the smile and paused a moment before he resumed his steps, falling in beside her again as she turned down a narrow street that led away from the city garrison.

Jacob cleared his throat several times, then managed, "I am fortunate that you live so near the garrison. I can see you every day."

Miriam lifted her eyes to his as they paused before the tiny thatch hut she shared with her brother and Esther. His hand tensed in nervous shock as one of her small hands reached forward and slipped into his. "You are not the only one who is fortunate," Miriam said, her blue eyes large.

"Oh?" Jacob's heart began to thunder in his chest, and he hoped that she could not hear it.

She nodded. "I am fortunate, as well. After all, you are as dear to me as a brother."

"Oh." He released a long breath, then lowered himself slowly to the ground, leaning his back against the stiff thatch. He unfastened the shield from his arm, and pulled his helmet off. He ran his hands several times through his damp hair and lifted his face to the cooling breezes that brushed over him.

A brother? he groaned inside his head. He closed his eyes and listened to the rustle of her skirt as she sat beside him.

"Nevertheless, the friendship that we do have is good for both of us," he murmured, his mouth moving before his mind could think.

"I think so," Miriam sighed, stirring the loose dust on the ground with her toe.

"But not all men would agree," he said, thinking quickly, his eyes snapping open as he forced a smile on his face. "The ways of you women are awfully confusing sometimes."

"I am not a woman." Miriam smiled. "I am just a girl, Jacob."

"But you are of marriageable age. According to the laws you are—,"

"I do not feel like a woman," she sighed.

Jacob studied her from where he sat, her eyes on the ground, her toe stirring the dust. Her face was turned demurely downward. The curve of her neck was smooth, her features soft, her skin flawless, her maturing form as near perfection as any mortal woman's could be. She seemed hardly girlish to Jacob. A warmth stirred within him, and he asked, "Miriam, will you ever marry?"

"Someday. Perhaps." She lifted her face to his and gazed into his eyes, the unwavering blue of her eyes was searing, and penetrating, and he jerked his face away, his eyes focusing on his hands.

Coarse black hairs rose on the backs of his hands and fingers like tiny forests, his palms were rough and callused, his nails brittle and broken. "I am not a man," he mumbled. "I am only a boy."

"Jacob, you are over twenty!" Miriam laughed lightly, resting her hand on his arm.

Jacob's heart leaped at her touch. "It does not matter," he said, forcing a smile onto his face. "I am a free man, and if I wish, I can choose to say I am a boy though I live ninety years."

Miriam laughed, which in turn made him chuckle as well and glance back at her, relishing the shining in her bright eyes. "I am glad we are friends, Miriam."

"I am too, Jacob. I feel safe, knowing you are near."

His pulse caught as he reached to cover her hand where it rested on his arm. "Truly?"

The softness in her eyes deepened. "Yes. Jacob, I—,"

She was cut short by the sudden, blood-chilling blast of a distant conch shell horn. She froze at the sound, but Jacob leaped to his feet, his face suddenly tight. His eyes locked with hers, and she could see the pulse, suddenly thick and fast in his throat. A moment later, the distant sound was answered by a closer piercing blare that froze her blood.

"I must go," Jacob exclaimed, grabbing his helmet and shield.

"Jacob—," Miriam scrambled to her feet. "Is that—,"

"The Lamanites have come," he affirmed, turning to her and pulling his helmet over his head, adjusting the leather strap under his chin. He touched the hilt of the sheathed sword at his side, and slipped the straps of his shield over his left forearm. He turned away.

"Jacob." Her voice was tight, frightened, and he turned back.

"Come back alive. Please," she begged.

"I will try," he stammered, his voice dry.

"I will pray for you," she murmured, gazing up at him with large eyes, her face pleading, filled with fear.

He reached out and touched her arm gently. His callused hand slid down her arm until he gripped her hand. He held it tightly for a moment, feeling it answer his squeeze. Then with one last furtive glance, he turned and dashed away.

CB

The wealth of adrenaline that poured into his arteries amazed Jacob as he and his men pressed upon the left flank of the Lamanites. The Lamanites had not expected such opposition as they were giving them, and for all their numbers, they were falling fast beneath the swords of the Nephites. The sun was high overhead now, baking the earth unmercifully below it. Many soldiers on both sides were beginning to tire, but Jacob clenched his teeth against his aching muscles and forced himself to press on. Sweat poured down his face as he shouted orders to the men beside him and struck out at brown skinned warriors who hurled themselves mindlessly at him, wishing he could ignore the groans they made as they fell. Their blood was bright on his sword, their dying prayers to their unknown war gods reaching his ears. They were not prepared to die, and Jacob was not pleased that he had to send them to their deaths. He could see the Title of Liberty somewhere far ahead of him where Teancum was cutting through the Lamanites' defenses like a wedge, splitting the Lamanite army.

He realized vaguely to himself that the group he fought against was cut off from any retreat. He wondered what that would do to the spirit of these men who would have no escape. Either it would make them submissive and frightened, or they would become savage as wolves, and fight until they cut through the Nephites with brutal force, or were all slain.

His thoughts strayed back to the Title of Liberty, mounted on its standard. Even from this distance, he could read the letters painted across the cloth, and felt a surge of energy in his blood.

He remembered the tears that Miriam had bravely blinked from her eyes, and the smoothness of her arm beneath his fingers. She had promised him that she would pray for him. He smiled grimly, letting that memory fill him with much needed energy as he raised his battered shield to block the blows of another foe. The Lamanite army had been cut in two, and the much larger half that had access to escape had done so, with the vast Nephite army on the other side of the valley, pouring after them.

The Lamanites in the group Jacob and his men surrounded had sensed that they had been deserted, and had little hope of escape. They were tiring, and some, Jacob could see, were simply falling on the swords of the Nephites, or upon their own, to avoid the shame of being taken as prisoners. Jacob parried the blow of a Lamanite, and drove his blade home as the man fell to the ground. He stepped forward again and held his sword pointed at the next Lamanite, a young warrior, who seemed hesitant to attack, and unsure. The boy's teeth were clenched in a show of courage, but Jacob could see terror in his eyes. The boy's frightened eyes sent a wave of compassion through his heart, and he sucked a lungful of air into his burning throat.

"Put down your weapons!" he shouted in the language of the Lamanites. "Yield yourselves to us, and I give you an oath that we will spare your lives!" His dry throat felt as if it was on fire.

Slowly, the glaring group of sweat drenched copper bodies heaved a collective groan of resignation, and one by one, each man tossed his weapon to the blood-soaked ground. The Nephites, hearing Jacob's shout, had backed away, ready with their swords. The boy who stood before Jacob let out a sigh that sounded like a moan, dropped his club, still bright and bloodless, at Jacob's feet and fell to his knees.

"What is your age, boy?" Jacob demanded, trying to hide the sympathy in his voice.

"I am fifteen years," he choked, glaring up at Jacob, his glistening copper chest heaving. His hands rested on his knees, and it was then that Jacob saw the wound on his left arm: a long gash gaped open from his shoulder almost to his elbow, and even now, the blood was soaking the ground beneath him.

"You are wounded," Jacob snapped. "If it is not dressed, you will soon faint from the loss of blood. You may even die."

The young Lamanite sniffled, and glanced down to eye the wound almost apathetically.

"I will see to it that your wound is dressed," Jacob finished, and the boy's eyes darted back up again, a look of disbelief on his face.

"You would save the life of your enemy?" he spat, his eyes betraying his lack of trust.

"Ahimaz," Jacob called to a soldier not far from him. The sergeant turned to Jacob, his armor smeared with blood, and a fierce grimace on his face.

"Sir?" he called, hurrying to Jacob's side.

"Bind the injured boy's wound," Jacob said, nodding to the young Lamanite. "Take him to the prison in the city until he is sufficiently healed."

"Sir!" Ahimaz glared, insulted. "Let him die. It will be one less prisoner to waste food on."

Jacob turned and looked Ahimaz hard in the face. "Do as I say, Ahimaz."

Ahimaz's jaw tightened, and he stabbed his bloody sword defiantly into the dirt. "Sir, I—,"

At that moment, a messenger pushed through the crowd of Nephites behind Jacob, and in between the two men. He was breathing hard, and was covered with sweat.

"Sir, I have a message from Captain Teancum," the messenger gasped. "He wants you and as many men as can be spared to join him down by the sea shore. They have engaged Amalickiah."

"Very well," Jacob said, glaring at Ahimaz. He started to follow the messenger, but turned back before he did, his eyes moving from the Lamanite boy to Ahimaz.

"Do as I commanded," he ordered, his eyes on Ahimaz. "Bind the wound here, then have a physician clean and bind it again, in the city. If he is not accounted for when I return, I will come to you to find out why."

"Yes, sir," Ahimaz spat as he saluted stiffly. Jacob glanced again at the young Lamanite one last time before he marched away.

ভ

Miriam wiped a bead of sweat from her brow as she sat in the hot sun watching the southern gate. Even at Esther's insistence that she come inside from the heat, she had been firm in her resolution to stay outside. Her gaze drifted back and forth from the gate to the work in her hand. She had been stitching a small tunic for little Jacob, but her mind was not on the work. She had made so many mistakes and had retraced her stitches so many times that the sun was past its zenith, and her work was only half finished.

"Miriam, they will be a long while yet." Miriam heard Esther's voice as her friend sat beside her on the small step and sighed, her eyes on the section of gate that they could see over the neighboring housetops.

Miriam studied her face for a moment, setting her sewing in her lap.

"You are worried for Jacob?" Esther finally asked.

"Yes." A small tear formed in Miriam's eye, and she glanced away.

Esther sighed and did not answer, so Miriam continued with her stitches, brushing away a tear every few minutes as they squeezed into her reluctant eyes. Now and again the sentries would pass along the visible top of the wall, but there was no other movement. Even the trees beyond the wall did not have a breeze to stir them. Her eyes lowered again to the work in her hands, dimming with unwanted tears. But when the sentries on the wall called down to someone outside the gate, Miriam's eyes shot up, her vision suddenly clear. She could hear the gate opening, and the rhythmic footsteps of soldiers coming through.

"Perhaps one of them is Jacob," Esther offered hopefully. But Miriam shook her head.

"It is not likely." Her voice sounded forlorn and hopeless and she lowered her eyes again to the work in her lap, ignoring Esther's sympathetic gaze.

At last, Esther rose, pressing a gentle hand against Miriam's shoulder as she did. "Little Jacob will be hungry when he comes home from school," she murmured. "I will prepare some food for him." And with that, she returned back into the house.

She had been gone no more than a few moments, when a shadow fell across Miriam, and she looked up with a little gasp. A small group of soldiers had stopped before her. They stood in a tight circle around something that panted like an animal, but choked quietly on emotion as only a human could.

"You speak the language of the Lamanites?" the leader asked gruffly.

"You know I do, Ahimaz." Miriam rose slowly, laying the unfinished shirt beside her on the step.

"We have brought a Lamanite prisoner for whom you must translate." Ahimaz pointed over his shoulder, but from the tightness of the group, Miriam could not see.

Miriam took a deep breath, and dusted her hands on her skirt. "But you speak their language, Ahimaz." She could hear the fear in her voice. "Why have you not—,"

"I have tried," Ahimaz growled, his impatience rising. "He refuses to answer me."

He turned slightly, and a few of the men parted enough for Miriam to see the prisoner. The Lamanite was young, near her age. He was not as tall as the guards around him, but his muscles were strong, and bulged out starkly beneath his copper skin. His left arm was bound tightly in cloth, blood seeping from beneath it and his hands were free, so that his right hand could support his wounded arm. But Miriam could see the shackles binding his ankles, restricting his movement to little more than small steps. His face was toward the ground, and the only movement he made, was of his brown muscled chest rising and falling with each breath.

Miriam said nothing, but the young man sensed her eyes and looked up. He studied her for a few moments, his face blank, and then his dark eyes flickered with recognition.

"Thobor—," Miriam whispered, her whole frame suddenly growing stiff and numb.

Ahimaz spoke. "Tell him that a physician will clean his wound. He will remain unhurt if he does not disobey us. Tell him that I am not the man who chose to let him live, and if I chose, he would be a corpse."

Miriam bit her lip and nodded at Ahimaz, forcing herself to speak. "He asks you to let them help. No man will hurt you if you do not fight against them."

Thobor looked fearfully at Ahimaz. He slowly opened his mouth. "I trust none of them."

"Do you trust me?" she whispered, ignoring Ahimaz's disapproving scowl. "You and I were children together. Do you remember?"

He gulped.

"You took me with you to hunt, but I could not hit the rabbit."

His eyes widened, and he drew in a deep breath. "Miriam?"

"Do you trust me?" she repeated.

He nodded sharply, and Miriam smiled, turning her eyes to Ahimaz who scowled but remained silent. "He will not hurt you. If he does, Captain Jacob will learn of it." She turned back to him. "I ask you to promise that you will trust someone to help you, so that you might get better."

Thobor paused a moment, then nodded slowly. "I promise."

Miriam turned her eyes on Ahimaz who glared with clenched teeth. He frowned, then moved, blocking Miriam's view of her friend, and the group marched down the dusty street.

Miriam shuddered and looked back at the gate. The weight in her heart was even heavier, such that she felt unable to bear it. Jacob was still fighting, perhaps injured, or even dead. And now, her childhood friend from what seemed a lifetime before, had come as an enemy to destroy her world. Yet she had seen the little boy she remembered in Thobor's eyes, and ached inside.

CHAPTER 13

$\mathcal{N}$ight winds blew out to sea as Jacob stood leaning on the spear in his hand, looking down through the trees. Far away and below him, off the bench along the sandy shore of the rolling ocean, he could see vague outlines of other tents. The full moon had risen in the eastern sky, laying its sliver tresses across the dark waters of the boisterous sea, and lighting the sandy beach until it glowed silver.

His armor was smattered with blood, and he had a bandage on his left forearm where the blow from an enemy's obsidian blades had split his shield. It was the last day of the year, and of all the days of the year, the Lamanites chose today to attack. Added to that, Teancum had ordered him to command the guards taking first watch. He glanced behind him at the tents where his fellow Nephites slept, exhausted from the long battle that had not ended until after the sun set.[8]

His eyelids were feeling heavier as the moon lifted itself out of the ocean and rose in the sky. Suddenly it was no longer there, and Jacob jerked his eyelids open with a sleepy snort, straightening his frame. He shifted his weight from one leg to the other. He tightened and relaxed the muscles in his shoulders. His sigh of frustration was audible, and a moment later, he felt a stern hand on his shoulder.

"Are you on watch, or are you sleep walking?" Teancum's fatherly voice asked him gently.

"Forgive me, sir, I do not mean to—,"

"No need to ask my forgiveness, Jacob," Teancum chuckled as he jostled his shoulder. "Everyone is weary from the battle."

"Yes, sir," Jacob agreed, trying desperately not to yawn.

"Jacob, you were on the watch all last night."

He shrugged, trying to force his eyelids to open wider as he lifted his face to see the moon.

"But you did not questioned me why I ordered you to take command of the first watch."

"No, sir. I trust your reasoning."

"Good, for I trust you as well." Teancum glanced at the spear in Jacob's hands. "I need a soldier I know I can depend upon to come with me down to the Lamanites' camp."

Jacob's weariness vanished, and he gaped. "Sir?"

"I need you to come with me, Jacob," he explained, his eyes dancing with excitement.

"For what purpose?" Jacob felt fully awake now.

"To kill Amalickiah."[9] Teancum's eyes flickered for a moment with pain and bitter distaste.

"What of his guards?" Jacob pointed out, wondering if the heat of the day had gotten to the captain's brain. "If they find us, they will kill us."

"True." Teancum nodded. "But they are as exhausted as we are. And Lamanites aren't as concerned with the threat of attack. I will wager that his guards have fallen asleep."

Jacob folded his arms across his chest, and looked out at the distant shadows of Lamanite tents pitched on the glimmering sands of the seashore. Jacob nodded, and took a deep breath.

"Tomorrow is the first day of the year," Teancum added. "The Lamanites believe that the events of the first day of the year determine all that will happen the rest of the year. If they find their king dead, they will take it as an ill-fated omen."

"They would abandon their plan to attack Bountiful to get to the lands northward." Jacob's thoughts flashed back to Bountiful, and to Miriam. If they were successful, the Lamanites would no longer be a threat to the city, and those in it.

"I will come with you, sir," he affirmed.

Teancum grinned gratefully. "I knew you would, Jacob."

Jacob pulled his spear out of the ground, and followed as Teancum beckoned into the cover of the trees.

As he followed his captain silently through the thick growth, and down the sloping land toward the seashore, Jacob tested the weight of the spear in his hand, feeling it grow slick with the sweat of his palms. But Captain Teancum seemed confident and unafraid, jogging silently ahead of Jacob, making no more sound than the wind that swirled around them.

Jacob's heart pounded furiously as they broke through the last of the trees and jogged out into the open, his feet sinking in the coarse beach sand. There was no cover now, and if there were any guards awake, the light from the full moon would show the black shadows of the two men easily. Nothing stirred among the tents. And but for the constant beating of the tireless surf on the shore, everything was silent.

Without a pause, Teancum started through the tents toward the center of the camp where feathered banners caught in the wind, easily showing the two men where Amalickiah slept.

Many of the doors of the smaller tents were thrown open to take advantage of the cooling breezes after the blistering heat of the day, and Jacob caught glimpses of their sleeping occupants as he passed them. Many were no older than the boy he had captured earlier. And several of them, many of the younger ones, had wretched wounds, hastily bound, and bleeding through the wrappings. Yet they slept with their weapons beside them as if they expected to fight again the next day.

Why did they insist on coming up to the lands of the Nephites to make war? Why did the thought of striking down those who had once been their kindred not repulse them? They only did it, Jacob hoped, because they knew no better. All they knew was what Laman had passed to his children, and them to their children down through the generations, that Nephi had wronged his older brother Laman and stolen his birthright from him. This lie was compounded doubly by dissenters like Amlici and Amalickiah who knew better, but gave no merit to truth in their greed for power. Already instilled with a deep hatred for the Nephites, it would take little more than skillful persuasion to convince the Lamanites to come up to battle against them. Jacob shook his head sadly as the two men slowed to a stop in the middle of the camp. Jacob could feel his heart throbbing in his ears, fearing that the sound of it alone would wake the

Lamanites. He parted the door of one of the largest tents, and peered in.

Amalickiah's girth had expanded since he had been among the Nephites, but Jacob recognized the ruddy skin, the black hair, and the heavy black beard. He had fallen asleep in his fine linen tunic, his feathered crown still on his head, and lay sprawled like a huge, beached whale among several pillows. His mouth hung slack, and saliva drooled into his thick beard as he wheezed noisily.

Jacob's chest swelled as his jaw tightened, and his mouth grew into a tight line. Teancum glanced in, angry fire rising in his eyes as he looked upon Amalickiah with disgust. Amalickiah had been the cause of this war, and the blood of thousands was on his head. Perhaps the death of Amalickiah would mean the end of the war, and no more blood would be spilt.

Teancum drew in a breath, and indicated to Jacob that he was to wait outside as he took the spear out of his hands. Jacob nodded and watched as Teancum went through the door and let the flap fall behind him. Jacob waited. He listened in the silence to the unending surf, his heart beating in his throat. He flinched when he heard a muffled thud from within the tent. Amalickiah's heavy breathing stopped abruptly. A moment later, Teancum emerged, Jacob's spear still clenched in his hand.

Indicating with his head, Teancum began jogging away from the tent, and Jacob followed behind him, knowing what he did not need to ask. His pulse began to slow and his blood cooled as they entered the shelter of the trees, concealed by the silvery dark shadows that filtered through the cover overhead. They hardly breathed as they moved silently away.

The Nephite tents stood out from the dark trees in the moonlight as they slowed to a walk and entered camp. Teancum's face was calm. "It is finished," he said quietly, his shoulders sagging as if released from a heavy burden.

慓

Ammoron's eyes snapped open, jerking him roughly out of a troubled slumber when one of his soldiers rushed through the door screaming inaudibly. He scowled up at his canvas ceiling.

"Calm yourself and speak slowly," he hissed brokenly in the warrior's tongue as he sat up. "You know I cannot understand such rapid babble."

"Your brother, my lord!" The Lamanite cried, dropping to his knees, his face contorted. "He has been killed by the Nephite dogs!"

Ammoron's hand went automatically to his tangled beard, and he tugged on it before he scrambled to his feet, pulling on his leather boots.

"My brother what?" He frowned.

"My lord, he is dead!" he howled. The arteries on his temples stood out on his face.

Calmly, Ammoron buckled on his metal sword. "Show me," he said in his most serious tone, brushing aside the tent door. As he stepped out into the bluish light of the morning, a gasp of disbelief tore from his throat, and his jaw dropped. The news of his brother's death had been carried to each man, and the camp had been thrown into a state of chaos. Warriors rushed about in a panic, the camp in tangled disarray. The tent had been taken down around his dead brother, his corpulent mass nestled among its pillows like a fat, beached manatee. To the west, against the green of the jungle, Ammoron could see glittering rows of Nephite warriors. Their flag, mounted high on its standard, rippled in the morning wind that came off the ocean at Ammoron's back.

Ammoron scowled. There was no way he could persuade the Lamanites to attack now. It was the first day of the year, and the Lamanites would take Amalickiah's death as a bad omen. Yet, he realized with a twitching smile, his brother's death had certain gains. He smiled to himself, and then, noticing two of his captains, called to them. "Mathani, Ahiah, come here."

The two light-skinned men looked worried as they came, their eyes focused on the line of Nephites. He laughed haughtily at their expressions.

"Sir, the Nephites are ready to come down upon us," Ahiah grumbled, fingering his sword hilt nervously as stray locks of sandy hair brushed against a red mark scarred into his forehead.

"You know they won't," Ammoron laughed, slapping Ahiah's shoulder roughly. "They are weaklings. They fight only in defense of themselves and their kind," he sneered. "This is but a small loss. We will return to Mulek and strengthen my armies."[10]

"*Your* armies?" Mathani asked incredulously.

Ammoron sneered. Then he moved to the inert mass that was once his brother and bent over it. Placing his foot on his dead brother's chest, he gripped the quetzal feathered headdress that indicated Amalickiah's station, and wrenched it off.

"This," he hissed, his eyes burning with greed as he set it on his own head, "is mine, now."

CHAPTER 14

26TH YEAR OF JUDGES

"*I* was told to bring the prisoner food and water," Miriam sputtered nervously to the guard who stood outside the heavy wooden door.

The guard eyed her, expressionless. "Yes, I was told you would come." He pulled the door open and the noise echoed ominously from within. From the door, steps descended into dark shadows. Miriam gulped and hesitated before she started forward. Clutching the food she held in her hands, she descended into the murky darkness. Her vision blurred, and she stood wavering at the bottom of the steps until her eyes adjusted to the darkness.

She moved deeper into the dim shadows, stopping when she saw her old friend. He sat with his back to the cement wall in the same position he had been in the night before. An iron fetter fastened around his ankle was linked with a long, heavy chain soldered into the stone wall at his back. His wounded arm had been cleaned and rebandaged, but he continued to cradle it, his jaw knotted with discomfort.

"Thobor," she tried to whisper softly.

His head had been lowered to his chest, and at the sound of her voice, raised up with a sudden snort. "Greetings, Miriam." His voice sounded forlorn in the empty, echoing chamber. "Such is my cursed luck, to find myself in this place on the first day of the new year."

"I brought you something to eat. Bread and cheese, and water to drink, for now."

"What I would do for a shank of roasted pig," he groaned, rising to his feet.

"Oh," Miriam shuddered and glanced away.

Thobor saw her expression and rolled his eyes. "Oh, yes, you Nephites do not eat unclean flesh," he snorted, disgust thick in his voice. But he stood and walked to her, as far as his chain would allow, and grumbled his thanks as he took the food from her hands.

"So you call yourself a Nephite now?" He bit a chunk out of the bread.

She cringed as he spoke, as if he was spitting out something vile. But she nodded. "Yes."

He glanced down and continued to munch on the bread. The loaf was nearly half gone already. His capacity to eat surprised her, and she studied him carefully, realizing how much he had changed since they were children. He was taller than she was now, and his once bony frame was bound in thick muscle. Most of his thick black hair had been shaved away except for a little crop that was bound at the top of his head like a sheaf of wheat. His jaw contracted rhythmically under his skin as he chewed.

"How is your arm?" she asked, releasing her gaze from his face as she studied his arm bandaged in clean, white cloth. He did not cradle it as he ate, but he did not use it, either. It simply hung at his side, like a useless, dead thing.

"I think it is better," he grunted glancing at his shoulder. He swallowed hard, steeling his face. "It hurts. The—the man who came to care for it, stitched it closed."

Miriam winced at the pain the memory brought onto his face.

"I hardly slept. When I did, I dreamed of my mother. She came and comforted me as she did when I was small, whenever I was sick. Once I dreamed of Grandmother Ishna."

Miriam smiled at the memories her name awakened. "Is Grandmother yet alive?"

"I do not know," Thobor shrugged. "The night you left, warriors and Nephite defectors came and took me, and boys my age away to train us as soldiers. I never saw Grandmother Ishna again. I got news later that she was midwife to my mother, you remember, she was going to have a baby—," He shook his head suddenly, stiffening. He glanced sharply away, his frame tightening.

"What happened?" Miriam whispered, but Thobor shook his head, violently.

"I owe no answer to a Nephite," he growled, his voice suddenly heavy with emotion. "Why do you ask all this of me?"

"I am your friend," Miriam gasped, retreating several steps. "Do you not—,"

"They sent you, did they not?" He jerked his head in the direction of the steps leading upward. "To gain my trust, so that I might tell you the plans of my army? You are a spy for them, are you not?"

"No, Thobor," she pleaded. "I am your friend."

"You are not my friend!" he spat, his eyes red and angry, his face swollen, as if holding back unshed tears. "The Miriam I knew no longer lives. You are a Nephite woman, a daughter of these pale dogs, who have taken me as their prisoner." Thobor's breath had grown labored, the tendons in his neck taut as bow strings. His eyes burned holes in Miriam's face. "My Miriam is as dead to me as my mother is."

"Your mother?" she whispered, her heart melting inside of her. She stepped up to him. "She is—dead?" She reached a hand up, and touched his face, feeling the hard sinew of his jaw beneath his cheek. "Oh, Thobor."

Thobor's wrath cooled at her touch, and his face crumpled. As it did, his whole frame seemed to lose its strength, and he sank to the ground, sobbing.

"Thobor," she murmured, dropping to her knees, and gathering his head against her shoulder. "My friend. I am here."

"My mother died in childbirth. Grandmother Ishna sent me word," he sobbed against her neck. "My masters, the Nephite dissenters never gave me a period of mourning. I was barely ten, but they told me that if I cried, they would beat me. I was a warrior, they said, and was expected to be strong."

"You can cry now, Thobor," Miriam murmured in his ear. "You have no reason to be ashamed of it."

Thobor nodded against her neck, his body continuing to jerk with fierce, wracking sobs, held in by years of staunch discipline, but that came spilling out now, like water over a broken dam.

Miriam held him this way for several minutes until his sobbing grew weak, and finally subsided, and he pulled back, his own expression open and vulnerable as he studied her face.

"Grandmother Ishna told me in her message that you had gone. That and the news of my mother's death were blows that took the heart out of me. She did not tell me why you had gone, or where." His eyes pled with her, filled with pain. "Why did you go? How did you come to be among these thieves and liars?"

"Grandmother Ishna herself sent me," Miriam returned, unable to ignore the hurt his last words had caused. "A Nephite dissenter, perhaps one of the dissenters who took you, wanted to offer me as a sacrifice to the gods."

He sighed wearily, "But to come here, among these ill-begotten dogs? Why did you not flee to another part of our lands where he would not find you?"

"He would have found me had I gone anywhere but here. And I am happy here, Thobor," she whispered tiredly, forcing herself to be patient. "There is much good among the Nephites. And I have learned much truth. You might learn as I have, if you are willing."

She drew back, and rose once again to her feet, gazing sadly down at her friend who remained kneeling dejectedly on the cold floor.

"I will come in the evening with more food," she promised, and turned away from him toward the steps where light spilled from the doorway, cascading down like a waterfall. Jacob's image returned to her mind, and her familiar ache returned to her heart. If only she could know that Jacob was safe!

"Miriam." Thobor's voice had softened. "Forgive me. I have hurt you."

She glanced back at him. "Of course I forgive you, Thobor."

He shook his head. "But you are a woman. My father always said that it is dishonorable for a man to hurt any woman, even with words."

"Thobor, you do not see things as I do. I too, believed all I had been taught about the Nephites, and was fearful when I first came among them. I understand a little, I think, what you feel now."

At her answer, his face softened, and he glanced down, blinking his eyes fiercely.

She barely heard the flurry behind her, but when a shadow blocked the light, she noticed the change. She turned back toward the steps, shading her eyes against the glare of the sunlight coming down around the man who stood silhouetted against the top of the steps.

"Miriam?" he called. He started down a few steps, shading his eyes. "Are you here?"

"Jacob!" she cried. Her heart leaped joyfully into her throat, and she dashed up the steps to him. He had shed his armor, but he wore his battle clothing, frayed and blood stained. He had a fresh bandage wrapped around his left forearm, and blood had seeped through it. She flung herself against his chest, ignoring the smell and sweat. "I was so worried about you."

She felt his strong arms circle around her, and squeeze her tightly. Somewhere underneath the thin cloth of his shirt, she could hear his warm, beating heart, and at that moment, it was one of the most wonderful sounds she had ever heard. She held herself close to him, relishing his nearness, his scruff-covered chin resting on top of her head. One of his hands stroked her hair gently.

"You worried about me?" His voice had deepened and softened, warming her to her core.

"Yes," she choked, pushing away to look up into his face. She could lose herself in his eyes. "I could think of nothing else."

"I thought of you, too," he sighed, and his hand came up to rest against her cheek, warm and gentle, though his palm and fingers were roughened. "I missed you."

Her heart leaped, and she pulled back suddenly, dropping her eyes as a flush came to her cheeks. *You are nothing but a child to him!* she reminded herself fiercely. *Do not be such a fool that you imagine he feels things for you when he does not.*

"Come Jacob, you must meet an old friend," Miriam stammered. And she took his hands in hers, pulling him down the steps into the cool shadows. Thobor sat with his arms folded across his chest. His back was against the wall, and he glared at the chain fettered to his ankle, his eyes burning with unbridled anger. The food was gone, and the water jar lay broken in pieces.

"This is Thobor," she stuttered hurriedly in the tongue of the Lamanites as Thobor lifted his eyes and glared at Jacob. "We were children together."

Jacob met Thobor's glare with equal strength of will. "Does your wound heal well?" Jacob's voice was sullen and guarded.

"I owe no answer to a Nephite," Thobor snarled.

Neither man's expression changed, and Miriam sighed. "Thobor, this is Jacob."

"Yes," Thobor muttered, stiff jawed. "The Nephite who saved my life." Miriam's eyes flickered from Jacob to Thobor. "I do not know if I should thank you, or curse you."

Jacob and Thobor continued to eye each other soberly.

"Jacob, Thobor, please," Miriam pleaded, her eyes flashing help-lessly between the two men who broke their stare to look at her.

Jacob sighed. "Very well. Let's go, Miriam." He smiled down at her, and caught her hand in his. Turning toward him, Miriam did not see Thobor's appraising eyes narrow as Jacob's hand circled her own.

Miriam tightened her hand within Jacob's hand, large and rough, yet gentle and comfortable to hold, and lifted her eyes to his as they started toward the light.

Even in the dim light, his golden brown eyes seemed able to see into her soul, and she diverted her gaze, fearful of the feelings stir-ring inside of her.

Think of him as a brother, and all will be well, she reminded her rac-ing heart.

A small shudder escaped her, and she turned her face forward as Jacob's hand released hers, and his arm slipped around her shoulders. She did not see the sadness behind his eyes as she lowered her face, and mounted the steps toward the sunlight.

○

Daylight was swiftly fading from the sky as people scurried about the street, eagerly finishing their daily tasks. Each person seemed intent on getting somewhere. At the doorway of her little house, however, Esther felt safe and at home, and had no desire to go anywhere else. Her arms were folded as she leaned against the doorjamb, savoring the lingering twilight and the cool evening air, remembering home in Melek as a child when her parents had been alive. Life had been like this with them. She sighed, a smile crossing her face. She felt like a child, like one of the little ones, who played kickball before her in the street, as they flew, screeching joyfully, after the ball as it bounced wildly away. She had not felt such freedom as a maid to Lylith, Pachus's daughter, who treated her more like a slave than a servant. But that life was far behind her, and a new one was before her.

Before the house, in the wide dusty street, the excited shrieks of young Jacob at play with his friends rose easily into the calm evening air as they raced up and down between the houses and stone fences. Someone had kicked the rubber ball in a wild arch, and the boys raced after it. Young Jacob was the swiftest of his friends, and cried in childish delight as he closed in on the escaping ball. Miriam, his sister, sat below Esther on the steps, watching the game as she twined cotton thread onto a spool in her lap, humming softly to herself. Esther smiled as she hugged her arms tightly. She had nearly everything she wanted in her life, safety, friendship with Miriam, a child to help care for. But—something was missing. She sighed, and pressed a hand close to her heart, impatient with herself. She had all she needed, she reminded herself, and even more.

The noise in the road had died down, and she heard Miriam rise to her feet. Esther glanced in the direction Miriam was looking, to see a soldier approaching them through the dusk.

"Jacob!" young Jacob bleated, running toward the man and throwing himself into his arms. "I kicked the ball through the basket three times!"

"Good for you. You will make it four next time." Jacob set him back on the ground, took the boy's hand in his, and together they came toward the steps where the women waited, his smile lifted toward Miriam.

"He played very well," Miriam agreed, her hands fluttering nervously before she clasped them behind her back. "His legs are as swift as a jaguar's. Someday, he will be a great warrior."

"Like Jacob," little Jacob grunted, using Jacob's arm to catapult himself up onto his back.

Esther smiled and turned her eyes down as Jacob drew closer to Miriam, ignoring the energetic boy clambering on his back.

"Young Jacob," Esther murmured as she descended the steps, and reached for the boy's hand. "Come."

Without argument, he slid from Jacob's back, and reached for Esther's hand, following her up the steps, and through the door. Young Jacob continued on into the house, but Esther waited just beyond the doorway, her breath arrested in her throat.

"It is almost time for me to go out to command the night watch." Jacob voice was low, but filled with animation.

"I will wait for you at the gate in the morning when you return," Miriam replied, her own voice even and soft.

He smiled, and his eyes sparkled as he lowered his face. "As you always do."

A long moment passed, and Esther could not help but roll her eyes, and let her hands fall against her skirt in agitation. Still she remained quiet as the two spoke, still lengths apart, ignoring her and all else around them.

"I also thought I must tell you," Jacob continued, a hint of breathlessness in his voice, "We have formed a plan to retake Mulek."

"Yes, I have heard," Miriam answered softly, but then her voice grew coarse. "You will—be in the battle."

He gulped and nodded slightly. "I have command of some of the men under Teancum. We will have our final strategies planned within the week, and we expect to make an assault very soon."

"Then I will pray that God will be with you." Miriam's voice was heavy, near tears, but she made no move toward Jacob. And while Jacob's posture betrayed his desire to move toward Miriam, he remained where he stood, his hands hanging heavily at his sides.

After another long moment, he stirred, and looked away. "I must go now, Miriam. Rest well. May God be with you."

"May God be with you, as well, Jacob," Miriam murmured to his already retreating back, then turned, and clambered slowly up the steps.

Esther folded her arms, and glared at her as she shuffled through the doorway.

"Miriam," she ground out, a hard edge to her voice.

Miriam glanced at her eyes, and sighed, "I have told you, I am just a little girl to him, Esther."

Esther sighed. "Have you never wondered why he looks at you the way he does? Why he spends all his free time with you, simply so that he can be near you?"

"I told you, Esther. I am nothing compared to Lylith, or even the mere memory of her—,"

"And I have told you, Miriam, I knew Lylith! She is nothing compared to you! Jacob did not want her! Why can you not see that?" Esther hissed, her patience gone. "And if you doubt that, why do you not ask Jacob? Speak to him about your feelings! Surely he feels the same for you."

"I cannot speak to him about such things. I am a little sister to him. Nothing more."

Esther groaned audibly, and glanced toward the fire where little Jacob waited, staring at them over the top of the bubbling stew pot.

Drawing in a deep breath, she turned away and stepped toward him, folding her legs beneath her as she sat before the fire, opposite him.

She heard Miriam come quietly from behind her, and sit between them. In the firelight, Miriam's face was sober, almost sad. "I am almost sixteen. Most girls are married by my age, and mothers," she sighed, and let the words hang in the air a long moment before she spoke again, wistfully. "Perhaps I will never marry."

"I am seventeen," Esther offered with a shrug, her eyes crinkling into an amused expression. "But there is hope yet for us both."

"Yes, there is," Miriam sighed, but her eyes did not agree with her words.

CHAPTER 15

28TH YEAR OF JUDGES

*B*lue tendrils crept across the dissolving gray of the early morning sky as Miriam sat before her loom, her fingers flying nimbly as her shuttle moved back and forth. The cloth she wove was not as fine twined as some others she had seen, but it was durable, and of good quality. And if she sold it for a good price, perhaps she would have enough to buy a length of the lovely blue linen she had seen and admired in one of the booths at the market. And if Jacob came home from the battle alive—she shook the thought out of her mind and glanced at Esther.

Her friend sat nearby, busily spinning thread, but from the look in her troubled eyes, she could see that her mind was not on her task. As Esther's eyes turned to hers, they quietly traded a glance that needed no words.

"You are worried for Jacob," Esther finally murmured, and Miriam quickly turned her face back to her loom, not wishing for Esther to see the reaction on her face.

"Yes, I am," she admitted.

She lifted her eyes to the southeast horizon. As she did, her heart tightened and tears clouded her vision. She blinked them quickly away, and turned back to her loom, her hands resuming their work, though she noted that they trembled now, a little. Her eyes remained on her hands and the cloth they wove, but her thoughts were far away, beyond the city walls and the nearby hills, to where a company of soldiers waited to do battle. Almost of their own volition, her silent lips began to murmur a prayer.

At that moment, far away to the southeast, Jacob was taking advantage of a moment's rest to sharpen his sword. The metal sang as he rubbed a stone along the blade that lay across his knees. He paused a moment and looked up as if he heard something, turning his eyes to the northwest. He saw nothing and dropped back to his work, locking his eyes on his task. In truth, although he was indeed sharpening his weapon, in his mind's eye he was watching Miriam, studying the tenderness of her eyes, the softness of her tanned skin, the curve of her mouth.

He finished sharpening his sword, so he set the stone on his knee, and wiped the blade smooth with a light cloth before sheathing it, and picking up a spear from the ground beside him. As he began to grind the stone along the short, barbed head of the spear, a slight frown creased his countenance. He could gain nothing from such foolish daydreams. She had said, many times, that she saw him as nothing more than a brother. A momentary pang of frustration shot through hm. The metal vibrated as he raced the stone up the edge of the blade with furious energy, instantly repenting of his emotion after the tip of the blade nicked the edge of his thumb, drawing a small, red bead of blood. He blinked his eyes several times, shaking his head to clear it as he wiped the blood away against the cloth of his kilt.

But her eyes, when she looked at him, were large and soulful as if they could see into his heart. And when he allowed himself the luxury of daydreams, he imagined the look in her eyes as something more than friendship. She had been easy to understand as a child, but the woman she was becoming was vastly different than the child she had been, and her sea blue eyes haunted him as they gazed through the window of his mind. And he wondered, and hoped.

He was jarred out of his reverie by someone's voice. "Sir, they have seen us." The man's voice held an edge of tension, and the look in his eyes matched it as he pointed. Jacob lifted his face and looked to where the city of Mulek lay to the west of Teancum's army.

In the distance beneath the gate of Mulek's east wall, a dark horde of men streamed toward them. A chill ran through him, but Jacob's heart mustered courage, and a slight smile touched his face.

Gripping the shaft of his spear in his hand, he leaped to his feet as he heard Teancum's shouted signal to march at full speed. Even as a distant roar of confidence rose from the army of Lamanites, Jacob did not feel the same desperate urgency that other battles had brought to him. As they had hoped, their small army had drawn out the greater part of the Lamanite forces who did not know that an army, led by Moroni himself, was advancing toward the west side of the nearly deserted city. Or that Lehi, with his own numberless troops, waited beyond the distant rills toward which Teancum's army led them.

CB

Night unfurled its raven wings across the sky as the last of the evening's light faded to a dark purple against the western horizon.

Jacob lifted his weary head as he passed under the large open gate into the city, glancing down the rows of buildings. Dozens of anxious women crowded the street, or filled the light that streamed out through doorways and windows as they gazed out over the crowd of soldiers, searching for husbands, sons, and brothers. It was a moment before he saw a face he recognized, and drew to a stop, lifting his hand in greeting. Miriam's eyes found him and she waved before she darted toward him.

He started eagerly forward through the crowd toward her. A moment later, she squeezed between two portly men who had been blocking her way, and threw herself into his arms in spite of the sweat and grime caked into his clothes.

"Jacob," Miriam breathed, lifting her brilliant blue eyes for a moment. "Where you hurt at all?" He smiled at her, studying the expression in her eyes as he held her close, wondering again if there was more behind her words than what she said.

"I am unhurt," he assured her. "We led the Lamanites away from Mulek while Moroni came from the west side, and took the city they had left unguarded."

"Yes, yes," she hurried on, breathlessly, "then with Lehi's army, you turned and trapped the Lamanites between you and Moroni's army that had come from behind them," she sighed. "I heard Moroni was wounded."[11]

"He will recover," Jacob reassured her as she studied him with worried eyes.

She pressed again, "And you? You were not wounded?" With her hands in his she stepped back and appraised him as if searching for wounds, and his heart flopped rapidly in his chest at the thought that perhaps what she saw pleased her. But her hands fell from his, and she stepped back.

"I am glad you are not hurt," she murmured, suddenly demure, as a soldier, not two paces away from them, scooped up a giggling girl in his arms, and kissed her soundly.

An empty ache settled in Jacob's heart. His feelings of exhaustion and hunger seemed suddenly overwhelming, and nothing but his own needs concerned him now, drained as he was.

"I must go now, Miriam," he muttered, and turned, trudging the rest of the way to the garrison alone.

A crestfallen look came over her face as she turned, and gazed after him, gnawing her lip. "Jacob," she moaned to herself. "Wait. Turn back. Come back to me."

He did not look back, and in a moment, he was gone from her view.

Her shoulders drooped. Sighing, she turned and shuffled away.

გ

The sun had set only moments before, shooting a plethora of reds and purples into the sky. The plumes of fire touched off the gathering clouds, filling the land with light. Even without the sun's direct rays, Thobor could feel the heat against his back, and a drop of sweat suspended at the tip of his nose as he hacked at the soft earth with his pick.[12]

Frustrated, he rubbed away the sweat, smearing dirt across his face. He glared up at the guards who stood above him, opposite the sheer wall of the city as he flung another shovelful of dirt on their feet. The one who was the leader, the tall one with the dark hair and the light brown eyes, was the one called Jacob, who had saved his life. He glanced down at his arm where the jagged pink scar extended from his shoulder to his elbow. It would not have taken long to bleed to death from such a wound.

He frowned as he flung up another bite of dirt. Why had the Nephite not left him to die? It would have been easy enough. Why had he not done it? He flung one more shovelful of loose earth up, purposely hitting Jacob in the legs, and then straightened and stared at him defiantly, waiting for a curse or a reprimand. Jacob merely stepped back a pace, his eyes fixed on Thobor, his hand resting on the hilt of his sword.

Thobor finally glanced away, returning with his pick to his work.

"You are thirsty?" he heard Jacob ask him, and he glanced back up again.

Thobor ran his tongue over dry lips. "No." He bent back to his task.

"Here," Jacob said. He picked up a heavy water skin, fat and bellied with water that had been lying at his feet, and tossed it down to him.

Thobor straightened, caught the heavy bag in both hands and glared suspiciously up at Jacob as he uncorked it, and lifted it to his lips, pulling long hungry draughts down his parched throat until his thirst was satiated. "What of my comrades?" he gasped, wiping his mouth, pointing with his head at the other prisoners.

"Let them drink until they are full," Jacob commanded. "We have more."

Thobor nudged the man beside him with his elbow and handed him the water skin. The man snatched it, and drank deeply, before brushing his forearm across his mouth, and handing the skin to the next man.

Thobor raised his face to the sky, realizing the brilliant color had faded. The clouds, now black and threatening, were clamping down over the sky like a hard metal lid.

Jacob had seen the lowering clouds as well. "Put your tools up!" he shouted. His powerful voice carried easily down the long line. In obedience to his order, the prisoners tossed their digging tools up on the bank, where a handful of soldiers ran down the line gathering them up. Thobor waited at the bottom of the trench with the others, feeling the first spatterings of rain, while the soldiers carried the tools away. The dirt under his feet would soon turn into thick mud, and Thobor eagerly obeyed the command when Jacob finally gave them permission to climb out of the trench they had been digging along the city's wall. The dirt was slippery, and he imagined himself a fly, trying to climb out of a honey jar. He grabbed at the solid grass that lined the top of the trench. His feet kicked helplessly against the mud soaked side, and he sensed himself beginning to slip back, when he felt the solid grip of someone grasping his forearm, pulling him up to his feet.

He glared in surprise and indignation at Jacob as he shook his arm off.

"You lost your foothold," the Nephite declared calmly, his expression unchanging.

Thobor said nothing as he turned and followed after the others along the edge of the trench.

"Miriam speaks of you often." Jacob's words startled him, and he glared over at him.

Thobor did not answer at first, glaring in his accustomed way, silent. Then he spat, "Why does it matter to you, Nephite?"

Jacob stared straight ahead. "She thinks highly of you. She believes you are trustworthy and honorable. And though you strive to prove otherwise, I am not blind. I believe Miriam is right."

Thobor turned his eyes to the Nephite's face. The rain was coming down harder now, the boiling clouds growing black, and Jacob's brown hair was plastered to his forehead.

"Are you?" the Nephite persisted. His light eyes bore into Thobor's.

Thobor rolled his eyes. "Miriam was a friend to me when we were children. Her opinion of me would be marred, because of that. It is true, I have never killed a man, but that does not mean I am not wicked."

"A truly wicked man would not admit his fault." Jacob's voice had dropped.

Thobor glanced at the Nephite. His eyes were down, water dripped from his hair, but there was tenderness in his eyes, and a thoughtful smile on his lips. The sneer dropped from Thobor's face, and his eyes narrowed. "Why do you speak of Miriam?"

"I have known her since she came to our lands," returned Jacob, without looking at him. "She is a good friend to me."

Thobor tightened his jaw, studying the Nephite's chiseled features. His face, like all other Nephite men, was covered with a shadow of scruff that would grow into a full beard if he allowed it. He was well favored, for a Nephite. It was no surprise that Miriam looked on him with tenderness. And as beautiful as Miriam was, it was no surprise to him that this Nephite looked on her with equal favor.

"Like you, Nephite, I am not blind," Thobor heard himself say gruffly, his eyes focused on the prison gate before him. "Miriam is dearer than a sister to me. I want her happiness, and could never endure to see her hurt." He turned one last glance at the Nephite. Jacob's light eyes appraised him, his face pondering and reflective, then he turned away with the rest of his men.

A guard, drawn sword in hand, mumbled something Thobor could not understand, and pushed him along through the heavy, black mud where the other prisoners were waiting for the guards to hand out their evening rations. Those Lamanites who had their meager bowls of gruel and flat corn bread had collapsed exhausted, ignoring the rain as they ate.

Several of his fellow Lamanites looked up when they saw him. Others, their heads bowed in shame and defeat, glanced at him with apathetic eyes, and then looked away again. A few of them, with similar spirits as Thobor remembered in himself, kept their heads up as if they were completely unaware that they were prisoners. Their eyes were bright and ever dancing around, looking for a chance to revolt against their captors.

One Lamanite, older and larger than himself, his face hardened and scarred by numerous battles, had his face up, studying his surroundings, and Thobor gulped and cringed inwardly as he saw the murder in the man's dark eyes. A young armored guard stood near him, dwarfed beside the prisoner he guarded. The Lamanite's hands, large paws for a man, were slowly clenching. Intense hatred blazed in his angry eyes.

He could see the shifting in the man's eyes, and without thinking, Thobor stepped from his place in line and started forward moments before a war cry erupted from the Lamanite's lips.

The huge man hurled himself at the young guard, and in a moment's time, had shoved him to the ground, wrenching the sword from his hand.

Warning shouts echoed across the compound, and the pounding of running feet came from all directions as the Lamanite lifted the sword above his head to slice it into the soldier's body.

Before the blade could descend, however, Thobor wedged himself between his fellow Lamanite and the Nephite soldier. In a single motion, he caught the descending fist of the Lamanite in one hand, bracing its downward swing. He held it there, his eyes focused on the dark, murderous eyes of his comrade as the Nephite soldier scrambled clumsily away.

"Traitor," the Lamanite hissed. His dark eyes narrowed and his pungent breath caused Thobor's throat to tighten. He twisted out of the younger man's grasp, and lashed the sword at Thobor's stomach. Thobor leaped nimbly back, feeling a biting sting slice across the taut skin of his belly, and with as much agility, plunged forward, bringing his fist sharp into the Lamanite's jaw, causing him to stumble backwards. He tumbled into several other prisoners who fell with him into an almost comical dog pile.

In his fall, the man had dropped the Nephite's sword. Thobor picked this up, and slapped the hilt into the hands of the young soldier who came forward to claim it, gaping in awe at Thobor. The other Nephite guards arrived and pulled the fallen prisoner and his companions who had stumbled after him, to their feet. A harsh, shouted command silenced the grumbling crowd of prisoners, though many turned back to glare at Thobor. But he clenched his jaw, his chest heaving from his fight, and glared back, barely aware of the thankful hands the Nephite soldiers clapped onto his shoulders.

Thobor only shook his head and scowled, wondering why he had done it. He had passed up so many chances to cause mischief in the last year that he had lost count of them. There was something here, though, beyond his understanding that stopped him. What it was, he was not sure. It seeped into his soul, a sort of whispering that filled his heart with peace, and he thought that if he stayed, he might discover a secret hidden here that seemed to live in the air about him, only just beyond the reach of his thoughts.

Thobor sighed and turned his attention to the cut on his stomach—a clean, shallow slice across his abdomen. With his bare hand, he mopped at the long streak of red, not noticing a familiar figure approaching him with a quick, energetic step.

"Thobor?" He looked up to see Laman approaching him. "Do my eyes lie to me? Did you truly fight another prisoner to save the life of one of us?"

Thobor spread his bloody hands, to show the wound across his stomach. "I did not wound myself."

Laman gaped. "Why?"

Thobor shook his head, shrugging.

Laman studied Thobor thoughtfully, and after a time, Thobor looked away, disconcerted by Laman's pensive stare. At last he spoke to the young man whom Thobor had saved, who stood a few steps away. "Take him to the garrison. Tell them what has happened. Captain Jacob will arrange for quarters for him."

Though Laman had spoken the Nephites' tongue, Thobor had understood, and his eyes shot up. "I am a prisoner. You dare not trust me."

"Yes, I do. And you cannot stay here. Every Lamanite here is now your enemy."

The young soldier nodded, and beckoned with his head. "Come," he ordered. The bright glint of gratitude was in his eyes as he trotted away, his helmet in his hand, and his sword now safely sheathed. Thobor followed him hesitantly out the prison gates, and turned his feet in the direction of the torch-lit garrison.

Ω

"Miriam!" Esther cried. "Do you know what this is?"

Miriam saw her friend waving a scrap of paper, but she turned away and continued to examine bolts of cloth stacked in the narrow wooden booth, only one of many that lined the busy and humming market place. One bolt of soft blue cloth caught her eye, and she touched a hand to it, fingering the cloth gently from both sides.

"Miriam, look." Esther's brown eyes were alight as she thrust the paper at her. Miriam sighed, but obligingly took the paper from her friend, and read. It was a notice for all those who had lived in Mulek to prepare to return to their homes and help to rebuild the city.

"What is this for?" she wondered, looking into the eager eyes of her friend, her face aghast with confusion. "We are not from

Mulek." Miriam shook her head slightly, and turned back to the booth. The large woman was growing anxious, wondering if Miriam would make a purchase, or simply drive the rest of her customers to other little shops.

"Why do you want to go to Mulek?" Miriam asked, indicating to the woman that she wanted to make a purchase of a length of the blue fabric. "Are you not happy here?"

Esther was silent, and Miriam cleared her mind of the matter as the woman cut the desired length of cloth, wrapped it for her, and held out her chubby hand for the money.

"Thank you," she murmured to the woman who rolled her eyes and did not answer, relieved to see them leave.

"Of course I am happy here." Esther's voice carried a hint of distress in it. Miriam stopped with a sigh, and turned to her friend.

"Esther, what is it?"

"We have been so blessed here, and so safe," Esther sighed. "Should we not help do something, so that those who have come from Mulek can have their own city again?"

Miriam lowered her face. "But we help here as well," she protested. "We have woven and rolled bandages, and even cared for the wounded several times."

"Yes, we have," Esther agreed tiredly. "But I think you should know—Captain Lehi, who was given charge of Mulek, has asked Teancum to relieve Jacob of his duties here so that he could take command under Lehi in Mulek."

"Jacob?" Miriam's hands suddenly tightened around her package.

"Miriam," Jacob's voice called as he broke through the crowd at Miriam's shoulder. She caught a gasp in her throat, and her eyes darted about, as if looking for an escape before they lifted to his. "Captain Moroni has given Captain Lehi charge over Mulek and I have been—,"

"Yes, I heard." Miriam drew in a long, slow breath, and glanced at Esther who had taken several steps away, and was pretending to be interested in the clay jars covering the table of one of the booths nearby. "Esther and I wish to go to the land of Mulek as well." She held up the paper Esther had given her.

Jacob snatched the paper, his eyes dancing over it. "There will be much to do. We will have little time to see one another."

Miriam sighed, and looked away. "But at least we will be near each other."

Jacob's eyes turned to her as she said this, and her eyes flicked to his, then lowered as she felt the heat rising to her face.

"It will be good if you come to Mulek," Jacob offered softly. Miriam lifted her gaze, stiffening at the look in his warm, golden brown eyes.

"I hope so," she murmured before she dropped her eyes again. She could feel Jacob's eyes on her, and within her, she could hear the excited beating of her heart.

CHAPTER 16

The evening wind blew softly across the parapets of the west walls of Mulek as Miriam climbed the creaking wooden steps and leaned out over the battlements, drinking in the wonder of the land around this new city. From the wall where she stood, the land fell away and rolled down into a valley below her, where evening mists were already beginning to swirl. It appeared almost as if it was a lake, filled with shimmering water. The sky was splashed with crimson, purple and orange, and reflected down onto the misted valley, brightening the mixing fog with as much amber and rose colored light as was burning against the clouds in the sky.

She leaned against the parapet, drawing a long, slow breath, grateful for a few moments of rest. She and Esther had been in the city for several days, helping along with the others, to repair the damage caused by the Lamanite occupation. The men were reconstructing many of the damaged buildings, and portions of the wall needed repair. Miriam and the other women worked at their own tasks as diligently as the men, doing numberless, tiring chores beginning with the sun's rising and not finishing until it had set. She sighed again, her heart warmed by the brilliant fire in the sky, wishing for someone to share it with. But since they had come to the city, the soldiers had little time to eat or sleep, let alone speak to the women. She smiled, remembering her quick glances at Jacob when she was certain he was not looking. Once, she had caught him with his gaze following her, and when their eyes met and lingered, a warmth coursed through her blood.

A gentle breeze sprang up, bringing her out of her thoughts as it caught strands of her hair and played with them, tossing them about her shoulders. It caught at her dress, pulling at the soft blue material, quietly brushing over her as it cooled the city from the day's heat of the sun.

She sighed, pressing her fingertips into the craggy, grainy surface of the stone, feeling its rough coolness before she pulled her hands away, and folded them to herself against the warmth of the blue cotton cloth.

Heavy footfalls coming up the wooden stairs alerted her to the soldier's presence. She straightened and turned to utter a hasty apology, but the words froze in her mouth when she saw his face.

"The view is beautiful, here," Jacob murmured, his eyes on her face as he came to join her at the parapet.

"Yes, it is," she agreed, turning her face from him as she gazed over the scene below her, watching the light fade to darker reds and purples. Slowly she unfolded her arms again, resting her hands against the grainy surface of the stone.

Jacob rested his arms against the parapet and shifted his weight so that his muscled arm brushed against her shoulder. She shuddered as a pleasant chill shot through her.

What were these strange feelings surging through her veins as he smiled at her? She hardly dared to hope.

Jacob turned back to gaze over the reddened valley, leaning close to Miriam. Their arms touched lightly, sending warmth through her. A moment later he slowly moved his large, warm hand to cover hers. She heard him exhale a great breath.

"I am glad I found you." His voice was soft. "Esther and young Jacob said you might be here."

"Why were you looking for me?" She could barely squeeze the words out.

"I have something important to tell you." She turned to him in the moment he turned to her. Their faces were mere inches apart.

"Captain Lehi is leading a group of men up to Gid to spy on the forces there. I am going with him."

"Oh." She studied the sober lines of his face. "When do you leave?"

"Tonight." He turned to look out over the valley, his jaw tightening thoughtfully.

Miriam said nothing, but she knew that her face reflected the worry she felt inside.

"We will not be gone long," he assured her, turning toward her. "Then I will come back to you. I promise."

Her heart gave a fierce throb, and her blood pulsed like hot lava through her veins. "I will miss you, Jacob." Her words were so soft, she wondered if he could hear them.

"And I will miss you." His voice was a warm caress, and she dropped her eyes.

He remained silent for several seconds, then he drew in a deep breath. "I have something for you." He straightened again, and opened a tiny pouch at his belt. "Here, I have saved this."

Miriam caught her breath. Jacob lifted a long, thin leather band from the little pocket, and held it out for her inspection. It twisted, something glinted in the wane light, and she drew a deep breath as she studied the polished smoothness of the blue drop-shaped stone bound to the leather string, which Jacob held out to her. Its ends still hung loose.

"I remember," she stuttered, embarrassed. "Though I wish I did not. I do not deserve—,"

"There is no one else I would ever give it to." He begged her, "Will you take it?"

She hesitated, surprised at the intensity of his question. "No one? But I thought—," She could feel tears coming into her eyes, her throat constricting. And finally, she blurted the words she had been holding inside for so long, "But what am I to you, compared to Lylith, Jacob?"

"Lylith?" he whispered in disbelief. "Surely you do not think she means anything to me?"

"But I saw you—and her. She was with you—in the trees. The night in Moroni's camp before I left to go to Lehi," Miriam whispered timidly, her head down. "I saw you—, I saw you kiss her, Jacob."

Jacob's face blushed red, and he glanced downward. "Yes, I remember that night, and the kiss. But I did not want it. She caught me off guard. I never wanted someone like her for my children's mother. If anything, her kiss that night reconfirmed that she was not the one I wanted."

"But she was so beautiful. How could I compare—,"

Miriam felt the soft brush of his hand beneath her chin, his callused finger gentle as he lifted her face. His eyes, ringed with an edge of dark brown, were the color of soft, sun-warmed leather, flecks of gold and green catching in the light where the fading sun touched the side of his face. The tender look in his eyes deepened, and he drew closer to her. "You are beautiful, Miriam. And your beauty goes deeper than the surface of your skin. Your soul is as beautiful as the rest of you." He paused, his eyes filled with tenderness, then lifted the necklace again in offering.

She leaned her neck forward in a silent acceptance of his gift, and felt his warm hands against her skin as he slipped the necklace around her throat, deftly binding the loose ends beneath her thick hair at the back of her neck.

As he drew back, his hands brushed against the soft flesh of her throat.

"Jacob, I—," she swallowed, "I have something for you, as well."

Reaching beneath her collar, she withdrew the beads that had been resting there since the night Ishna had given them to her when she had been a child. Drawing the leather thong over her head, and gently pulling her hair free of the long cherished gift, she held it in her hand a moment, and gazed at the blue and silver pattern in the beads where they lay in her palm before she offered it to Jacob.

Jacob took the beads that still held the warmth of Miriam's skin, reverently into his own hands, running his thumb gently over Miriam's hand where it lingered within his. She looked up, and her eyes met his, which were warm and dark, and shone in the fading twilight. "Jacob," she finally murmured, "am I only as a sister to you?"

"Miriam." He smiled, and his voice grew tender. "When we first met, when you were a child, I loved you as a brother would a sister, but now, over these last few years as I watched you become a woman, I came to see the beauty and sweetness of your spirit as well as your physical beauty. And I have grown to love you as a man loves a woman."

"Oh, Jacob," Miriam choked. She turned away, pressing her hands hard into the grainy surface of the stone, crushing her eyelids tight against the tears that spilled from beneath them. "I—," she drew in a shuddering breath, "love you, too."

She felt his hand cover hers, and lift it slowly, holding it tenderly between his own large hands as if he held something infinitely precious. Slowly, she turned, and looked up at him, losing herself in the warmth of his closeness, and the depths of his eyes. She glanced timidly downward as a hand came to her face and cupped her cheek. Barely aware of what was happening, she closed her eyes and tilted her face toward his.

Men's voices penetrated the stillness; a group of them were approaching the gate and Miriam started, her eyes snapping open.

"That would be Captain Lehi and the others," Jacob murmured, his mouth enticingly close to hers. He drew back, shaking himself, and gazed down at her, his eyes pleading forgiveness. "I must go now, Miriam."

"I will wait for your return," she breathed softly. "May God be with you, Jacob."

"And you, Miriam." He lifted her hand, and pressed his lips against her open palm. She shuddered deliciously at the warmth of his mouth against her flesh as he silently conveyed his tenderness and longing before he released her, turned on his heel, and did not look back again as he marched down the steps, his footsteps fading into silence.

She shuddered, suddenly cold under the darkening sky. The first few stars began to twinkle through the veil of the firmament. The creaking steps echoed in the stillness as she descended to the ground, seeing again the angles of his face softened in tenderness, the scar of the jaguar's claw across his shoulder.

He had been barely more than a boy when he had gained that scar, risking his life to save hers. She had been a child herself, but the affection that had grown between them had been real. And now, he was a man. And she had become a woman. And their friendship had grown from the seed that had been planted in their young hearts into a magnificent flower, the bud of which had begun to bloom.

ଔ

Jacob crept along the ground under the clear night sky, as silent as a prowling jaguar as his taut muscles paused. Beside him, a twig cracked, and he swiveled his head.

Ahimaz's eyes glowered like an angry animal's in the darkness. And as Jacob turned, Ahimaz shrugged and scowled. Jacob gritted his teeth. Jacob knew of Ahimaz's deeply burning hatred for Lamanites, and that he thirsted for battle, resenting Lehi's orders to stay secreted in the wilderness. And since Jacob intended to carry out Lehi's orders, Ahimaz directed his anger at him. Jacob's frustration twisted in his belly like a coiled serpent. But this was the fifth night, and soon they would return to Mulek, and he would be with Miriam again.

The thought brought a wry smile to Jacob's lips as he came to a bank of earth hidden from the southern road.

Jacob turned, seeing a hungry glint in Ahimaz's eyes. He signaled him to stay down, hoping desperately that he would obey. Ahimaz nodded and dropped to his belly on the soft earthy soil as both men peeped over the top of the ditch onto the silvery gray dusted road. They could see troops of Lamanites through the dark veil of trees, ten men abreast, marching toward the city. Jacob began to size them up, counting as each row filed past him. Ahimaz noiselessly removed his bow from around his shoulder, and fitted an arrow to the string.

As swiftly as they came, they were gone, and Jacob began to push his way from the ditch, but Ahimaz stayed where he was. "There might be more coming, sir," he mumbled.

"We are going, Ahimaz," Jacob grated, his hands balling into fists.

"Fool," Ahimaz rasped. "Why must we go when they are here, unsuspecting, in our grasp?"

"There are only two of us, and many of them," Jacob seethed.

"Sir, if we leave them alive, they will continue to do to us what they have done to our people for centuries." Ahimaz's voice was taut. "You do not understand, sir, nor does Captain Lehi understand. Like our chief captains, you think you can win this war by showing them mercy. But when have they shown us mercy? They showed my wife and children no mercy when they came to my village and slaughtered them."

Jacob glowered at Ahimaz now, confusion roiling within him as he saw the anguish on his face. "I understand your pain, Ahimaz," he grated, forcing patience. "There was a time when I thought the dearest person in the world to me was dead, that the Lamanites had killed her. But even if it had been true, I cannot hate the Lamanites. Not for their sake, but for mine. It would canker—,"

"Your children are not dead," Ahimaz sneered. "Or the woman who bore them."

Jacob shuddered at the look in Ahimaz's eyes, and could only stand by his orders. "We were given the order not to harm Lamanites," he reminded him. "You agreed to obey."

Ahimaz glared at Jacob, enmity seething like venom from a snake's fangs. "I lied."

Jacob clenched his teeth. "Ahimaz, we must return now."

At that moment, a soft sound floated toward them from the road, and they turned back. Jacob turned with alarm while Ahimaz grabbed his bow again, fitting an arrow to the string. Jacob glimpsed three Lamanites through the trees, who straggled behind.

"No, Ahimaz!" But Ahimaz had already released the arrow.

Jacob watched in horror as the arrow parted the thick leaves and slammed into one Lamanite with a thud. The blow spun him violently before he fell to the ground with a scream of pain.

Ahimaz sucked in a wild breath, suddenly aware of what he had done.

"Come," Jacob ordered as he tugged on Ahimaz's arm, and sprinted away as the wounded Lamanite's companions plunged into the undergrowth, long obsidian knives in their hands.

"This way, Ahimaz," Jacob puffed as he tore through the thick jungle, hoping to put enough distance between himself and any pursuers that they would not be able to catch him.

As he rounded the fat trunk of a tree, he would have crashed into a wall of rock if he had not tripped over a thick root, and gone sprawling face first into the soft soil. He could hear his pursuers crashing toward him, blocking any escape. As he scrambled to his feet, and unsheathed his sword, he saw with a sinking feeling that Ahimaz was no longer with him. At the same moment, he realized that two Lamanites alone could not create the noise that came tumbling and crashing toward him through the darkness like some unseen wild thing from a nightmare.

Finally, the trees shuddered, and he was surrounded in an instant by over a dozen Lamanites, clenching cimeters lined with glittering obsidian blades in their fists.

"He has no bow," he heard one of them say. "It was not him."

"Let us take this one prisoner."

"You cowards!" a voice with a Nephite accent growled, breaking the stillness of the night. "You could kill him easily. Do not leave him alive." After a moment, as Lamanites were flung left and right, a man with strong Semitic features and a mark tattooed into his forehead pushed his way through to face Jacob.

"If you do not kill the Nephite dog, I will," the man growled.

Jacob held himself steady, his sword gripped in his hand. His heart pounded in his ears.

The man sensed Jacob's apprehension, and his mouth twisted. The night was only half in shadow, but as the man drew a metal sword from its sheath and stepped forward, the jungle seemed to fade into the darkness. All Jacob could see was an odd, unnatural light glinting from the man's cold, blue eyes.

ଔ

The light of the distant dawn was beginning to reach up into the sky, giving it a clear bluish-black hue that made Lehi feel as if he was walking on the bottom of the sea. The trees around him even swayed lazily as if stirred by some underwater current.

The lines on his face were deeply etched, and weariness dragged at him like a heavy weight. His silver hair was plastered to his head beneath his helmet, but he patiently fought his fatigue.

"This was where they were to be," he grunted, staring steadily through the cover of trees at the walls of Gid.

"But where are they?" the young soldier at his side whispered. "They weren't at our meeting place. They could have—,"

"Wait." Lehi's whisper was harsh. "Look." He nodded to a large, heavy leaf. At first, it seemed to have nothing unusual about it, but upon closer inspection, he could see that the stem was torn and bruised on one side as if someone had brushed past the leaf, tearing the thick stem.

He saw now, a clear path made by many men as they crushed the undergrowth beneath their feet. Drawing in a great breath, he began to follow the path gouged through the forest. In spite of the crushed and broken plants, the forest growth was still heavy and as he pushed his way beneath overhanging vines, his foot snagged on something and he barely caught himself before he toppled to the earth.

"Sir." The soldier nodded at something on the ground, and Lehi glanced down.

The man whose arm Lehi had stumbled against lay unmoving, face down. Lehi involuntarily stepped away, but then forced himself to bend over the body, checking for a pulse though they both knew he was dead. He turned the head enough to look at the face, then let it drop.

He muttered something under his breath, then straightened and said it again, "Ahimaz." He felt the color drain from his face. "If they found Ahimaz, they surely found Jacob."

"Where is he, then?"

Lehi felt a sick heaviness filling his stomach as he spoke. "Perhaps they dragged him off somewhere, and despoiled the body."

The two of them continued with some trepidation along the path, their eyes scanning the floor of the trail as well as the depths of the thick jungle around them. After a time, they found themselves in a small clearing, surrounded on three sides by a sheer cliff of rock that thrust into the air, several times higher than a man's head. Mossy green plants, and low, fern-like bushes had once covered the little clearing, but had since been savagely trampled into the ground. The two Nephites stared in disbelief at the sight. Their eyes did not miss the massive red stain that had soaked into the crushed and trampled earth, nor did they miss the glimmer that caught their eyes from the depths of a mass of broken leaves, crushed against the ground. Glancing about with caution as he crossed the open clearing, Lehi reached the spot where they had seen the glint of light, and parted the leaves carefully, his heart pounding in his chest.

"It's Jacob's sword," he gulped, lifting the notched and bloody weapon.

"But where could the body be?"

"We cannot stay." There was an urgent tone to Lehi's voice. "The Lamanites know we are here. We must go."

"What of Captain Jacob's body, sir? Should we not find it as well?"

"His soul is with God," Lehi choked. "That must be enough for us." Then he turned and, with heavy footsteps, made his way back into the thickness of the jungle.

CHAPTER 17

There was something wrong. Even in her deepest sleep it woke Miriam when she felt it, and she sat up on her pallet, clutching her hand to her heart. She gasped, choking for air as the pain throbbed deep inside of her soul. Her own body was unhurt, yet a part of her was bleeding and in pain, and it frightened her. Sleep would no longer come to her, so she slipped into her sandals, and rolled to her feet. She glanced down at Esther and young Jacob, still sleeping, and felt a spasm of unexplained tears rising in her throat. She stepped out into the cool air.

The morning star shone brightly over the eastern sky, heralding the rising of another day, gray in the distance. A hint of ominous dark clouds rolled from the south. She hugged her arms, beating away the chill, and glanced over her shoulder at the full moon that was falling behind Mulek's west wall. In the thick smoky sky it glowered down on her, dark and red as blood.

A guard over the west gate called down to someone outside the gate, the sound carrying easily through the still air. The gate began to creak slowly open and Miriam's heart leaped, her pain forgotten in an instant. Jacob was returning! "Esther! Wake up," she gasped, rushing back into the tent, and dropping down beside her sleeping friend. "Jacob is back!"

Esther opened her eyes, and rose to her elbows, her face alight. "Then go meet him, silly girl!"

Quickly, Miriam scrambled to her feet, flinging the door aside, and rushing out to meet the returning soldiers.

Her breath coming in short gasps, Miriam ran eagerly toward the gate. But in an instant, her anticipation was crushed by a return-ing wave of pain and fear as she saw Captain Lehi emerge from the dark shadows beyond the gate.

Lehi reminded her of her father, Aaron, and he always had a smile or a kind word to say to her. But this morning, his worn, fatherly features were drawn down in a weary, unreadable expression. His eyes lifted and he saw her, turning his steps toward her as the other soldiers filed past, as somber and silent as a funeral procession. The last two men came out of the fog, a sturdy pole hanging between their shoulders. Lashed to both ends of the pole was a large skin wrapped tightly around something heavy that bent the thick pole as it swayed in time to the marching feet of the men.

Lehi bore something in his arms, wrapped in a skin. Miriam's hand rose without her bidding and touched the blue stone that lay warm against her throat. Dropping his burden to the ground, Lehi reached out, and took her chilled hand in his. He held it for a long moment, not moving or speaking. The skin had fallen away from the long, narrow object he had held in his hands, and Miriam moved forward, hesitant, her heart clattering in her throat. It was then that she realized it was a sword—Jacob's sword, notched and smeared with dried blood. Her eyes rose slowly to Lehi's and saw a deep weariness there.

"Who?" Miriam nodded to the lifeless sway of the skin lashed between the ends of the pole.

"Ahimaz," he answered, his eyes barely meeting hers.

"But this is Jacob's sword," she moaned, her voice hollow, coming as if from a distance.

"Yes."

"Where is he?" she demanded, her voice filled with anguish.

"We had no time to search for the body."

Miriam closed her eyes tightly as she drew forward a step. Lehi sensed her need, and opened his arms to her. Her throat tightened and as he pulled her close, she gave way to her grief and wept, her sobs muffled against his chest.

೧೫

He stumbled weakly against the stone steps that rose impossibly high toward the top of the terraced pyramid where a shadow stood waiting in the cold blue light of the early morning.

The steps of the pyramid that rose out of the jungle in the land of Siron were steep and broken, worn with wear, and he took care to step with caution. He did not have his arms free to catch himself if he fell, yet his guards impatiently hurried him, prodding him ever upward. He could hear the murmuring of the crowd below him, gathered at the base of the steps.

He barely felt the throbbing pain on the side of his face, or the swelling bruise on his cheek where they had struck him to wake him that morning. His guards had heard of his fierce battle with the dissenter, Ahiah, and in spite of their rough treatment of him, there was fear in their eyes. Ahiah was rumored to be the greatest swordsman among all the Lamanites. Yet he had beaten Ahiah, cutting a slash deep into his leg, slicing through an artery, spilling Ahiah's blood onto the trampled ground where they had fought, only to be overcome by Ahiah's men who knocked his sword from his hands, and pinned him down.

There were three warriors now, two in front and one behind. The two in front had shaved heads save for a patch of hair at the top, bound together and cropped flat. They both carried heavy cudgels set with blades of black obsidian. They were naked except for their loincloths and beaded leather shoes. The one behind was dressed in similar fashion and wore a headdress, high and pluming with the golden-green feathers of the quetzal. He also carried an intricately carved obsidian knife sheathed at his waist, and a staff, which he jabbed repeatedly into the Nephite's back.

The top of the pyramid was drawing closer, and the waiting figure came into focus. He realized with some surprise that it was a woman, an old woman bent and haggard with age and disease. She backed away slowly as the first two guards gripped his arms and pulled him up to the flat surface of the pyramid. Her eyes carried an empty, haunted look, and she was emaciated, a skeleton with a thin sheet of skin stretched over her bones. Her clothes were in rags, and the long stringy hair that scraped her skull was dull and dirty gray.

Behind her was a long flat altar, which had once been a cold, stone gray, but its surface had since been stained a dark color, and dark stains ran down its sides. The Nephite's blood ran cold.

One of the men in front called a greeting to the woman who slowly came forward, examining the Nephite with cold, piercing eyes.

"Adequate," she breathed in a hollow voice. "Bring him to the altar."

The woman moved slowly to the side as the first two warriors jerked him forward and forced him onto the altar, tying his feet down. They untied the rope from his arms, and fastened his wrists against the sides of the rock. The priest with the headdress moved into his view, and unsheathed his obsidian knife slowly. The blade was sharpened to a glistening point. The Nephite clenched his fists, his eyes focusing on the blade.

Miriam, forgive me, he thought as he raised his eyes to the face of the man who towered above him. The priest smiled, light dancing off of his teeth. *I promised you I would return.*

"Open up his heart," the man ordered the two who stood by.

Obediently, they approached him, each taking a corner of his soiled, bloody collar. The rotting cloth tore easily. The two men smiled to themselves, and moved away.

The Nephite felt his heart thundering within him and stared again at the man's eyes as he slowly raised the knife above his head.

Out of the corner of his eye, he could see the woman coming forward, perhaps to get a better look. *She may watch if she wants,* he thought. *After I die, they will have no more power over me. But Miriam— I promised her I would return. She trusted me.*

The priest grunted softly as he lifted the beaded leather thong from the Nephite's chest and examined it coldly for a moment, before he sneered and wrenched it viciously away, tearing the leather thong, and flinging it to the ground at the woman's feet where it landed with a soft clatter. The woman looked down, then bent and picked up the broken necklace as the priest began to raise the knife above his head.

Despite his hardened will, the Nephite closed his eyes as the knife reached its apex, clenched in the angry hand of the man who held it. *I love you, Miriam,* his mind whispered calmly, awaiting the feel of the cold stone slicing through skin and bone, into his chest.

∞

The half moon above Mulek softly illuminated the city and the surrounding forest in its silver light. A thin shadow slipped in and out of the moon's view, gliding noiselessly through dark streets. The gentle breeze stirred her long dark hair, tossing it as it caught and glittered against the moonlight. Her expressionless face was soft with the appearance of a mature woman; her full lips were parted slightly, and her eyes were filled with a deep unspoken pain.

She lifted her face to the cloudless sky. Countless points of light shone down on her, aloof and cold. The city walls, lined with sentries, came into view as she rounded a corner, the bright yellow torchlight shining in her face. Affronted, she pressed herself back into the shadows, not wishing to be seen.

As she turned back the way she had come, a figure stepped from the blackness of the deepest shadows, and caught her by the hand. Abruptly, she pulled her hand back, catching a sharp gasp in her throat.

"Thobor," she whispered, hiding her choking anguish. "Why do you follow me?"

"Why do you wander about in the dark, giving me a cause to follow you?" he whispered, releasing her hand.

She lifted her chin defiantly. "Thobor, you know why." She turned from him.

"Yes, Miriam, I do." He let out a long breath, and caught her by the hand, again pulling her to a gentle halt. He placed his hands on her shoulders and turned her toward him. "Miriam." His voice was mild, and he squeezed her thin shoulders, unsure if he wanted to continue. "Miriam, Captain Jacob is dead. Captain Lehi saw what happened—his sword and the blood on the ground—you cannot bring him back."

"Yes, I know." She cut him off with a quick wave of her hand, picturing the scene of Jacob's death in her mind. "But my grief is such that I cannot bear it." A sob rose in her throat, but she bit it back, feeling the comforting squeeze on her shoulders. "I love him, Thobor."

She shuddered, holding back sobs, and did not resist as he pulled her against his shoulder.

He stroked her hair, shushing her gently until she shuddered and pushed away from him.

Miriam bit her lip, tasting salty tears. Her eyes were down, but rose again to his face as his hand cupped her cheek, his thumb drying away the bitter tears.

"It would not be right for you to grieve out your days, alone, and sad," he began.

At the tone of his voice, and the penetrating look in his eye, she shivered and backed away.

He gulped, and stepped toward her, catching her hands in his. His heart was so full, he did not know how to make the words come out. But as he searched her eyes, seeing the anguish in them, he knew that the time was not yet. He could not enter into her sorrow now.

"I thank you for your care, my friend," she whispered sadly, her eyes large and shining.

He paused, tightened his jaw and almost spoke again, but she had already turned and moved out of his reach, gliding away through striations of light and shadow, as silent as a ghost, lost in her boundless sadness. Behind her, Thobor stood alone, watching her graceful, silent movements as she faded from his sight in the darkness. He drew a deep breath and released it slowly before he turned away.

His head was down as he walked back toward his quarters, but a shouted command brought it snapping up.

"You, there. Lamanite." A sentry on the wall had spotted him.

He stopped and glanced up.

"Why are you not in your quarters?" the man demanded, his deep voice reverberating through the silent city.

Thobor paused, not wanting to reveal Miriam's pain.

"It is no matter," the man growled, impatient when Thobor did not answer him. "But Captain Lehi has been searching for you. He wishes for you to speak with him. Go report to him at once."

"What is it he wishes?"

"Now!" the man returned.

Thobor tightened his jaw at the soldier's caustic words, but said nothing. He merely gave a nod of assent, and turned his feet in the direction of Lehi's tent.

"Sir?" Thobor questioned as he stood across the rough hewn desk from the grizzled Nephite Captain. "One of the sentries said you wished to speak to me."

"Thobor." Captain Lehi lifted his weary, war scarred face, which seemed even more deeply lined in the flickering light of a single tallow candle. He rose and came around the table to stand in front of him. "I am grateful you have come. I wish to speak to you of things that have happened here in Mulek these last weeks."

Thobor shifted his weight.

"I have noticed that you have done much to help us rebuild our city. You are as diligent as any of the other men, and although there are those who do not trust you because you are a Lamanite, most of the men speak highly of you. And I have seen by your actions, and also believe in my heart, that you are an honorable man. I have come to trust you as I do my own men."

"Thank you, sir." Thobor smiled at the praise.

Lehi paused and put a hand to his head, massaging his graying temples.

"Sir?" Thobor asked, his brow furrowing.

Lehi frowned thoughtfully and shook his head. "Twenty of my men, myself included, went up to spy on the forces of Gid. Only eighteen returned. We lost a sergeant, and a young lower captain who showed much promise. It is difficult for me to lose good men."

Thobor's face betrayed a pained look. "Yes, sir. I knew Captain Jacob well."

"Yes, you are a friend to Miriam." Lehi shook himself, and lifted his eyes to Thobor. He forced a smile on his face. "I have thought much about you, and what to do with you. You are still considered a prisoner of war, but—,"

Thobor ran his tongue along his lips, and shifted his weight, waiting as Lehi paused.

Lehi took a deep breath. "I have chosen to release you to return to your people, if you will make an oath that you will never come again against the Nephites to war."

Thobor's jaw stiffened. He stuttered, "I will make the oath— gladly—but I do not wish to leave."

Lehi's eyes traveled over his face searchingly. "You wish to stay and live among the Nephites?"

"Yes, sir."

"Will you bury up your weapons, as the Ammonites have done?" Lehi asked carefully.

Thobor gulped nervously. "I desire to join your ranks and fight—as a Nephite."

Lehi leaned back against the table and folded his arms across his chest.

"It is not the first time that such a course has been taken," Thobor pressed. "My friend, Laman, was once one the guards of the king of the Lamanites who reigned before Amalickiah. But he is now a loyal Nephite. There is no other man more loyal or trustworthy among all of Moroni's army."

Lehi grinned. "That is true, Thobor," he murmured, and stepped forward to clap Thobor's shoulder. "I will be proud to call you my comrade."

匣

"Esther, are you awake?" Thobor's soft voice came through the door of the tent, and Esther's eyes fluttered open. Her eyes focused on young Jacob, sleeping peacefully on his mat, then flashed to Miriam's bare pallet, and she sat upright.

Scrambling to her feet, she threw the canvas door open, blinking in the dim light of the early morning, to see Thobor waiting for her, Miriam's sleeping form cradled in his arms.

Esther breathed with relief as she beckoned him inside. "Where was she?"

"She cried herself to sleep in a doorway near the east wall," he said, laying her down on her bedroll.

"Again?" Esther murmured, kneeling at her friend's side, stroking her tangled dark tresses. She lifted her eyes, and found Thobor studying her face intently. She drew in a breath and rose to her feet, feeling the heat rising in her cheeks.

"Jacob's death has devastated her," Thobor muttered, rising until he towered over Esther.

"It has," Esther agreed with a nod. She glanced down once at Miriam, then turned away, her feet taking her out of the door. Thobor followed behind her, letting the flap fall closed behind him.

"I do not know what to do for her," Esther murmured, once the two of them were outside.

"Nor do I," Thobor agreed, folding his arms across his chest. "I fear we have no choice but to let her grief run its course, and be there to comfort her if she needs us."

"It will be difficult for her. She loved him deeply, and he her." Esther glanced up and studied Thobor's face. His raven black hair had regrown, and fell now about his face like a mane, accentuating the masculine angles of his jaw and cheek bones. She could feel her face flushing, and ducked her head, wishing her heart would not pound so noisily.

Thobor sighed. "Watch over her, both you and young Jacob. She will need your care today. Farewell, Esther." He turned away, and as an afterthought, turned back. "May God be with you."

"And you, Thobor," she murmured, watching him stride away. The muscles in his broad back shifted beneath his brown skin like quiet ripples on the surface of a still pond, and she put a hand to her cheek, feeling the heat there. Chagrined, she turned and ducked into the shadows of the tent.

CHAPTER 18

29TH YEAR OF JUDGES

*T*he afternoon was scorching, and the sun in the brassy sky over the city of Bountiful beat down with relentless cruelty. Miriam brushed a hand against her damp face, then dipped it into the bucket of cold water, and brushed it across her forehead before pouring the water into the clay jar on the stone lip of the well.

She smiled to herself as she lifted the heavy jar to her shoulder and started back. Footsteps from behind jerked her out of her thoughts, but she did not have time to turn before she felt someone's chin resting on her shoulder, and heard a chuckle in her ear.

"Thobor," she exclaimed. "You almost frightened me. I could have spilt all this water."

"But I knew I would not." He grinned, coming into her view. "I never have before." He eyed the water jar on her shoulder. "May I carry that for you?"

"You may." She smiled, gladly surrendering the heavy jar to his capable hands.

Effortlessly, he lifted the jar to his shoulder, and continued along at her side, content to keep silent, his eyes on her face.

"I received a good price in the market yesterday for my cloth," she offered after a moment, beginning to feel the pressure of silence.

"You have become an exceptional weaver," Thobor said. "Your skill rivals women who have been weavers all their lives."

She smiled tiredly up at his dark eyes. "I cannot match Esther, though. She is a far better weaver than I am."

Thobor agreed with a shrug as they slowed to a stop near the tiny house she and her brother shared with Esther.

"Esther has gone to walk young Jacob home from school. He is at the age where every day is an adventure, and he would forget to come home until nightfall if he was not reminded."

Thobor chuckled, and allowed Miriam to take the jar from his hands. Softly, she pushed the door open, set the jar inside, and rejoined him in the shade the little house created. She lowered herself to the ground, and sat back against the scratchy wall, running a hand through her hair as Thobor sat beside her, and watched her.

"Now, I have a new tunic to stitch for young Jacob. He is growing so fast these days, we can barely keep him clothed. I need to go to the market to buy the cloth, and while I am there, I cannot forget to buy more raisins and honey to make that sweet bread he likes."

"You try to do more than you should, Miriam." She could hear the smile in his voice.

She released a tired sigh. "Yes, I suppose so," she admitted wearily.

The smile stretched across his face as a mischievous look came into his eyes. "Let us go out to that old dead tree beyond the south gate. It has been months since you practiced."

Her eyes widened. "Thobor, I could not do that. I have so much to do—," She felt his hand cover hers. "Oh," she murmured, and pulled away. A distant look glazed her eyes, and she turned away from him, remembering the gentle touch of another man's hand. The poignancy of the memory stung her.

"Please?" Thobor's voice reached out to her as if over a great distance, and she shook herself back to the present.

She turned to Thobor, smiling. "I have enough time to take a few hours."

Thobor leaped to his feet, and Miriam gratefully took his offered hand. "You can borrow my bow." Miriam squeezed his hand, and let him pull her up after him.

Gentle forest noises echoed around them as Thobor and Miriam came to a stop in the grassy clearing where the old dead tree stood, stubbornly rooted in the earth. Miriam sighed, memories again flooding her mind and heart.

"It has that old mark you painted on it," Thobor noted, handing her his quiver of arrows and his bow. He moved a few paces away and sat on a fallen log to watch her.

She tested the feel of the bow in her left hand as she fitted an arrow to the string. She drew the string back to her cheek, and after sighting down the arrow's shaft, released it. It struck the tree, but out of the faded circle.

Thobor rose to his feet, and came again to her side. "Remember the flight will carry it up a bit." She felt the gentle pressure of his hand at her back.

She nodded, and took another arrow. Fitting it to the string, she drew it back to her cheek.

The string sang as the bow sprang back into shape, and Miriam smiled at her arrow, buried near the center of the red circle.

"Well done." The quiet tone of his voice, as well as his hand at her back confused her, and she pulled gently away, turning to him.

He was smiling again, his mouth curled shyly. The warmth in his eyes had softened.

"Thobor, what is wrong? Does something trouble you?" she asked.

"Nothing at all," he assured her, his eyes studying hers.

"Then—," her mouth twisted into a smirk. "What is it?"

"I only wanted to say, you look well, Miriam."

A smile turned the corners of her mouth up. "I look *well*?" she inquired.

"Yes, and happy. You are at peace with yourself."

"You hint that I have not always seemed this way." Her smile faded and she stepped back.

"You have not," he admitted. "Ever since—,"

"Ever since Jacob died." She nodded, and turned her face away from him. Instinctively, her hand reached just below the hollow of her throat and touched the blue stone that lay there, threaded through with a thin strip of leather, warm against her skin.

"Miriam, forgive me," he pleaded. "I did not mean to bring back unhappy memories."

"No." She lifted her face and smiled bravely. "Not unhappy memories. They were very happy ones. Jacob was a wonderful man.

I only wish—," Her brow creased before she shook herself. "What are these words coming out of my mouth?" she laughed. "I should not wish for things that never were, and never can be." She released a choppy sigh.

Thobor smiled gently. "You have the future."

She looked up into his face, her lips pursed, sensing that he would continue.

He released her shoulders, and looked down. "I have always liked you, Miriam. I cannot remember a time when I did not," he murmured, forcing himself to lift his head and look into her troubled blue eyes. "Truly, you are one of the most beautiful women I have ever known. And in the past years that I have been here, I have also noticed an inner beauty that is as beautiful as the rest of you. I have not told you for the longest time, out of respect for your memories, but I—I love you."

She stared at him, numb.

"Miriam." His eyes were pleading as he stepped closer to her, taking her hand in both of his. His hands were warm, and clutched hers with trembling urgency. "I would make you my wife."

"Oh," she breathed, studying his hopeful, pleading eyes. She had always wanted to marry a good man, and she had always hoped, a handsome one, and Thobor was both. His form was sinewy and strong, his chiseled features comely, and his heart was good.

Her own heart however, was empty of tender feelings for him, but surely they would come with time. She forced her mouth into a smile. Opening her mouth, she tried to answer him in the affirmative, but to her surprise, she heard herself say, "I—I cannot."

The sudden look of pain in his eyes wrenched her heart. "But—why not?" he pleaded.

Why not indeed? she asked herself. Jacob was dead, after all. And Thobor was someone she could easily come to love. She turned away and dropped her face into her hands, ashamed of herself. Thobor was her friend. Why did she feel it necessary to refuse him like this? In time, if she let him, surely he could fill her heart.

"Forgive me, Thobor." Her voice was a whisper. "Surely you must hate me now. But I cannot marry you. I do not know why, I only feel that I should not."

She waited in the silence that followed for Thobor's response, wondering whether he would lash out at her in his pain, or plead pitifully with her to forget her own feelings and marry him for his sake. Instead, she felt his gentle hand on her shoulder. Slowly, she let him turn her toward him.

"No, I cannot hate you," he murmured softly.

She drew in a slow breath. "You are a good friend, Thobor," her voice trembled. "I do not wish to lose your friendship."

"Nor I yours."

Several moments of silence passed between them, and finally, Thobor opened his mouth. "If you ever feel differently, please—," his voice grew soft, "tell me."

Miriam lowered her eyes and nodded.

"Very well." His hold on her arm loosened, and he leaned down, gently kissing her on the cheek. His lips were soft and lingering, his breath warm against her face. Without another word, he pulled away from her, and marched back toward the city gates.

Miriam remained where she stood, both hands clasping the blue stone at her throat desperately, drawing what comfort she could from its smooth, familiar touch. Her eyes searched the ground as she asked her heart questions it could not answer.

☦

The angry hateful whip rose again and flashed under the hot sun, snapping as it came down across his naked back. His ragged tunic, torn away from his chest and back, was soaked in blood. Rivulets of blood ran down his legs, dripping into the discolored sand beneath his knees. He clenched his teeth, letting out a muffled cry. Another slash quickly followed, knifing like a blade of fire across his back, catapulting him across another threshold of pain. He summoned enough strength to glance up, and saw the pitying eyes of one of the Lamanite soldiers, the one called Tuloth, at the edge of the crowd. They both flinched as another lash ripped across his back, tearing a deep throated groan from him as his head dropped against his chest. He crushed his eyelids closed, and took himself away, remembering a time when there had been less pain to cloud his mind, but he had been as sure of his coming death as he was now.

He waited, bound to the blood-covered altar as the priest raised the knife above his head, and he had closed his eyes, seeing again the beautiful face of his beloved, knowing it would be the last thing in his mind as he died.

"No!" A shriek stung his ears, and his eyes flew open to see who had cried out. Whose voice had that been? It seemed almost as if it had been Miriam's voice, and by some strange design, she was here on top of the pyramid with him. But as his eyes focused, he realized that it had been the woman who had cried out.

"Give that to me!" she cried, jerking at the knife in the startled priest's hand. "Give it to me, I said!" she yelled fiercely, finally wrestling the knife away.

"What has possessed you, woman?" the man cried, grasping her wrist to seize the knife.

"Fool," the woman growled hotly. "Can you not see that this is an unworthy sacrifice?"

The other two men and the priest stood in awkward, stunned silence for a moment, and the woman turned her eyes to the bound Nephite.

"I speak your tongue," she muttered in his language. "Do you want to live?"

"Yes," he gasped, beginning to realize that the woman, at least, had no desire to kill him.

"Then tell me," she demanded, "where did you get this?" She bent over him, and shook the torn beaded necklace in his face.

He studied her gnarled face, a face that at one time, must have been beautiful. His chest drew in great breaths. His heart pounded. "The woman I love, the one I hoped to marry gave it to me."

She uttered one word as she straightened her twisted figure, the knife still in her hand. "Miriam?"

His eyes widened, and a breath stopped in his chest. He nodded, astonished.

Her mouth curled up in a haughty smirk, but quickly dropped into a thoughtful frown. "I am her—her aunt, Isabel." She leaned her weak frame against the altar, and looked him over carefully. "The gods have been good to her." She fingered the knife, and laughed resentfully. "There are no gods for me. If there are any, they have forgotten me. There is no hope for me. From the moment I was born, I was marked to this end."

"That is not true," he insisted. "There is hope for you, and anyone who will take it."

"You are as foolish as old Ishna was," Isabel whispered angrily, and turned toward the priest. "This Nephite will make an unworthy sacrifice. He has a blemish."

"A blemish?" the priest snorted, snatching the knife back. "Where?"

Isabel looked desperately at the Nephite's eyes, scanning his face. "There." She pointed at the mark of the jaguar's claw across his shoulder.

"Ha!" the priest balked. "It is nothing—,"

Isabel snapped, "The gods will be angry if you dare offer such an unworthy sacrifice."

"Very well," the priest argued back. "But who will the sacrifice be if not the Nephite?"

She straightened her wizened shoulders importantly. "Me."

"What?!" he blurted. "That can never be. Ammoron ordered that you be here so that the blood of the sacrifices might strengthen you as it strengthens the gods."

"Do you deny me the right to immortalize myself with the gods? This syphilis that is eating me slowly will kill me soon. Why not make some use of my death?"

"No," the Nephite mumbled to himself in his own tongue. "She is not prepared—,"

"Shut up, dog!" the priest barked impatiently. "The gods have made their decision. No Nephite blood will defile the altar today." He turned to the guards who waited silently. "Get him off the altar and take him back to Lord Ahiah. He will find some use for him."

The guards again had the Nephite on his feet, his arms twisted behind his back, and were marching swiftly down the steps of the pyramid. Anxiously craning his neck, he twisted his head back and watched in disbelief as the old woman climbed onto the altar. The priest clenched the knife in his hand, already beginning to raise the blade high. The guards jerked him roughly, and the Nephite lowered his eyes to the steps.

Worried eyes from the crowd turned to him as his guards parted the mass of people. They stared after him, their faces beginning to show confusion. But after the guards had shouldered their way through, a cheer escaped from the lips of the crowd behind him. The Nephite did not dare to look back. If he had, he would have seen a dim figure at the top of the pyramid who had come to the edge, holding up a distant object, that trembled in his hand, for the inspection of the sun god and the ecstatic crowd below.

Another lash burned across his back, and he grunted, awaiting the next crack of the whip. But Ahiah had tired at last. He was coiling his whip now, and coming around to face the Nephite who summoned enough strength to lift his head, and stare defiantly into the eyes of the dissenter.

"I am impressed," Ahiah puffed, his lips curling into a snarl. "Most men would be screaming by now. Many would already be dead."

The Nephite held his tongue.

Ahiah allowed his whip to uncoil to the ground, and flicked it around in the dust like the tail of a venomous snake, grinning into the defiant Nephite's light brown eyes. Ahiah kept his eyes locked, waiting for the prisoner to drop his gaze, and when he did not, Ahiah angrily lashed the Nephite across the cheek. "Did you truly think you could escape us, Nephite?" he snarled. "When you broke from your guard and fled, did you not realize we would catch you? You had no hope."

"As long as my God is with me, there is hope," the Nephite murmured.

Ahiah laughed, his fists resting on his hips. "And where is your god now? I could kill you, and how shall he stop me?"

"If He allows you to kill me, I will accept it, as I know He would stop you, somehow, were it His will that I continue to live."

"Where is he?" Ahiah demanded, beckoning about him at the ravaged city, the crowd of Lamanite soldiers looking on. "Does he stay my hand that I cannot end your life now? If he is with you, why does he not help you?"

"He helps me, even now."

Ahiah sneered. "How?"

"'He giveth power to the faint, and to them that have no might, he increaseth strength.'"[13]

Ahiah's eyes narrowed. "You quote Isaiah," he growled.

The prisoner's light hazel eyes met his, unwavering, disconcerting him.

With an angry snarl, Ahiah stepped back, and backhanded him across the face, sending the salty taste of blood sliding down his throat. The young man's head lolled to the side. "Take him away," he roared to the two guards who stood nearby. "I will end his life tomorrow when I have returned from the city Omner. Then we shall see if his god will help him."

"Lord Ahiah," a voice spoke up, and the Nephite lifted his now barely conscious head to see Tuloth coming forward. "The loss of this Nephite will hurt us tremendously. He is very strong, and does the work of five men—,"

Ahiah chuckled. "He has the strength of ten. You saw how he broke away. It took seven dogs and more than that many men to pull him down."

"Yes my lord, but—,"

"I would not test my patience, were I in your position," Ahiah hissed, his jaw tight. "I do not easily tolerate those of my men who give prisoners more food than they need."

"They work better when they have something to eat."

"We feed them enough."

"Not the children," Tuloth muttered.

"Silence!" Ahiah finally roared. "Speak no more, or you will meet the fate of this Nephite."

Tuloth glared challengingly at Ahiah, his glance sliding momentarily to the Nephite whose light, penetrating eyes studied him. Tuloth lowered his face, clenching his fists. The muscles of his jaw were knotted.

The Nephite fought to keep himself awake, and to keep his face out of the dust as they unbound his wrists and began to drag him away.

The guards dropped him into the dust at the door of his cell, and he heard a distant clank of metal as they opened his door. The musty smell of aged darkness brushed his face.

"Go in," one of them commanded, shoving him roughly in the side.

He scrambled to his hands and knees as he crawled slowly through the door. The door behind him shut with a resounding slam.

Now, he was alone. Slowly, he crawled toward the square beam of light beneath his window. He stretched out beneath it, his chest against the dry earth, and drifted into welcome blackness.

Out of the darkness of his mind, her form, undimmed by the years, took shape, and he saw again the gentle gaze of her sapphire eyes, and tasted again the sweetness of her flesh when he had kissed her palm. A smile came to his dry cracking lips.

☙

"Who goes there?" Tuloth shouted angrily into the darkness at the four shadows that stood before the gate, heavy barrels hefted on their shoulders. He was irritated and angry tonight, and the other guards assigned to the night watch avoided him.

Lord Ahiah always applauded aggressiveness, even if it meant that his soldiers expressed hostility toward each other. *Learn how to hate, hold it inside you until it burns in your belly, and when you go to battle against the cursed Nephite dogs, let it give you strength that you might slaughter them.* Ahiah's words echoed in his mind. But Tuloth was not angry to impress his pale-skinned overlord. He thought only of the Nephite who was to die the next day when Ahiah returned from the city the Nephites had called Omner.

"I am Laman, a Lamanite by birth," the shout echoed up to him in his language, strong and steady with no accent. "I and my friends have escaped from the Nephites as they sleep, and we have brought some of their good wine with us."[14]

The thought of Nephite wine swept away Tuloth's previous cautions. "Wait, and we will open the gate," he shouted to the invisible shadows as he moved away from the wall. But he soon realized that the newcomers would not wait at all. The mention of Nephite wine had brought several others running, and before he reached the ground, they had begun to open the gate. Soon it was swung wide, and the little group came through. In the flickering light of the torches, it was clear that they were indeed Lamanite. Although their years in captivity had grown their hair out, and they were wearing the same odd tunics that the Nephites wore, their distasteful appearance was forgivable, for each man balanced a barrel of wine on his shoulder.

"Will you allow us to drink of this wine now?" one guard asked as the four men set the barrels down, and stretched their tired muscles.

Laman, the leader of the group, shrugged. "Not yet. It is night, and we have traveled far."

Hurriedly, Tuloth spoke. "Give us some of your wine," he spouted. "We are glad you have brought wine with you, for we are weary."

"Let us keep our wine until we go against the Nephites to battle."

"No," Tuloth begged, joined by several others. "We are weary," he repeated, wishing that he could drive away the pain for at least a few hours. "Let us have some now, and later, we can receive wine for our rations so that we might be strong when we go against the Nephites."

Laman released a great breath of air, and traded a quick glance with one of his companions, a young man, whose gaze was sober and unreadable. "Very well," he said, and his massive shoulders sagged wearily. "Do whatever you desire, then."

 C3

Pahoran sat on the stone window ledge of his throne room, looking out over the dark city, dotted with light as if someone had plucked the stars from the sky, and scattered them across the land. It was such a restful scene, the calm of the night concealing the surging political unrest that rocked the city with the force of an earthquake.

He sighed, gazing over the same familiar view. He had not been outside for days. Even surrounded by loyal guards, the streets were no longer safe. Even in broad daylight, it would take only an instant for an assassin's knife to find him.

He remembered with glad thoughts his wife and children, who had gone to Melek to escape the unrest of the capital city. At least they were safe.

The door squeaked imperceptibly behind him, and he swiveled to meet Micha's familiar eyes.

"You cannot sleep, sir?" he asked, nodding to the cot in the corner.

"I cannot," Pahoran answered. "I feel it in the air."

"I, too, can feel it," Micha agreed. "There isn't much time left." He moved to the window, and gazed out.

"Do you think the Lord will allow us to be killed?" A nervous tremor was in Pahoran's voice.

"I doubt it," Micha muttered. "I feel as if we are surrounded by wild animals, but somehow the Lord will lead us out of it, or at least, you. You are valuable."

"So are you, Micha," Pahoran added. "A more loyal captain I have never had."

Micha smiled gratefully.

Pahoran grinned back, and the two men turned back to the darkened, sleeping city. There was no more need for words.

C3

The light was dim. His eyes were closed, and he felt strange bluish warmth against his eyelids. He was lying on his chest as he was before he fell into unconsciousness. But instead of earth, he was sleeping against soft animal skin. He shifted slightly, and felt the stiffness of bandages wrapped around his chest. At the same moment, he felt a flash of pain across his back where his wounds healed beneath the bandages.

"Jacob?" The word sounded strange to him, and it took a few moments for him to remember that in a time before, long ago, it had once been his name. "Captain Jacob, are you awake?"

Jacob, for that was what he now remembered his name to be, stirred again, wishing he could open his eyes. Was this all a delusion of his feverish brain? But the bandage, the warmth, the softness of the skins he lay against were too real to be a dream. With a great effort, he shook himself, pulled his eyelids open, and lifted his head.

"Jacob!" the voice exclaimed, and a hand gingerly touched his shoulder where there was a spot unscathed by Ahiah's whip.

Ignoring the pain, he pushed himself up, scowling at the speaker as he folded his legs under him. It was a Lamanite. A shock of anger burned through him, but faded as he scrutinized this younger man who studied him with worried intensity. His skin and eyes were dark, but he wore the uniform of a Nephite officer, and Jacob's muddled brain struggled to take it all in.

Jacob spoke, and the words came out of his dry throat as a hoarse whisper. "Thobor? A Nephite solder? A lower captain even?"

Thobor nodded and made a great effort to smile as he grabbed a water skin that lay nearby and held it out to him. "Captain Lehi saw promise in me. He commissioned me himself. It was only recently that he made me into a lower captain."

Jacob lifted the water greedily to his lips, moistening his parched throat, then focused his eyes on Thobor. "Is all well in Bountiful? How much has changed?"

Thobor's mouth twitched, but he continued to grin. "Your namesake, young Jacob, is as energetic as ever. That has not changed."

Jacob laughed, and the sensation felt good in his lungs. "I lost count of days. How long have I been gone?" He tugged at the mass of growth on his face.

"Two years, and some days," Thobor answered, guessing his next question.

"What of Miriam? How is she?"

Thobor's grin faded. "It would be a lie to say that she took the news of your presumed death well. In truth, Miriam became a shadow of herself when we were all certain you had been killed."

Jacob's face darkened. "Miriam is well, now, though? She has made peace with her pain?"

"After many months," Thobor muttered. His eyes were no longer on Jacob.

Jacob dropped his eyes now, too. His next words would be painful, but he knew he needed to speak them. His words were measured, sober and sullen. "Does the man she married care for her well, and love her? Is she happy?"

"She has not married." Thobor lifted his eyes, and in their dark depths, Jacob thought he saw a hint of pain.

He studied them a moment, then spoke. "She is betrothen then."

"No," Thobor answered flatly.

Jacob's eyes lightened, his face brightening with a sudden hope. "Truly?"

Thobor nodded, his own face now sullen, and looked away.

Jacob did not notice, for his thoughts and heart had turned suddenly toward Miriam and his reunion with her. He let out a breath of air, looking out the billowing tent door into the bright afternoon sunlight while Thobor cleared his throat vehemently and turned his eyes down.

CHAPTER 19

"Young Jacob, watch the stew for us while we are gone to get water," Miriam called over her shoulder as she and Esther stepped through the curtained doorway into the golden red light of the late afternoon.

He looked up from where he sat on a mat in a corner of the sparse room, studying the figures on his clay tablet, gnawing at the end of his stylus, and nodded agreeably. "Of course."

Esther smiled once they were out the door, lifting the jar to her shoulder. "It will not be much longer before our boy will become a man. He is already making friends with many of the soldiers, especially Thobor."

"Yes." Miriam nodded, surprised at the pang the mere mention of Thobor's name brought to her heart. She smiled bravely at the young woman beside her who balanced the clay jar gracefully on her head as they walked through the red light of the lowering sun. Esther was now nineteen years old, a year older than Miriam, and still unmarried. But she was beautiful. Her hair was a dark, raven black, and hung glistening to the middle of her back. Her skin was a soft brown, and her eyes were warm and dark, much like Thobor's, Miriam thought.

Why had she not accepted his offer of marriage? There was no one better for her than Thobor. He would be a wonderful husband to her, and she could grow to love him, if only she gave him time. But for all her reasoning, she could not force her heart to accept him.

"Miriam!" Esther's bright voice brought her out of her thoughts, and Miriam lifted her eyes in the direction she was looking. A crowd of exhausted men had gathered around the well, their clothes and armor dusty, their faces and limbs glistening with sweat. "They may have come from Gid! Perhaps Thobor is among them! Come!"

She grasped Miriam's hand tightly, and rushed toward the crowd of men, addressing the closest one. "Is Thobor among you?" she blurted. "He is a lower captain."

The young man scratched his sweaty brown hair, more concerned that he get a drink. "Uh, I do not know. There are many of us. Ask them." He pointed to another group of men. One of his friends nudged his shoulder, holding a dipper of water, and the young man turned away.

Esther moaned in frustration as she turned, and began to approach another soldier.

"Miriam! Esther!" a voice cried out above the hum of male voices.

"There is Laman, Miriam!" Esther cried, turning to the voice to see Laman striding toward them from the head of the street. She waved frantically and started toward him as fast as she could with the pitcher on her head.

"Laman!" Esther gasped, slowing to a stop when she reached him. "Where is Thobor?"

A grin stretched across Laman's face, and his eyes flashed between the two young women. "He is not far behind me," he answered, his eyes twinkling at the relieved smile that came to Esther's face. "But now, I am going to your house. Thobor and I promised young Jacob that we would come straight to him and tell him all our stories, once we returned."

"Miriam," Esther said softly, "perhaps I should go with Laman to meet Thobor when he comes to our home."

Miriam's eyes darting over the crowd of men. "Perhaps you are right. It will take only one to get the water, but I cannot get those men to move for me."

"You might go to the well in the market," Laman offered. "It will surely be faster to bring water back from there."

"Very well." Miriam took the pitcher from Esther as the two started away.

Miriam watched them leave, then turned toward the market-place.

The road was dusty and narrow, and empty now that she had moved beyond the crowds of soldiers. She was passing through what had earlier been a busy marketplace, but now that evening was coming on, and shadows were growing longer, the merchants had packed up their wares and had gone home. Tables were left empty, and a few of the shops still had their bright cloth awnings stretched out over empty enclosures. She smiled with relief as the well came into view, encircled by a stone barrier in the center of a circle of small buildings with empty booths scattered before them.

A deep sigh escaped her as she drew to a stop and set the pitcher upon the lip of rock surrounding the well. She rested her hands against the rough stone and tilted her head back, drinking in a long breath of air as she felt the breezes caress her, and toss her long, unbound hair about her shoulders. The tightness in her throat slowly relaxed and she released a sigh as she grasped the rough hempen rope knotted to a protruding stone, and lowered the wooden bucket into the cool water. She drew it up to the lip of the well again, moist and dripping before she poured the water down the mouth of the clay jar. She smoothed her damp hands against her skirt, and rested them again against the stone. With her eyes closed, the wind gently whispering across her skin and through her hair, she took herself back in time to the last moment she had seen him, the sunset over the wall of Mulek, the boundless love she had seen in his eyes. She bit her trembling lip, remembering the soft sweetness of his mouth against her palm, and the painful yearnings that had stirred in her heart. His image appeared again in her mind, the sharply honed angles of his face, the pleasing curve of his mouth, and the infinite depths in his golden brown eyes. Somehow, though her mind knew otherwise, she could never imagine that Jacob was dead. Her heart had never allowed her to truly believe it.

At the edge of the circle of booths, two men paused. Jacob gulped, his eyes following her movement as she filled the pitcher with water. She set the wooden bucket on the lip of the well once the pitcher was full, and brushed her damp hands softly against her skirt. All traces of the girl he remembered were gone. Her movements were softened with the natural flowing grace of a woman. Her eyes were the clear blue pools they had always been, and her skin, a golden honey brown, shone flawlessly. The shiny dark tresses of her hair fell sparkling over one shoulder as she grasped the pitcher and lifted it to her shoulder. She straightened, slowly, gracefully, her full lips parted slightly. The blue drop-shaped stone still lay just beneath the hollow of her throat, cool against the warm tones of her skin. He wiped his palms, which were suddenly sweating, against his gray kilt, and released a deep breath that had been swelling in his chest.

"Jacob." Thobor's voice made him jump. "Go speak to her."

Jacob's heart pounded in his chest, and he nervously straightened the sweat-soaked rumples of his dusty shirt. "I—I will not know what to say."

Thobor managed a weak grin, and his teeth sparkled against the dark copper of his face. "Yes, you will. Wait here." Thobor started toward her.

Miriam sighed as she gripped the smooth handles of the heavy pitcher, lifted it to her shoulder, and straightened, worrying lest the jar should tip. Such indulgent daydreams of what could never be could do no good for her, and she needed to return with the water. With a sad sigh she turned away from the well. Lifting her head, her eyes looked into those of Thobor.

"Thobor," Miriam laughed softly, surprised. "I did not hear you coming—,"

"How are you?" he blurted.

"Very well." She nodded. "And you?"

He shrugged, letting his hands hang limply at his sides. His eyes were down.

"I heard that you and two others who are Lamanites by birth, helped Laman."

He nodded, but did not speak.

She continued, desperate to fill the silence with conversation, "You took wine with you into Gid, and the guards became drunk. Then the other soldiers brought in weapons to the prisoners. You captured the entire city[15] without shedding one drop of blood."

"Yes." He did not seem eager to talk, and Miriam bit her lip.

She set the jar down on the edge of the well, and gripped the cool, solid stone behind her to hide her hands' trembling.

"If it is too heavy, I will carry it for you," he offered, lifting his eyes.

"It is not necessary, Thobor," Miriam pleaded, remembering the day he had asked her to marry him. He had carried the water then, and this would only bring him painful memories.

"I brought someone to see you, though," he spouted in a rush, "from Gid." He allowed a weak smile to touch his lips, and beckoned behind him with his head.

Furrowing her brow, she glanced past Thobor's shoulder to see a man standing under a dusty brown awning stretched over one of the many empty booths lining the street. His face was in shadow while his fist gripping the support pole was clenched tightly.

"Miriam?" the man in the shadow asked, stepping forward. His voice was full of emotion, and strangely familiar. Shuddering, she nodded as he stepped into the light.

She gasped softly, and stepped back, catching herself against the lip of the well. She knew that what she saw could not be, even as her heart leaped within her. He was dead. He had been for two years. Yet here he stood before her, his warm eyes gazing at her with painful longing.

"Thobor?" she gasped, desperately glancing around for an explanation. But her friend had disappeared along with the clay pitcher she had filled. Turning quickly back, she blinked her eyes and looked again. His hands hung heavily at his sides, opening and closing. The cloth of his linen shirt thinly disguised his firm, muscled chest, which rose and fell with emotion, and narrowed to his flat, sinewy stomach where his sword was belted across narrow hips.

She whispered his name, letting the word roll deliciously over her tongue. Then she took command of her voice. "Jacob?" She managed to take a few faltering steps toward him, her heart thumping wildly within her.

"Jacob, how did you come to be here?" she pleaded, her voice husky. "I thought you were dead. Captain Lehi came back. He brought your sword." She pointed to the sheathed weapon at his waist, the same one Lehi had brought back from Gid, dented and blood encrusted. "He said you died, Jacob. How did you come—," she paused to breath.

"Dare I believe it is you, Miriam, and not a dream?" his voice choked.

A warm shock raced through her, and tears started instantly to her eyes. Without further hesitation, she flung herself, sobbing, into his arms.

She felt his arms circle around her and pull her tightly against him, his warmth permeating into her. With her face against his chest, she could hear his heart pounding, and felt the heat of him against her cheek. The touch of him was fulfilling, and real, unlike the vague, faint shadows of dreams that had tormented her at night, only to disappear when she awoke. This time, there would be no waking, and no loss. For a long moment, Jacob said nothing as they held each other, but stroked her hair, sending pleasant shivers along her skin. At last she felt him bend his head, and bury his face in her hair, and then she felt him shaking, and heard his soft sobs. He was crying, holding her as if he needed to know of the reality of her as much as she needed his touch to assure herself of his.

Emotions surged through her soul like tempestuous waves, threatening to overpower her, and after a long while, she finally pulled away, wanting to see his face.

"Jacob," she breathed, as she reached up, touching her fingers against his lightly stubbled cheek. He had changed little, yet he seemed to be a whole new man. A new light shone in his eyes, giving him an air of wisdom beyond his years. Yet the same smile she remembered turned the corners of his mouth, the same warmth lit his countenance.

Jacob caressed her brow and her cheek, his eyes growing moist as he gently touched the blue stone that lay warm against Miriam's soft flesh. "You've kept it," he whispered, stroking it gently.

"And I will all my life," she answered softly.

He sighed, feeling sudden shame. "I lost your—,"

"You have returned to me," Miriam interjected gently. "That is what matters."

"Miriam," Jacob murmured. He said her name again, letting the word roll over his tongue. "Miriam, have you any idea how I have missed you? How much I have dreamed of you, and longed to be with you?"

Her breath quickened as Jacob's lips kissed her hair, and her brow.

"Do you remember the night I left for Gid?" he asked softly.

"I could never forget." She released a jagged sigh.

His hand came beneath her chin as it did so long before, and he tilted her face up. His eyes studied hers intently as he spoke. "I love you now, as I loved you then, and more. If you love me, will you have me?"

Gently pressing against the firmness of his chest, she drew back, and gazed up at his face, aware of the movement of his breath beneath the soft cloth. Her mouth parted slightly. "Yes," she whispered.

It seemed natural now, that they should draw even closer together. Her heart fluttered as she tilted her face toward his, and closed her eyes. She felt his breath against her face, and the warmth of his lips brush her forehead, then her cheek.

A moment later, his warm mouth gently covered hers, causing a rush of heat to surge through her body. As his lips tenderly plied hers, her mouth softened, becoming more yielding, and for the first time, she tasted the intensity of his emotions. Her arms slipped up and around his neck as she began to answer his implorations with a warmth all her own. His own arms circled around her and tightened, pulling her to him, and she melted against him, her heart overflowing.

◌

Esther could not sleep. Instead, she sat at the window, drinking in the salty sea breeze that flowed through the quiet city. Moonlight flooded the air, and she turned to look over the other sleeping forms. Miriam's lovely face, even in sleep, smiled with a soft contentment.

Esther sighed and pushed herself away from the window, her eyes on the blackness of the street outside the little house. The street stretched away in the distance, up nearly to the temple that sat in the center of the city. It rose in the darkness, shining silvery in the moon's light.

Softly, so as not to wake Miriam or young Jacob, she rose to her feet, and opened the door quietly. She stepped out onto the wide street, peaceful and empty, and she found herself walking slowly, the cool wind coming easily to her nostrils. The sky was as black as a transparent opal. The stars smiled down on her as they wheeled in the eternity of space, guided by the finger of God. There was no other light but the moon, and the brilliance of the stars took her breath away.

She turned, walking slowly backwards, her face gazing upwards, unaware of her immediate surroundings until she bumped into something. She stumbled few paces before she caught her balance and turned, chagrined, her eyes coming down to rest on a man who still seemed unaware of her. His face was bent downwards. He was a soldier, a lower captain, she saw, from the rank insignia on his uniform.

"I am such a clumsy fool," she muttered in the tongue of her birth.

"No, I am the one at fault," he answered in her language.

She faltered, even more embarrassed than before. She knew that many soldiers learned the language of the Lamanites, but he spoke flawlessly, without the hint of an accent. His face was turned to the ground, and his hands were clasped behind him in thought, or perhaps prayer. It occurred to her that she might have interrupted a personal moment between the young man and God, and began to utter another hasty expression of apology as he lifted his face.

She stifled a gasp. "Thobor!"

"Esther." He managed a smile. "I am surprised to see you as well, at this hour. Forgive me, I did not expect to meet anyone."

"No, Thobor, I am at fault. The stars were—," Esther gasped, her breath coming faster. He was lean, with strong arms and broad shoulders, and his face was sharply chiseled, pleasingly masculine, his warm eyes softening his expression as he returned her open study.

"I did not thank you for the water earlier," Esther ventured. "It was good to see you. I had feared you did not feel well. You did not seem . . . yourself."

He shook his head. "I was . . . tired."

"You left before Miriam returned," she continued. "Jacob was with her. It is a miracle you found him alive. He said you saved his life."

Thobor gnawed his bottom lip thoughtfully, a gesture Esther had never seen before. She smiled quietly, thinking it endearing.

"Do you know that he and Miriam have announced their betrothal already?"

"I supposed it would happen." Thobor released a small chuckle, and thoughtfully rubbed his jaw. He glanced up at her. "I am happy for them."

Esther sensed the melancholy tone in his words, and the urge to see his smile welled within her with surprising strength. "Thobor?" His eyes upon her melted her heart, and she trembled as she spoke. "Why did you stay with our people, and not return to your own, when Captain Lehi offered you your freedom?"

He opened his mouth, and she imagined his voice saying, "So that I might stay where you are, Esther." But it was not to be. "I did not want to return. I no longer believe in the cause for which the Lamanites fight." He added sadly, "And as my parents are both dead, everything that ever meant anything to me, is here."

Esther swallowed her disappointment, and forced herself to smile gently. "Miriam says you are to be baptized tomorrow."

Thobor brightened, and a thrill raced through her heart. "Yes, I am. Laman agreed to baptize me, and afterwards, Jacob will give me the gift of the Spirit."

"I will come."

"I had hoped you would, Esther." He pointed over his shoulder. "I should return to the garrison. If the others learn that I have been out with a pretty girl, they will be jealous." He smiled fleetingly. "Farewell."

She watched him turn and stride away, and let out a long sigh before turning around, and retracing her steps. He had called her pretty. Thobor, whom she thought would never notice or acknowledge her beyond a polite greeting, had called her pretty. No one in her life besides her parents and Miriam had used such a word to describe her.

At home, she touched her hand against the door lintel and paused, seeing the kind eyes of Thobor again in her mind before she slipped quietly inside. She unrolled her pallet, and knelt upon it for her evening prayer. She closed her eyes and sighed, allowing the warmth she remembered in his eyes to fill her heart.

og

The sun was high overhead as Ahiah silently parted the thick, water heavy branches and glared with undisguised malice at the couple who walked hand in hand through the dappled shade of the jungle. He could not see the soldier's face, but the woman's eyes were alight with joy as they gazed up adoringly into the man's. Ahiah scowled, nausea rising in his throat.

He had not been in the city the Nephites called Gid to rally his warriors when the Nephites had retaken the city. But if he had been, he would have ordered them to fight back. He had been a Nephite once. He knew their ways and he knew of their weak, powerless god who only subsisted on the blood of small, unblemished animals. He hated their feebleness. The Nephites were never on the offensive, never aspiring to crush the Lamanites under their feet. They stayed, out of cowardice, in their own lands. Surely his warriors could have crushed the Nephites.

He turned back on the man and woman who had paused, and were talking softly, their words barely perceptible.

The woman sighed and stepped back a pace. "Even though I was only a daughter, my father always told me he loved me as much as he loved young Jacob, and that he would never have traded me for a thousand sons, even if they were of his own flesh."

"Is that not the way it is, though?" The man grinned, coming to the woman. "Men always want sons, but when we have daughters, we cannot help but favor them, and spoil them."

The woman smiled playfully, tilting her head to gaze up into the man's face. "I hope you do not spoil our daughters," she teased, pulling demurely away.

"If they are as beautiful as you are, I won't be able to help it." The man smiled, coming to her and sweeping her into his arms.

She surrendered to his embrace, draping her slender arms about his neck with a soft sigh of contentment.

The rest of their words, spoken between soft, intimate kisses, were too quiet to reach his ears, but Ahiah had no interest in what they had to say. The young woman, dressed in the common garb of an unmarried Nephite maiden, with her long dark hair unbound and shining in the narrow spears of light that penetrated the thick, plaited branches overhead, looked almost as if she could be a Lamanite. But she was too fair. Ahiah narrowed his eyes, seeing in the form and figure of the woman someone he remembered from years past. How could such a thing be? Surely the child she had borne him, the one he had searched for in Siron, had been torn to pieces and devoured by some beast in the wilderness. He glared at her. But was it her? Ahiah shook his head to himself. It did not matter. He drew a knife slowly from its sheath at his waist. He could easily kill the man, then he would return to Ammoron with the woman as a present. That would restore him to the king's good graces, and he would not be executed for losing the city of Gid.

At Ahiah's quiet movement, however, the Nephite warrior released the woman from his arms, and turned toward Ahiah, reaching for the knife at his waist. "Miriam, I heard something."

Ahiah's lips curled up angrily as he saw the man's face, and recognized him.

"What is it?" she wondered, her blue eyes blinking as she gazed at the dense undergrowth surrounding them. "A wild boar? Or a snake?"

"I am not sure." The warrior frowned, his eyes peering through the shadows at Ahiah. He began walking toward Ahiah's hiding place.

"Be careful, Jacob."

Ahiah bared his teeth as he slithered back into the darker parts of the shadows. That whelp was in love with his daughter, and she with him! That could never be allowed. He was almost tempted to attack now, but remembered the deep slash the Nephite had left across his thigh. He did not desire another encounter with such pain again. He would have to wait for a better time.

"Daughter of Ahiah, you will discover your true birthright yet," he hissed as he clambered silently back into the deeper shadows of the forest.

CB

Thobor stood after binding his gear to his pack, and breathed in the cool night air. He sighed and looked down at the ground, crushing a clod of dried mud under his heel as he glanced back at the other men finishing their own preparations for the march they would begin that night. Laman strode among them, and Thobor grinned as he watched the older Lamanite bend down to help a young soldier bind his pack closed. It had been only a few weeks before that Laman had baptized him, and Jacob had blessed him with the gift of the Spirit. He would be marching with Laman and this band of soldiers until they met a group of nearly sixty young Ammonites, fresh from Melek. And then it would be only a few days before he would join in the fighting beside the first two thousand sons of the Ammonites, led by the prophet Helaman. The thought made him dizzy with anticipation. He would meet Helaman face to face!

"Ow!" Another young soldier kneeling almost at his feet, had caught his finger as he tied his pack, and Thobor dropped to a knee.

"Let me help you." He grinned, freeing the young man's finger as the young man mumbled his thanks, then stuck the sting in his mouth.

"Thobor." He glanced up at Laman, framed against the twilit sky. "Do you feel ready?"

Thobor rose. "I have prepared as well as I can, but I do not believe that anything can truly prepare me fully for what lies ahead."

"It is times like this, the calm before we face war, that I remember the words that many of the mothers of the first two thousand Ammonite youths told them before they left."

"What was it?"

"That if they had faith, God would deliver them." Laman sighed, "Whether it meant that their sons would be saved alive, or only that their faith would remain strong in spite of tribulations, I am uncertain. But I do know that so far, God has kept each of them alive for some purpose, just as he spared you, so that you could come to learn all that you have."

Thobor nodded thoughtfully, and rose to his feet, stretching, his eyes surveying the darkening sky. "It is a marvelous thing, the way the Spirit influences in ways that we are not even aware."

"I wish you had a mother of your own to tell you this."

As he said this, the younger man's eyes rose to his, and Laman sensed a sudden tension.

"I do have a mother," Thobor muttered, "though she and my father have died, she still watches over me as surely as she did when she lived."

Laman's face grew penitent. "Forgive me, I did not mean-,"

Thobor recognized Laman's remorse, and clapped his shoulder quickly. "No, forgive me. It is only that my mother died in child-birth after I had been taken away when I was a child," he explained. "The message the midwife sent me said that the baby was pale-skinned, and had green eyes and red hair. It was clearly not my father's. My father, Amran, went after the man who had defiled my mother, and never returned." Thobor shook his head sadly. "Nephite dissenters thought they were gods where we lived, and took what-ever they wanted, including women, married or not."

"Whatever happened to it? The baby?" Laman asked, leaning forward.

"I would that I knew. The midwife took it away to another vil-lage after our mother died, and our father disappeared. I wonder myself from time to time."

Laman clapped Thobor on the shoulder, and squeezed, thought-ful for a moment before he lifted his eyes, and saw someone beyond Thobor's shoulder. He brightened, and stood up, pulling the closest soldier up with him.

"Come, friend." Laman pulled the young man along with him, and trotted off toward the greater body of men who were making their final preparations, leaving Thobor standing alone, watching them, his brow furrowed.

Thobor's confusion fell away when he heard a quiet voice behind him. "Thobor?"

He tensed suddenly and turned. Esther stood at the edge of the shadows, then moved toward him with a natural grace he had never noticed in her before, almost like liquid in the fading light. "I came to see you, before you go. You have become a good friend to me, and much time will pass before I will see you again."

Thobor's jaw contracted, unable to form words in his suddenly dry throat.

Esther's smile grew faint. "I will be here until the end of the war. Miriam and Jacob will have their own home after they are married, but I will stay with young Jacob."

Thobor opened his mouth to speak, but his voice refused to come out.

Cowed by his lack of response, her eyes glanced downward, and her smile fell. "Farewell—," She turned away, her head drooping.

"Wait," Thobor blurted, suddenly finding his voice as he reached after her, and caught her hand. Her hand tensed within his, and she glanced back at him with such hope shining in her dark eyes, that he did not think as he grasped her other hand and pulled her closer to him. "I will come back to see you again, Esther." He paused and added shyly, "If that is your wish."

"It is." Esther's eyes dropped demurely as she smiled. "I will look forward to your return. I will miss you, Thobor." She glanced up as she spoke, and Thobor studied her eyes as they sparkled in the torchlight. Why had he never noticed before how beautiful she was? Almost without thinking, he reached out, and gently brushed her face with his hand, feeling the softness of her cheek beneath his fingers. He held it there for a moment before slowly drawing his hand back.

"And I will miss you, Esther. Very much."

She stepped back, lifting a hand to the cheek he had touched. He noticed a tear beginning in the corner of her eye. "May God go with you, Thobor." At that, she turned and hurried away into the twilit streets of the city, and then she was gone.

Bring me back alive, he prayed with a sigh as he hefted the pack to his shoulder. *If only to see her again.* He turned and trudged toward the torchlight to join the others.

CHAPTER 20

30TH YEAR OF JUDGES

$\mathcal{M}$iriam's hands were clasped tightly in her lap as Esther carefully plaited small flowers into her braid. Her white dress whispered with every small movement as she fidgeted nervously.

"Jacob will be speechless when he sees you." Esther tucked a sprig into the rope of her hair.

Miriam bit her trembling lip, and looked at Esther's reflection. "Do you truly think so?"

"I know so." Esther smiled.

Miriam blushed. Releasing a deep breath, she clasped a hand over her heart. "My heart beats so quickly, I am surprised you have not heard it."

"Oh, was that thundering noise your heart?" Esther teased, rubbing her ears.

Miriam pouted, glancing at Esther in the mirror. "Your time is coming, Esther."

A soft smile came to Esther's face then, concealing a sweet thought. "There!" she declared and stepped back. "You are ready now."

"No, I am not!" Miriam spouted, wringing her hands. "I will never be ready. I do not understand it. I have waited for this day for so long, yet now I am so frightened, I do not know what to do."

"Come." Esther helped her to her feet and led her out into the cool blue shadows of evening.

Miriam could see the light of the flickering torches in the plaza around the corner of the building, and hung back as Esther pulled her along.

As the scene opened up to her and she saw Jacob, dressed in a new linen tunic, standing near Teancum, all her hesitancy fell away. He was smooth shaven, and the flickering light accentuated the angles of his face. Never before had he appeared so handsome.

His eyes were focused intently at the ground, but at an affectionate nudge from Teancum, he lifted his face, and his eyes met hers across the plaza. She noted the sharp intake of breath that caused his chest to swell. He gulped quickly before he took another deep breath. Her own heart had again begun to thunder inside, and if it had not been for Esther's gentle shove, she would not have started forward.

She hardly felt the ground beneath her feet as she moved toward him, and slipped her small hand into his large, rough hand.

"You are beautiful, Miriam," Jacob breathed, his voice full of awe.

She blushed and dropped her eyes, lifting them to Teancum, who offered her a kind smile as he moved to stand in front of them. She blinked, and again turned her gaze to Jacob. He smiled softly, almost shyly. His hand was strong and steady as it clasped hers, helping to calm her own inward trembling.

She was barely aware that Teancum had addressed them, but she heard Jacob's affirmative answer, then a moment later she heard her own voice whisper "yes." She felt Jacob's hand squeeze hers, and drew in a quick breath of air as she returned his squeeze.

The sky above them was glowing with the last remnants of sunset, and the stars had begun to appear in their places in the cool darkness. Jacob's face fairly glowed with devotion, and she felt as if her heart would burst.

Miriam kept her eyes down as she stood near the wooden, rough-hewn table that was one of the many gifts Jacob had presented to her, along with the house he had secured for the two of them. She heard Jacob release a nervous breath as he softly closed the shuttered window, leaving the outer room they occupied bathed in soft candlelight. She glanced over her shoulder through the open doorway into their bedroom. The window in that room was shuttered, but silver moonlight was still able to spill in, illuminating the soft sheepskin pallet they were to share. She remembered laughing and enduring Esther's teasing as the two girls had woven the linens and coverlets, and had carefully gathered soft down for the pillows she had so carefully and lovingly made in anticipation for this night, but now that she was here, alone with him, she was frightened, and confused that she would feel that way.

She felt his eyes on her as Jacob turned slowly, and came to stand over her. His hand touched her shoulder gently, and she could feel the warmth and softness of his hand through the cloth of her wedding dress.

"Miriam?" he questioned.

Miriam bit her lip and looked down at the table top, chagrined.

"Miriam," he murmured, softly now, as he reached for and took her hand in his. "Don't be ashamed that you are suddenly afraid. I feel as you do." She lifted her eyes to his, and drew in a long breath. His eyes grew soft and pleading in the candlelight. "This is new for us both. If it is your wish, I will be content to do nothing more than gaze at your beautiful face."

Miriam smiled shyly, and Jacob returned a smile as he lifted her hand, and softly pressed a kiss into her palm. His touch was warm and sweet and gentle, igniting a warmth in Miriam's veins.

Slowly, she leaned into him, and sliding her arms around his neck, softly pressed her mouth against his, finding it warm and responsive. As they parted, and she gazed up into his gentle eyes, filled with love and longing, her fear quietly faded into oblivion.

"This is my wish," she murmured softly in return.

"Miriam, my wife—," Jacob whispered longingly. The candlelight touched off the angles of his face, heightening the new flame she could see in his eyes. She went into his embrace eagerly, feeling the mingling of their rapidly beating hearts as he circled his arms about her and pulled her against him. He kissed her again with all the passion he had for so long denied, and had kept locked in his heart for this one moment, and for her alone.

Beyond their window, the sky above the darkened peaceful city was cloudless. The moon hung luminous in the sky, and the stars shone brightly, the windows of heaven open to the eternities. A calm breeze had begun to stir, blowing over the city from the east, carrying with it, the smell of the sea.

⚮

Morning sun streamed generously through their window as Miriam woke surrounded by warmth, snug on their soft pallet of sheepskin, and stretched her arms contentedly above her head. She reached out for Jacob, only to find his side of the bed empty. Startled, she sat up in alarm, but then heard the cheerful whistling beyond the door.

She laughed softly to herself as she rose from the bed, and began dressing. Never before had she heard Jacob whistle. She brushed at the front of her tunic and ran her hands furtively through her long dark hair before she released a breath, and brushed aside the curtain. Jacob sat at the table, pulling on his boots. His face, full of quiet contentment, gazed out the open window into the bright sunlit world.

As she came into the room, his head shot up, and his whistling stopped as his eyes gazed into hers. For a moment, they shared a wordless intimate glance, and she drew in a quick breath.

He grinned then, and rose to his feet, coming to her. "You are even beautiful in the morning, Miriam."

"Jacob!" she laughed, coyly pushing his arms away as he tried to put them around her. "Did you think I would not be?"

Her gentle teasing only charmed Jacob all the more, and he finally encircled her in his arms and pulled her against him. As their eyes met, Miriam's smile faded, and her flesh shivered warmly at his familiar touch.

Jacob's grin fell away, and the look in his eyes deepened with tenderness.

"I love you," he whispered, the words carrying more meaning now that they were truly husband and wife.

"And I love you," she murmured.

At this, a knock sounded at their door, soft and hesitant at first, then louder with more purpose.

Miriam groaned and buried her face against Jacob's neck, wishing the sound would stop, but it only increased in intensity, and this time a voice accompanied it. "Captain Jacob, forgive me. Teancum is asking that all officers meet him immediately." The soldier's voice sounded distant beyond the thick, wooden door.

"Teancum said you had a few days leave." Miriam moaned, lifting her head.

Jacob's eyes found hers. "I know. But when Teancum says he needs me, I must go."

Miriam frowned and backed away as Jacob turned toward the door.

"Very well. I am coming," he shouted.

Reluctantly, he reached for his sword belt hanging from a peg on the wall. He buckled it on as he strode purposefully toward the door and flung it open.

A young soldier stood in the bright sunlight beyond, his face pained. "Forgive me, but—,"

Miriam impulsively started after him. "Jacob, you cannot go—," she pleaded, imposing herself between the two men. "Not the day after our wedding." She turned to face the soldier. "Please. Surely there is another who can fill his place—,"

The young man sighed, his face furrowed. "Teancum has received an epistle from Captain Moroni. The kingmen in Zarahemla have revolted, and Pahoran and his supporters have fled to Gideon."[16]

Miriam stiffened. She spun toward Jacob, her face frightened. His own apprehensive eyes studied her helplessly, already pleading for forgiveness.

He grated, "Then I have no choice. I must go." His eyes glanced at the floor, his muscles tensing in protest to the emotions that rallied within him. Then he regained control of his face, steeling his expression to the familiar, concentrated look of a soldier. His warm, expressive eyes cooled and grew shallow.

Miriam sighed, knowing that his thoughts were already far away from her. "Then go with God," she breathed, and began to turn away.

Jacob's expression softened momentarily at her voice and he turned again toward her. "Miriam, I must do this. For you, and our country, for our unborn children. Please understand."

She nodded wordlessly, and let him pull her close, feeling already the sweet pain of separation.

Jacob breathed deeply, pausing before letting his breath out again. "I love you, Miriam."

"I love you," she managed through her tightened throat. "I will pray for you."

"And I for you," Jacob said as he lowered his face and gently kissed her, tasting the salt of her tears.

As his mouth released hers, she pushed away from him, and ran back into their bedroom, falling in a heap on their pallet, allowing her tears to run free.

Behind her, the door closed, and feet pounded away, the sound fading as they went. She buried her face in the pillow Jacob had slept against. It was still warm, and lingered with the faint, musky scent of him. She stayed there a long time until her tears were dry, and she had cried herself to exhaustion.

ભ

The early sun shone cheerily down on her head and the trilling calls of thousands of birds outside the walls filled the air, as Miriam wordlessly followed Esther through the marketplace lined with countless shops.

"That is a good duck." Esther pointed at a robust duck squatting nervously in a wooden cage.

"Yes, it is." Miriam nodded absently, turning her face toward the south, hardly having heard what Esther said. She tucked a wisp of hair behind her ear. She had let her hair hang free today, not plaited against her head as most of the other married women.

"We have rarely eaten meat, you and I and little Jacob, but I know many ways to prepare duck. I could teach you—Miriam, what are you looking at?"

Miriam jerked, and turned her face back to her friend who was watching her curiously. She smiled sheepishly. "Esther do you not worry for Thobor?" she asked.

Esther turned to her, ignoring the shopkeeper who was beginning to shift his massive weight anxiously. Esther sighed. "I try not to worry. I must endure, as every woman does. We cannot keep them here, safe with us, or else there will be nowhere safe for anyone."

"Miss?" The sudden interjection of the shop keeper interrupted them.

"Oh, forgive me," Esther gasped to the distressed man whose fuzzy brown arms folded across his generous chest. "I would like that fat one right there." She pointed at the caged duck, and counted her money, dropping it on the wooden table with a hollow plink.

"Thank you," she said mildly, and the man nodded in return, and turned away as Esther took the caged bird in her hands. "Miriam, this is heavy for me, would you help—," She turned. Miriam had disappeared. But she did not have time to wonder where she had gone as she caught a familiar young face dash through the crowd.

"Oh, young Jacob!" she cried as the boy pulled to a halt and looked in her direction.

"What?" he yelled, trotting toward her.

"Could you help me carry this?" She asked, as the dark haired boy reached her side. "It is heavy for me, and I do not know where Miriam has gone."

"I suppose so." He took the duck, and hoisted its weight by himself. "Where did she go?"

"Oh, I do not know. Perhaps she has gone to join the army."

"Truly?" he opened his eyes wide.

She laughed. "Of course not."

"Oh." Young Jacob frowned, disappointed. "The more kinsmen I have who fight, the greater chance I have that one will do well," he pointed out. "Since Jacob is my kinsman now, and Thobor is almost my kinsman, I would have bragging rights at school if they fight well and if they aren't killed."

Esther's smile quavered as her eyes dropped. Young Jacob cringed. "Esther, forgive me. I—,"

"It is nothing, young Jacob. Let us just get this duck back home."

CB

The streets near the garrison were as quiet as an abandoned city when Miriam passed beneath the south gate. As she passed under the shadow of the gate, she raised her eyes to the line of guards who stood at the top of the wall. Their eyes were focused on the hazy distance. She moved on past the barricades, trenches, and the wide strip of bare ground into the trees, tightly clutching the bow in her hand.

This place between the southern wall and the old dead tree that she had filled with so many of her arrows, was a second home to her. She knew each tree and rock as well as she knew the streets of the city. As the shadows of the trees grew dense, however, the odd feeling that she was in an unwelcome place began to creep into her heart. She could almost sense the devilish glee emanating from a blackened heart that she should fall into his hands as easily as this.

She shook her head and blinked her eyes, trying to see something familiar in the harmless trees and rock-strewn ground around her, but it all seemed so alien now. Something inside her was beginning to scream to her to go back. Warily, she drew a slender arrow from the quiver at her back, and fitted it to the bowstring as she began to back away.

She did not see the figure out of the corner of her eye until he was almost upon her.

As she turned, her heart leaping in her throat, she barely had time to release the arrow from the string as a powerful arm knocked the bow out of her hand, and pushed her stumbling back several paces, landing painfully against the rocks. Her quiver crumpled flat between her back and the unforgiving ground, arrows scattering everywhere.

A man with wild eyes stumbled toward her, and she caught sight of a red scar tattooed into his forehead. The arrow had pierced through the flesh of his arm, but he merely ripped it out and flung it away.

"Daughter," he hissed, "is that any way to greet your father?"

She found strength in her legs to scramble desperately away as a scream rose in her throat. But the man, with lightning reflexes, leaped at her, and a chilling hand clamped over her mouth.

"You will not escape from me this time," he snarled, uttering foul epithets as she twisted desperately to pull away. *What did he mean?* she half wondered. She had never seen the loathsome monster in her entire life. The touch of his clammy hand over her mouth made her stomach lurch, and she shuddered before she bit down hard on his hand, her mouth filling with the salty, acrid taste of blood. She heard him curse between his teeth as he grabbed a handful of her hair. The next moment, she felt her head strike against a cold, flat stone on the forest floor. Lights exploded in front of her eyes bringing a floating sensation, and then black numbness.

As she melted into nothingness, she seemed to hear the man's voice above her growl, "I will teach you to obey me, Daughter." *Daughter?* she wondered, and was lost to oblivion.

Ahiah stared down at the unconscious woman, an ugly purplish bruise already beginning to form on her temple. So this was Miriam up close. She bore little resemblance to either him or the woman who had borne her, and this again disappointed him. Her face, even unaware of reality, had an odd glow about it that frightened him. He remembered though, why he had come for her, and braced himself, hoisting her up to his shoulder. She was very light for a girl who had put up such a heated fight, and had bitten a chunk of skin out of his palm. Painfully, favoring his wounded arm, he hefted her to his shoulder like a freshly killed deer, and bent down, retrieving her bow and quiver, and gathered the scattered arrows together. He glanced about the shadowed trees, gathering his strength. Satisfied that he had not been seen, he began running silently toward the west.

CHAPTER 21

The world was a mass of fuzzy green and brown, and she slowly came to her senses, a throbbing pain in the side of her head, her face against something soft and moist, earthy smelling. Some had gotten in her mouth, and she spat the dirt out, trying to sit up to rub the painful spot on her forehead. As she tried to move her hands from behind her, however, she realized that they were knotted together with rough, sinuous rope, and her ankles were roped together with the same sinewy fiber.

Realizing her desperately hopeless situation, she sucked in a sudden breath of panic, choking on more of the dark earth, as she struggled to wriggle to her knees, coughing violently.

"Do not strain yourself, Daughter," a low, sinister voice breathed close by. "I do not wish for you to ruin yourself before we get to Zarahemla."

With a high, frightened cry, she struggled to her knees, and began to crawl desperately away from the voice. A foot roughly shoved between her shoulders sent her sprawling on her face.

"Do not make it harder for yourself," the owner of the cruel voice barked, leaving his foot on her back.

With a wild gasp, she twisted her face out of the suffocating soil so that she could breathe. She spat out another mouthful of dirt. "Who are you?" she demanded, her voice frightened.

The voice above her laughed out loud. "Your father," it said.

"You are not my father," she choked. "My father is Aaron."

The voice laughed again, and he reached down a heavy hand, grabbing her by the arm. He hauled her violently up and shoved her back against the bark of a tree. She slid slowly, helplessly to the ground, staring wide-eyed at the man with the mottled red scar on his forehead.

She glanced at his hands, the manacle-like paws that had captured her and brought her here. His hair that looked as if it could be sandy blond beneath the dirt, hung greasy past his shoulders. One of his massive arms was bound with a dirty cloth, a spot of blood showing through it where her arrow had penetrated.

"Why do you do this?" she asked, looking away from his steely blue eyes. They felt as though they were piercing daggers into her soul, and it hurt to look at them.

By the position of the spears of light that angled through the jungle canopy, she could see that it was evening. The man who sat across from her, his face grinning like an empty skull, had seated himself with his back against another tree, weaving a long rope of rough coconut fibers.

"Because you are my daughter," he repeated, glaring at her as if she should already know the answer. "You are my property. You have been stolen from me, and I came to get you back."

Miriam said nothing. She held her tongue, glaring at the man's worn leather shoes. His tunic was ragged and gray, and he wore leggings, in the same condition. A metal sword was belted at his waist, and lay across his thigh, while her own bow lay on the ground beside him. Her quiver of arrows lay propped up against the tree, their feathery fletching sticking up out of its opening.

"You seem to have taken on quite a few airs since you have been on your own," he continued when she did not speak. "You have forgotten your heritage." He set his unfinished rope beside him, and rose, crossing the little clearing to stand beside her.

"You will not touch me!" Miriam threatened, though she knew that as she said this, being bound hand and foot, her words would hang empty in the air.

"Ammoron prefers maidens, so you have nothing to fear," he sneered, "from me."

"You said you would take me to Zarahemla," Miriam sniffed, her eyes down. She shivered against the chill of the air, wishing Jacob's arms were around her again.

Ahiah laughed as if he were humoring a small ignorant child and sat down, picking up his work again. "I have some old friends in Zarahemla who could help me."

"I do not wish to go with you," Miriam stated flatly.

Ahiah laughed again, low and cruelly. He lifted the fibrous rope. "You have no choice." He finished his work, and tied the end off, then rose and came toward her. "It is your birthright. You cannot escape it." Ahiah's face twisted into a triumphant grimace, as he put a hand over his heart. "I am your father. This Aaron you spoke of is no more your father than your weak Nephite god is."

"Aaron is my father," Miriam insisted. At that, she felt a hot lingering lash across her face. Her head bobbled and she realized that Ahiah had struck her.

"I will not hear that name again," he hissed.

He towered above her, his eyes seething with hate. She kept her face down, and sections of her hair, stuck with dirt and bits of twig, hung over her burning face.

After a moment, he continued. "There is no escape for you from the path your mother followed. Nothing the Nephites told you will change who you are. You are the daughter of Ahiah. From your birth you were marked to this end. Being your father, I will see that you will fulfill your destiny. You will be Ammoron's concubine."

"You cannot tell me what to do! That is wrong!"

Ahiah laughed. "I decide what is right and wrong." He slipped a knotted circle of itchy rope around her head, roughly yanking her long hair out of the way before he secured the stubborn fibers against the tender flesh of her throat.

"Are you more powerful than God to decide right and wrong?" Miriam demanded.

"I am my own god, Daughter. And the god of anyone weaker than me."

"You are an evil man!" she shouted, pushing clumsily away from him with her feet. "You speak blasphemies!" He moved to stand over her, and with a quick motion, unsheathed the metal sword from its scabbard. Miriam flinched.

He reached down, grabbed her ankles roughly, and severed the scratchy rope.

"Now get up and walk." He jerked on the knotted rope around her throat, and for a moment, the air to her lungs was choked away. She scrambled to her shaky feet, tiny needles of pain beginning to stab into her legs. She gasped in air as she kept her eyes down, trying to regain her balance.

"Come." Ahiah gave the rope two quick pulls, and grunted with a grin of satisfaction. He started off through the darkness of the trees following a dim animal path.

☞

An old woman parted the cloth hanging at the door of her wooden hut, and squinted her aging eyes at the distant sky hanging low over the lands far to the north of the land of Amulon. Her hand, steadying herself at the door, was wrinkled and mottled with age, a quiet courageous strength shining behind her dark eyes. It had been nearly ten years since she had come from the land of Siron to the land of Amulon, and it was time to move on again.

"I pray that Miriam fared well," she whispered softly to herself before she turned inside and moved to the tiny fire where their dinner of fish was slowly steaming on sticks.

"I caught a good supper, did I not?" the child, Rachel asked as she knelt at the fire.

"You caught an excellent supper." Ishna patted her amber hair. "You take good care of me."

The young girl grinned proudly, her green eyes shining with delight at the complement. "As you have taken care of me, Grandmother."

Ishna smiled at the child as Rachel turned the sticks to cook the fish evenly. She reached a gnarled hand out and touched the fire colored hair as Rachel looked up and smiled at her. Her green eyes were set like gems in her face as she sat with one leg pulled into her chest.

"Miriam was near your age when she went to the land of the Nephites," Ishna remembered fondly as Rachel nodded, familiar with the story. "Soon it will be my time to go on, and there will be none left to teach you, and you are now strong enough to travel through the forest. That is why we must go now to find the Nephites so that you might learn the truth that they have, and be baptized, and I can join my own people before I die."

"Grandmother," Rachel breathed. "Do not say such things. You will always be with me."

Ishna tapped a wrinkled finger on her lips. "Yes, but not as I am now."

Rachel blinked sullenly and looked at the door, her imagination carrying her far to the north, though her eyes could not see beyond the blanket that hung across the doorway. "Is it true that I look like a Nephite?"

"It is." Ishna nodded.

"Am I Nephite or Lamanite then?"

"You are a child of God." Ishna smiled, patting her on the shoulder. "If we all lived as we should, there would be no manner of 'ites' at all. We would all be the same."

"Is it true that Nephites are ugly? Pale as death?" Rachel fingered a curly auburn lock.

"They are not. Some of them have eyes blue like sapphires, or as green as jade and emeralds, as your eyes are. Some few have hair like gold and some, like you, have hair the color of the sunset."

Rachel nodded, though her eyes worried as she looked over into the corner where her pack lay as Ishna had prepared it. She looked across the flames at the gentle weathered face of the old woman, and slowly rose to her feet.

Ishna rose carefully to her own feet, plucking the speared fish from the fire as she straightened. "Put your pack on, Rachel," she murmured. "We will pray now."

Rachel hefted the load in her arms, and pulled the rough woven straps over her shoulders. "I am ready now, Grandmother."

"Good girl." Ishna handed her one of the speared fish as she folded her arms to herself.

"Grandmother," Rachel whispered before she began to speak. "Do you suppose the rest of the village will search for us when they find that we are gone?"

"Perhaps, but they will not find us." Ishna smiled, looking at the child with one eyelid closed.

Rachel smiled and closed her eyes, lowering her head and folding her arms to herself as Ishna had taught her, listening to Ishna's reverently whispered words.

When she finished the prayer, Rachel whispered, "Amen," and looked up expectantly.

"It is time, Rachel," Ishna said with a crinkled smile, holding out her hand. "Are you ready?"

"I do not think so." Rachel slipped her hand into Ishna's old gnarled grip. "But I am not afraid."

Ishna smiled, and together they stepped out the door as she parted the curtain. The jungle was not far from the door, and walking hand in hand, they were soon hidden in the trees.

Rachel ate her fish slowly as she walked beside Ishna. She did not look back as she pushed with determination through the thick growth. She lifted her eyes to the patch of sky she could see above her head, stars beginning to shine their weak, token lights down on her. She turned her gaze to Ishna, who smiled encouragingly at her.

"I am not afraid, Grandmother. The god of the Nephites watches over us."

"He is not only the god of the Nephites, He is also mine and yours and anyone's who chooses to follow Him," Ishna gently reminded her, squeezing her hand as the darkness enfolded them.

"Yes," Rachel agreed with a nod. "And He will watch over us, and keep us safe."

"That is right," Ishna added softly, slipping her arm around Rachel's shoulder.

ഗ

The darkness surrounded him, cold and chilling, and Jacob shivered, tightening his cloak about him as he walked slowly along the edge of camp, his eyes studying the grayish-green darkness of the jungle. Beyond the calls and shrieks of the night animals, the jungle was silent, and he shuddered, gripping the smooth wood of the spear tightly in his hands.

The cold air rushed steadily in and out of his lungs, and he stamped his legs, forcing warmth into them as he tried not to feel sorry for himself. After all, many of the other men had left young wives in the city as well. But that thought did not comfort him. He missed Miriam with a loneliness that penetrated to his bones as intense as any physical pain. And he could not rid himself of a heavy feeling of foreboding. He shook his head, reminding himself that she was safe in Bountiful. She was the one worrying for him. Perhaps it was only that they were apart from each other after only one day of marriage, and that he had left her so quickly.

Frustrated at the tense feeling of fear in his heart, he raised his eyes to the sky, studying the patterns of the stars. "Please," he whispered, "keep her safe. Let her know that I love her."

Almost immediately, warmth entered his heart, and he drew in a deep breath, nodding thankfully with the quiet knowledge that wherever she was, she would be watched over, and kept safe.

愉

Stars were beginning to peep overhead. The shadows of the jungle around her had faded to a color somewhere between grayish-green and black when for no reason she understood, she lifted her trembling voice. "He will find me and save me, and you will regret what you have done."

Ahiah laughed under his breath. "Who?"

Miriam shut her eyes, and turned silently away.

"Your father?" he mocked when she did not answer. He waited a few moments, the leaves underfoot crunching as he marched swiftly, dragging her behind. He laughed to himself, speaking again. "Who is your father?"

Miriam opened her eyes and braced herself. "I am the daughter of Aaron."

Expecting it, she ducked as he turned to strike her, and fell clumsily to the spongy ground.

"Who was your father before that?" Ahiah hissed, his lips curled in angry frustration.

She struggled with her bound wrists to sit up, biting back tears. She looked up into the bitter depths of his eyes, her glare unwavering. "The God of Abraham."

Surprisingly, Ahiah did not strike her. He backed away a few steps, reeling. He wavered for a moment, and then glared back at her, his eyes glowing with hate. "Get up," he hissed between clenched teeth. "I do not have time to play childish games. We must be to Zarahemla within the week." He jerked viciously, and she rose and stumbled after him down the dark path.

CHAPTER 22

$\mathcal{R}$achel tramped shivering, through the cool blue quiet of the early morning, clapping her arms to herself against the cold. Her long, freely hanging auburn hair was barely enough to ward off the chill from her slender neck. It had been many days since she and Ishna had left the land of Amulon. Ishna had forbidden her to build a fire, and the nights were bitterly cold. The two weary travelers had huddled together for warmth, wrapped in a thin woolen blanket.

Rachel had woken early, and had left Ishna wrapped alone in the blanket. When Rachel saw the long wall of gray stone peeking through the trees several hundred paces to the north, her insatiable curiosity refused to let her follow the caution tugging at her mind.

Now she stood less than fifty paces away from the massive stone wall, peering from around a large dew heavy leaf, at the soldiers who lined the top of the wall. The towns in the land of Amulon had no need for such walls as this. The irregular blocks were cut at perfect angles to fit into each other, and masoned with such skill and exactness that there was not even a need for mortar.

Her heart pattered in her throat as she crept forward to the edge of the trees to look across the wide strip of treeless ground. Surely these were Nephites, for these young men were dressed unlike any men she had ever seen. They had full heads of hair, unlike the half-shaved heads of Lamanite warriors. They also wore tunics, all of the same color, and thick, quilted armor to protect their chests. She had never seen anything like this before. No wonder the Nephites were great warriors. They wore so much, it would take great skill to get any weapon to their flesh.

She smiled at their ingenuity, and crept closer to the massive wall. She slowed and lay on her belly, watching from under the overhanging leaves of a low bush. A steady drip of morning dew splashed with well-timed accuracy against the crown of her head as she gazed up at the wall and the dark skinned men on it. Her face fell. These men were no different than her own people!

She pushed herself off the ground, and turned to retrace her steps, not seeing one of the guards atop the wall as he stopped and cocked his head as if listening for something, and turned alarmed eyes in her direction as she stumbled blindly away.

He squinted as he saw the fleeting figure of a child dash into the cover of trees, then raised a hand to summon several of his companions.

As she stumbled along, tears heavy in her eyes, and her head hanging down, she did not see the copper skinned young man until she almost butted her head into his stomach. Sensing something in front of her, however, she stopped and lifted her head. She gasped in shock, her once heavy heart leaping into her throat as she stared up at what seemed to her a towering giant. All in the space of an instant, her mind took in his tall stature, his broad chest, and his thick, muscular arms that rested in fists at his hips. He wore a light brown tunic of thick cloth, a pattern of red stitched into the cloth of his sleeves. The tightly stitched armor that looked like thick cotton was tied to cover his chest and back. Thin leather shin guards protected his legs. And for the first time, she noticed a sheathed sword, fashioned in the form that she had heard of Nephite swords, at his left hip where his right hand could draw it easily. His face wore an amused half smile, his eyes asking unspoken questions. And then she opened her mouth and released a scream that rent the silence of the forest and startled a flock of birds overhead.

Her own scream threw her into a panic, and she dashed to the side in an attempt to run around the young Nephite. As she did, a second warrior stepped from between the trees, and caught her shoulders in strong hands, speaking quickly to her, in strange, garbled words.

She stopped screaming to open her eyes and focus them on the man who held her, dressed in the same fashion as his companion.

He was speaking kindly to her, seeming as if he meant to assuage her terror, but she understood nothing. She screamed again, kicking at him violently.

"Release me! I do not understand you!" she managed to cry as she took a breath to replenish her lungs. She closed her eyes and screamed again, unaware of the young men gathering around her, barely able to suppress their laughter as the young man who held her, lifted her and held her out at arm's length to avoid her thrashing legs.

"A Nephite who does not understand her own language," one of them said at last, in words she understood. "How is this?"

At this, Rachel's tired legs fell limp, and dangled beneath her like sticks. Her voice quieted as if her mouth had been stopped with a cork, and she blinked her eyes, looking around. "You understand me?" she gulped, staring in wonder at the small group. "How is this? You are Nephites. Why do you speak my language?"

As she said this, several of the young men burst into laughter, including the one holding her, who had to set her back on the ground, though he kept a heavy hand on her shoulder.

"Were you raised in the middle of the wilderness with a monkey for a mother?" He laughed.

"She has lived in the land of Amulon," a familiar voice snapped behind her. "Release the child, and let us go in peace."

The young men fell silent, and turned, seeing the form of an old Lamanite woman shuffling through the trees, a look of alarm on her face, a thin blanket draped about her bony shoulders.

"Grandmother!" Rachel cried, breaking from the young man's hold, and rushing to the old woman. "I found the Nephites!" She circled her arms around the frail old woman's waist, and looked back at the group of young men.

"They are not Nephites." Ishna shook her head.

"We are Ammonites, Grandmother," the young man offered with a polite bow.

"How can that be?" Ishna asked. Her hand gripped Rachel's shoulder tightly. "The Ammonites made a covenant never again to go to war. You would never break your oath."

"Those of us whose fathers took that oath, were children, and are not bound by the same promise. Some of us were not yet born."

Ishna released a slow breath. Her grip on Rachel's shoulder relaxed and fell away. Taking a few tentative steps forward, she looked at the speaker, her old eyes squinting hard to see him. "You were not born an Ammonite," she murmured, softly. "What is your name?"

The young man glanced down. "Thobor, the son of Amran."

Ishna gasped, her hands flying to her mouth, and she appeared suddenly weak. Rachel hurried to her side to support her, her jade green eyes gaping at the young man.

"My name is Ishna," she whispered, a smile forming on her thin lips as tears began to fill her eyes.

"Ishna?" The young man's eyes shot up, and he came forward, his eyes wide, his hands tentatively outstretched. "Grandmother Ishna?"

"Your father was Amran and your mother was Zana," Ishna breathed, her hand gripping Rachel's shoulder heavily. "How did you come to be among the Nephites?"

"I was captured in my first battle, and taken to the city of Bountiful," Thobor breathed. He studiously fixed his eyes on the girl at Ishna's side, as the thoughts that were tumbling around in his head played out on his face. "Miriam was there."

"Miriam is safe then? Alive?" Ishna pleaded.

"It is because of her that I was finally converted and baptized," Thobor said, then added as an afterthought, "and she has married."

Ishna's hand went again to her mouth.

"Grandmother has waited all her life to be with her people," Rachel managed in a weak voice, sensing that Ishna was too overcome with emotion to speak. "We have come to find them."

Thobor drew in a long breath and held it for a moment before he spoke, his eyes fixing on Rachel. "And you are my sister."

The silence that followed confirmed his surmise. He started toward the child, an expression of wonder written on his face. Rachel allowed him to take her tiny white hand in his, cradling it gently as he studied it, nestled in his brown palm. He lifted his eyes and studied her solemn features, recognizing their mother in the child's fair face. "My sister," he repeated, his voice an awed whisper.

"Blessed be the God of Israel," Ishna murmured under her breath as tears streamed down her weathered cheeks. "He has led us to you."

"Come," Thobor said soberly, reaching forward, his hand still clasping his sister's and taking Ishna's elbow with great reverence. "Come back with us to Manti. We will take you to meet Helaman, our commander."

ଓ

Ahiah cast a sideways grin at Miriam as she strode miserably beside him on the road toward the capital city of the Nephites. She could see it before her now, the long alabaster walls in the distance, the glittering of the Sidon river to the east. It seemed so peaceful from a distance, but the knowledge that it was no longer in Nephite hands darkened her frightened heart, and intensified the dull ache of nausea that gnawed at her. That morning, even the scrap of dried meat that Ahiah had shoved into her mouth, would not stay down, and the heat rose to her face as she remembered his cruel laugh when she had doubled over beside the road, her stomach retching violently.

Bile again rose in her throat, when, from out of the grass around them, leaped six men. They were dressed like soldiers, but different from any kind she had ever seen. Their skin was fair, and they were obviously of Nephite descent, but were not in the familiar uniforms of Nephite soldiers. A confusing plethora of feathers of all colors covered their breastplates, and their faces were painted with a swirling mix of grays and blues. Five of them were armed with obsidian-lined clubs, like Lamanites, and the sixth, a young, muscular man who seemed to be the leader, had a metal sword. Miriam swallowed as she studied the man whose eyes traveled from Ahiah to her, and lingered.

"She is a rare beauty," he growled, his piercing gray eyes traveling over her. "How much are you willing to trade for her?"

"She isn't for sale," Ahiah snapped, taken aback. "Not to you."

The leader, followed by the other five, started forward, but Ahiah stepped toward them, wordlessly making a series of signs with his hands to which the soldiers stopped and gaped at him and each other.

"How did you know those signs?" the first demanded as his attention turned to Ahiah.

"I am Ahiah, a Lamanite overlord, commissioned by King Amalickiah. He taught me."

"A Lamanite?" The leader's gaze again strayed to Miriam.

"I was once a Nephite, as you were once Nephites," Ahiah admitted. "But I renounced them and joined the Lamanites in what you would reckon as the fifth year of the judges."

"You were a follower of Amlici, then," the leader asked warily. "Most of them are dead."

Ahiah brushed a stray shock of hair to show the blood red brand in the middle of his forehead.

At this, the doubt of the soldiers faded to awe. The leader took a step forward, and offered his hand, his eyes fastened on the mark. "We are honored to meet you. We are kingmen, loyal to King Pachus. He was a follower of Amalickiah before Amalickiah was driven from Zarahemla."

"I know Pachus," Ahiah affirmed. "He is the man whom I seek. He is the new king?"

The leader nodded. "And old Pahoran isn't pleased. He got away somehow, and then sent an epistle to his watchdogs. We expect them to come against us to battle any day now. The six of us were watching for signs of their coming. But our watch is over, and we are returning to the city."

"I would be pleased to come with you," Ahiah said, jerking on Miriam's rope, forcing her to step closer. "I hoped Pachus would be willing to help me."

"More than willing now," the leader assured him, his eyes turning again to study Miriam as he thumped Ahiah on the shoulder. "Pachus has opened correspondence with your people and wants to build an alliance. His wish is that there be peace between our people."

Ahiah smiled knowingly at the young leader. "Very noble," he hissed with a sly grin.

The leader nodded, and beckoned to his men, jerking his head in the direction of the alabaster city. They nodded, and started away. The leader again turned, and moved closer to Ahiah. "Who is the woman?" he whispered, eyeing her.

"My daughter," Ahiah breathed, a tight smile of warning on his face.

"Your daughter?" The leader looked at the rope in Ahiah's hand, and up again at his face.

"It will take much time to explain."

The leader nodded. "I am in the mood for a long story, but first I should introduce myself. I know who you are, but who I am, you do not know. I am Pachus's chief captain, and am second in command under him and next in line to the throne. Pachus is my father-in-law. My name is Nusair."

❦

"Captain Jacob, wake up." Someone was gripping his shoulder and shaking it.

"What?" He sat up on his ground blanket and looked up into a face lined with fatigue. He stiffened. "Yes?"

"A runner has come from Bountiful." The face of Micha, the captain of Pahoran's guard was filled with worry. "Come with me."

Jacob sat up, reaching for his boots and his sword belt, wondering what news would be so urgent as to send a man from Bountiful. Questions filled his mind, but he remained silent as he rose to his feet.

"I have awakened Pahoran, as well as Captain Moroni." Micha's voice was scarcely his own as he led Jacob into a brightly lit conference room. He blinked in the light. Smoke from lamps filled his nostrils. At the head of a huge table sat Captain Moroni, a lack of sleep showing on his face. Beside him sat Pahoran, who appeared to have aged dramatically. Behind the two men stood a younger man. He stood as still as a statue, his arms at his sides, and his bare bronze chest barely rising to breathe.

"Tuloth," Jacob began coolly, to which the messenger barely acknowledged him by blinking, and nodding slightly. "You have brought news from Bountiful."

"Yes, sir, I have." Tuloth's eyes were dark and impenetrable.

"Jacob," Pahoran began gently, leaning forward. "Please, sit."

He did as Pahoran bid him, his jaw tightening as he waited.

"Sir," Tuloth began in a deep baritone voice that seemed to vibrate the walls. "Your wife Miriam, the daughter of Aaron, has disappeared from the city Bountiful—," he paused as Jacob's frame tensed. "I followed the tracks left behind and read enough to see that she was stolen, and that her captor travels toward the city Zarahemla. I do not know with a surety, but I believe he is Ahiah."

Jacob's nostrils flared, and he clenched his teeth, listening in silence as Tuloth spoke. At last, he whispered through clenched teeth, "It cannot be."

"No, sir." Tuloth eyed him carefully, almost warily. "Though I wish it were not, it is true."

An angry protest froze in Jacob's throat. He had never been seized by such a wave of panic in his life, and he struggled against the urge to strike out at Tuloth for bringing such news. He lowered his face, his chest suddenly tight as he clenched his fists, reminding himself that the young messenger had no fault other than having to bear the bad tidings.

"Why would Ahiah come this far north, and risk capture?" he scoffed, hiding his fear behind his anger.

"The city that was in his charge was taken back while he was absent from it, and he might be ashamed to return to his king," Tuloth offered.

"So like the priests of Noah, he has stolen my wife for himself because he is ashamed to return to the Lamanites," Jacob growled acidly.

Tuloth dropped his eyes. "I do not believe that is why he stole her."

"Why else would he take her then?" Jacob shouted as he rose to his feet.

"Jacob." Moroni's voice was hard. "He is just the messenger. He is not at fault."

"Yes, sir," Jacob grumbled, lowering back to his seat, his limbs trembling.

"And sir," Tuloth cut in, "you must understand that there is another reason why Ahiah might have taken Miriam. Years ago, Ahiah had a daughter whom he wished to sacrifice to the gods, but she was taken far away from him. Perhaps he thinks Miriam was that child."

"He means, then, to sacrifice her to your—to the Lamanite gods?" Jacob demanded, his grief catching in his throat.

"Perhaps not," Tuloth offered. "The tracks were turned toward Zarahemla."

"And all you did was follow him," Jacob growled, glaring at Tuloth with poison in his eyes.

"The trail was already old," Pahoran added quietly. "And Tuloth has covenanted that he will never shed the blood of men again. We are grateful that he knows she is in Zarahemla."

Jacob forced himself to look down, his muscles trembling.

"Jacob," Pahoran spoke, and Jacob lifted his burning eyes. "Tomorrow, we retake Zarahemla. If Aaron's daughter is there, we will find her."

"She does not deserve this," Jacob snarled, fighting the tears that were stinging his eyes.

"We do not deserve this war," Moroni reminded him tiredly, "yet God will not take away man's agency, and often that means that good people suffer when bad people choose wickedness."

Pahoran rose, and came around the table, putting a comforting hand on Jacob's shoulder. "We will find your wife." He offered Jacob a hopeful smile. "Return to your pallet, and rest. You need strength for the battle."

"Sir, I cannot sleep after this."

"Then pray." Pahoran turned away slowly, sadly shaking his head, and left the room, followed by Micha and Tuloth.

"Jacob," Moroni spoke across the table, his voice echoing in the still room. "We will find her. Do not be afraid."

Jacob sneered and struck an angry blow causing the table to vibrate. "Miriam is my wife. I love her more than I have ever loved anyone. How can I not fear? How can I not hate myself because I do not have the power to save her now?"

"Can all your wishing change anything?" Moroni asked.

Jacob snorted and shook his head, glancing away.

"Jacob." Moroni rose slowly and came around the table until he stood beside him. He lowered himself to one knee and looked at Jacob levelly. "God will give us what we need. Trust Him."

"And you can say that even with what has happened?" Jacob raised his reddened eyes.

"I can say that because I know." Moroni reached out, and gripped Jacob's shoulder tightly. "Not everything that happens is what we expect or desire, but God gives us the strength to see through our trials, and we are blessed." Moroni's calm, wise eyes were bloodshot. "Come. I cannot sleep either. Let's pray together."

CHAPTER 23

The door opened, and she strained to rise to her feet as light from beyond the door enveloped her.

The silhouette of a young man blocked the light as he bent down and dropped a bowl of something near the corner of the doorway. She could see that he held a cloth over his face to shield his nose from the thick, pungent odor that had numbed her own sense of smell. "I am Jairus, sent by your father, Ahiah. He wishes me—,"

"Ahiah is not my father!" Miriam's anguished cry reverberated throughout the dank room, and in the darkness behind her, she heard the whisper of frightened rats' feet as they scurried away through cracks in the damp stone walls.

The silhouette sighed and his shoulders drooped. Miriam sensed something of pity in his voice as he spoke. "Ahiah wishes me to inform you that you will soon be taken up into king Pachus's home where the princess's maids will bathe and dress you to prepare you to be taken to meet your future husband."

"Ammoron will not be my husband," she spoke evenly.

The young man made a low sound in his throat and stepped out of her view. The door shut with an echoing shudder.

The light was dim now; only a tiny amount seeped through the corners of the door. But she could see the bowl that had been left. Cautiously she inched toward it, and knelt in the weak light. Nothing more than a bowl of water and a loaf of dried bread. Nausea rose in her throat, and she gripped her stomach, lowering her head until it touched her knees. She could not eat.

"I will die here in this darkness," she whispered. "I will never see Jacob or anyone I care about ever again." Her thoughts brought tears to her eyes, and they ran unchecked down her face, streaking through the layers of dirt that had settled on her skin.

At length, exhausted from her crying, she rolled into a crumpled ball on the floor, under the tiny sliver of light that came in at the door, and fell asleep.

A confusing mix of voices outside the thick door forced Miriam to wake from her shallow slumber and look up. By some miracle, the angry fires that had raged inside of her had subsided, and she rose to her feet, fighting the weakness that threatened to drag her down. For weeks, she had been unable to eat much, and being able to stand without fainting was a miracle.

The voices she heard were jumbled, almost afraid, and she began to wonder if perhaps the Nephites had come to take back the city. She reached a hand out and touched the crack of the door, gaining courage from the narrow sliver of light. If it was true that those loyal to Pahoran were laying siege to the city, she would not know for hours, perhaps days until the city was retaken.

She had resigned herself to this thought, when, with suddenness that made her gasp and leap back, the door burst open, flooding the room with torchlight. Confused and momentarily blinded, Miriam threw a hand up to shield her eyes when a pinching grip seized her around the wrist, and hauled her out of the cell.

"Worthless daughter," she heard Ahiah's cruel voice hiss as her eyes adjusted to the brightness around her. Ahiah, his vice grip fastened to her wrist, was dragging her farther down the narrow corridor toward the steps leading up and away from the cell behind her. He was wearing armor, and a sword was sheathed at his waist.

Panic gripped her heart. "What will you do with me?" she cried.

Ahiah leered over her, his face curled in a hideous expression of hate. "You are worth less and less to me, Daughter. Do not think I have not noticed how sick you are. You will surely be dead soon, but Nusair insists that you must come." He jerked her again down the corridor.

The movement twisted her stomach. "I am sick, Ahiah," she despaired. "Have mercy."

"They came upon us in the early hours of dawn," Ahiah spat angrily. "The Nephites fight like rabid jaguars, and even now are at the gates of the city."[17]

At that, Ahiah turned with an angry tug on her wrist, and began up the narrow stone steps, headed to what Miriam could see now was an open door halfway up the steps, through which an older man was looking out.

He was short; his height no greater than Miriam's. The fine clothes he wore seemed out of place on his barrel shaped frame. Tiny eyes like dark beads stared penetratingly out of a wine-reddened face. His feet were shod with well-crafted leather boots, and both a sword and a short dagger hung off the belt around his swollen midsection. He also had a tapering stick stuffed through his belt—a torch. The fat end was charred as if it had been burnt.

"Soon, the Nephites will have the gate battered down." The man's voice was low and angry as Ahiah yanked Miriam toward the wooden door set in the stone walls of the stairway.

With a rough shove, Ahiah pushed Miriam across the threshold where she stumbled, and almost fell, but she was caught by the arm, and hauled to her feet.

"It is a good thing that you bring your daughter with you, Ahiah. It would be a tragic loss to leave such a lovely thing behind," Nusair's familiar voice crooned, his grip tight on her arm. He was dressed in the same manner as the older man, both a sword and a knife on his belt. A bow and quiver of arrows were strung across his back and a torch was looped through his belt.

"She smells like raw sewage." The old man sniffed with unveiled abhorrence.

"It is only because she has been locked in that cell for days, Pachus," Nusair said calmly, his eyes traveling over her. "Beneath that filth is a rare gem."

"Nusair, she is to be Ammoron's concubine." Ahiah came between them and pushed Nusair back as he slipped a scratchy cord around her neck.

Nusair grumbled, and stepped away. Miriam drew a tentative breath, looking around the small room they were in. She realized with some surprise, that they were in a tunnel, reaching into lengths of unknown darkness beyond the light spilling in from the door. Behind her, she heard a sharp snapping sound, then a hiss, and suddenly, there was a bright flickering light. She shielded her eyes from the glare of the torch in Pachus's hand. Nusair held his own torch out to the flame as Pachus shut the door, and it was then that she noticed two other people in the tunnel with them.

Behind Nusair was a young woman, a few years older than Miriam. Her face, though expressionless with the hint of anger behind her eyes, was exquisitely lovely, almost as if her features had been carved and polished from marble. Her clothes, like the ones the others wore, were finely woven, silk, dyed in rich color. Her hair was golden, and was plaited back, reflecting the light from the torches. There was something strangely familiar about her, and Miriam could see by the way the woman looked at her, that there was something she recognized as well.

"Ema," the lilting voice of a child came from behind the woman's skirt, and she turned to the small person who voiced her name. "Will Grandfather give the Nephites their city back?"

The young woman reached behind her, pulling on the arm of a small boy who was dressed as richly as the others. "We will live among the Lamanites for a time, Zeram."

"And when we have gained the Lamanites' confidence, we will use their help to restore our kingdom," the large man growled at the child. "Then you will be king someday."

"I do not want to be king," the child whined.

"You are the son of royal blood, boy," Nusair barked at the little boy who ducked behind his mother's skirt. "Your ambitions should be higher than that." Nusair moved to step around the woman, but with silent threatening eyes, she moved to block him from the child.

"We must not waste time, my husband." Her voice showed submission, but her eyes did not.

"It is true," the large man conceded. "The Nephites are coming through the gate."

"Then let's go, Pachus."

"Did anyone see us leave?" Pachus asked, as he and Nusair started down the corridor at a swift march. Ahiah walked beside them, tugging on the rope, forcing Miriam after him.

"No one," Ahiah grunted.

"Why do you not wish for anyone to know you have left?" Miriam wondered under her breath. "Because you do not want your followers to know that you have deserted them?"

Nusair turned back. His eyes flashed indignantly, and he looked as if he would strike her. The young woman beside her tittered quietly at her boldness, and Nusair directed his anger at her.

"If you value your son's life, woman, you will be silent," he shouted at her.

At that, she was quiet, and lowered her eyes, placing a protective hand on the boy's head, whose eyes were upturned to his father, full of fear.

"Of course, Zeram has little to worry of from me," Nusair admitted, looking back at the child who followed behind his mother, clinging to her skirts. "He was born a boy, after all."

At that, Zeram started to cry. "Ema, hold me?" he begged, tears beginning in his little eyes.

"I cannot hold you, Zeram. You are too big," she muttered nervously, glancing at Nusair who had turned forward again.

"I—I think I am strong enough to carry him," Miriam suddenly heard herself say.

The young woman eyed her for a few moments, taking in her dirt-caked clothes, and her muddy face, but with a sigh, she finally agreed. "Very well," she said. With a grunt, she picked up the small boy, and shoved him into Miriam's arms. In spite of the weeks of dirt caked onto her face and clothes, little Zeram wrapped his arms tightly around her neck.

Zeram's mother walked sullenly beside her as they followed the men through the cavernous darkness, illuminated only a few paces in front of them and behind.

Miriam turned to the woman and murmured, "Is there any chance that the Nephites will know where we have gone, and follow after us?"

"No," the woman whispered. "Even before my father became king, he had powerful connections in the city of Zarahemla. He had this tunnel built beneath his home only by men who swore allegiance to him, and the Nephites know nothing of it."

Miriam turned her eyes toward the rough, jaggedly hewn walls, blinking away the tears.

"Look how little Zeram takes to you." The young woman smiled. "He is asleep on your shoulder already. I almost want to take you as his nurse, but your father will not have that. As I do, you have a special birthright. You are fortunate that you will be a wife to the king of the Lamanites."

"I do not wish to be Ammoron's concubine," Miriam murmured, to which the young woman blinked in surprise, and laughed.

"Of course you do. There is no greater honor for any woman." At this, she paused again, studying Miriam's features as if she was trying to remember something. "With your beauty, you will easily become his favorite. He will give you power. Everyone will bow to you."

Miriam turned her face away. "I will not choose to do something I know to be wrong. I will follow my Father's teachings, not Ahiah's."

The young woman's eyes were wide. "You mean Ahiah is not your father? Who is?"

Miriam bit her lip before answering. "Whether Ahiah is the sire of my birth, I do not know, nor care. My real father on Earth was a good man, who taught me who my true Eternal Father is. Before I was even born, or came to live with my real parents in Morianton, the God of Abraham was my Father."

As she spoke these words, a peace filled her heart, but the young woman did not seem to feel the same spirit. Her eyes narrowed. "What was your father's name?"

"Aaron," Miriam answered.

"You were in the camp of Moroni when the people of Morianton tried to make war on the people of Lehi?" The woman's voice had grown threatening.

"Yes," Miriam admitted.

At her answer, the woman's lips curled back in a snarl. With a violent grab, she pulled her little son out of Miriam's arms. "You are Miriam," she growled over her startled son's head. "Ahiah has not spoken your name, but I know you. You are the one who stole Jacob from me."

Miriam looked on in shock, confused by the young woman's sudden anger. She brooded for only a moment before she remembered. "You are Lylith!" she gasped.

"I am," she sniffed, raising her voice as her frightened son began to struggle and whine against her tight hold. "And someday I will be a queen, while you will be a mere concubine."

The scrape of a sword being drawn echoed through the narrow cavern. Nusair spun around, the sword in his fist glinting off the torchlight. "Lylith, silence that boy."

At that, she gasped, and thrust him back into Miriam's arms where he quieted and relaxed, again resting his head against her shoulder.

Hearing the stillness, Nusair sheathed his sword, and turned back.

Miriam fought the tears that rose to her eyes as she stepped carefully over the uneven stones illuminated by the flickering torches. Little Zeram snuffled against her shoulder, and she smiled weakly at the warm press of his cheek against hers.

"Ah, there, look!" Pachus cried, pointing ahead as they moved around a twisted bend.

Miriam lifted her eyes, a rough edged circle of light not more than a hundred paces ahead of her, lit the tunnel like a lamp in the darkness.

"At last," Nusair said, crushing his torch to death against the stones.

"How do we know that there are no Nephites waiting for us?" Ahiah wondered.

"We can send Zeram," Nusair offered. "If he is killed, we will know there are Nephites."

"Do not be a fool," Miriam snorted. "Nephites would not kill a little child."

Nusair spun angrily around, but Lylith stepped forward. "I will go."

"Even better," he smirked, moving toward her, and grabbing her roughly by the arm.

She jerked her arm from his, her eyes smoldering. "I do this for my son, Nusair. Though I, like Miriam, know that the Nephites would no sooner harm a woman than they would a boy."

She turned away from her husband and began walking toward the circle of light, her slender arms swinging rhythmically at her sides. Her smooth face was tilted proudly.

The rest of the group followed her, silent except for Nusair's subdued chuckle. Zeram twisted in Miriam's arms to watch his mother. The jagged opening grew closer.

Lylith continued to move toward the open cleft in the rock, through which Miriam could see sky. She braced herself against the two narrow sides of the opening, and peered out.

"I see rocks and brush, but no people," she called back excitedly.

The three men breathed a collective sigh of relief as they began to move forward again. Miriam stepped blinking into the light as she staggered out to find herself in a wide, river carved canyon. Several hundred paces from the cavern's opening, the river flowed placidly northward.

Behind her, in the distance, the stone walls of Zarahemla rose up. The army of Nephites rippled like the waves of the sea, and pressed up against the very walls of the city. A few kingmen lined the walls, even as Nephites poured through the battered gate.

The irony that their leader would be fleeing from them made Miriam sick with anger, adding to her own growing hopelessness. She had been so sure of it before, but now, surrounded by her enemies, cast almost as it were into the jaws of the Abyss itself, her surety that Jacob would find and save her was beginning to dim. She drew in a ragged breath and shook herself. She must not give up, she remembered. Tears stung her eyes, and fell against the fresh pink cheek of the child in her arms. Her hope was all she had left now. Quietly she turned her face into his soft golden hair, and began whispering, praying quietly for the peace she needed.

"What are you doing?" a soft voice whispered as a small hand touched her cheek.

She smiled through her tears. "I am praying, Zeram," she whispered.

"What is praying?" His eyes were open and trusting, and she smiled into them.

"When I pray, I talk to God."

"Who is God?"

"He is a very wise person who knows everything, and can do anything."

"Is He kind?"

"Very kind." She nodded. "And if you pray, He will give you good things, and help you."

"Oh, then let me pray also," he murmured earnestly.

A new flood of tears filled her eyes and she nodded to the small boy, pressing her face closer to his, and began her prayer again, whispering quietly so that he alone could hear.

CHAPTER 24

Jacob knew he must be a terrifying sight with his disheveled, wild appearance as he strode across Zarahemla's main plaza toward the palace of the chief judge. Blood splattered his arms, legs and armor as he surveyed the remnants of the battle. It was a sight that caused his stomach to twist into a hard knot. This city had once been his home, yet it looked like a scene from a nightmare. The moans of wounded men filled the air with their pitiful cries. He had traversed the entire city, yet there was no sign of Miriam. A broad set of stone steps swept down from the entrance, and Jacob mounted the first three to gaze out over the plaza, his fists on his hips as he furtively blinked frustrated tears from his eyes.

On the steps behind him, beside several other bodies, lay a young kingman, frightened, gasping for breath, an arrow in his chest. Jacob ignored him, continuing to scan the plaza, until the man spoke. "You are searching for someone," he said, his voice ragged and weak.

Jacob turned and looked up at the man through narrow, untrusting eyes. "Who are you?"

"My name is Jairus," the man answered. "Who do you wish to find?"

"A young woman, dark hair, blue eyes," Jacob muttered, and glanced away, doubting that the man would help.

"I think I know of whom you speak. A man named Ahiah brought her to the city, and kept her in a cell beneath Pachus's house."

Jacob turned to the man and began up a step. "Tell me more," he demanded.

Jairus shook his head. "Ahiah has disappeared, as well as Pachus and his family. I think they escaped down the tunnel beneath Pachus's home. It passes under the city wall and leads to the river. Few know of it. I only know because I myself helped dig it."

Jacob moved closer to the wounded man.

"Why should I believe you?" he asked when he stood over him.

"Pachus has abandoned us," the man gasped. "I was a fool to follow him."

Jacob straightened, scanning the plaza behind them. "There must be a medic near to come look after your wounds. Then you will be taken with the other prisoners we have captured." He turned back.

"Jairus—." He began to address the young man, but stopped himself.

The man's head had fallen back against the steps, and his ragged breath was silent.

ര

The walls of Zarahemla, glistening under the sweltering sun of the late afternoon, grew smaller behind them as the little group moved steadily southward. The river flowed placidly past them as they scrambled over piles of rock. Ahiah led the way, the knotted rope yanking Miriam along behind him. Little Zeram, dusty and exhausted, clung to her shoulder. Nusair followed, watching Ahiah with haughty stalking eyes, his hand fingering the dagger at his belt. Behind him marched Lylith, her forehead damp, her fine silken dress soaked in sweat. Further behind Lylith, came Pachus, his cumbersome frame tottering heavily, his hand on the hilt of the sword at his hip. His eyes nervously darted back and forth, squinting up at the rock around him. He flinched at every shadow, jumped at every unexpected sound.

He and Lylith were falling further behind, unable to match the swift pace Ahiah and Nusair kept. Even if he had breath to call out to them, they would not have waited, so finally, his lumbering scuttle stopped and he lowered himself to a stone, mopping the sweat from his brow.

"The Nephite fools do not know where I am. They cannot catch me," he reasoned under his breath as the flash of Lylith's golden hair disappeared around a bend of rock.

Nusair cocked his head to the side. Behind him, he could hear nothing but the soft flow of the river. He shook his head to himself, turning to see where Lylith and Pachus were. A sly half grin curled over his teeth. There was no one behind him. He did not know where they were, and he did not care. He was only glad they were gone. He turned his face forward, studying the woman Ahiah called his daughter. He smiled grimly as he pulled the bow and arrows from his back, and dropped them in the middle of the trail. He would have no need for any weapons but the sheathed dagger at his waist.

Pachus chuckled to himself. He supported himself with his hand as he clung to the branch of a scraggled bush as he passed it. He merely needed to follow the path before him, and sooner or later, he would come upon the others. No one else would find him here. Nothing could stop him now.

"Pachus!" the voice suddenly thundered as if from heaven. "Stop!"

He let out a long breath as he slowly turned. His eyes fell upon the warrior whose body shone with sweat, his chest heaving. Pachus's face crinkled into a sour, sarcastic smile.

Lylith glanced fearfully about, painfully aware that she was alone. She could feel her heart pounding within her as she scurried along the narrow trail, jerking in reflex to every whisper of sound that came to her ears. She remembered the greed in Nusair's eyes when he had looked on Miriam, and she shuddered. No matter what jealousy she felt for the younger woman, she still hoped for Miriam's sake that Ahiah had meant what he said when he told Nusair that his daughter would not be his.

When she stumbled across the abandoned bow and the quiver of arrows laying across the trail, she did not think as she picked them up, and slung them across her shoulders as she had seen men do.

Though she had never used weapons before, the smooth feel of the bow in her hand gave her some comfort.

"You were always a troublesome boy, Jacob," Pachus breathed, his sword slowly sliding out of its sheath as he stared into the young man's eyes. He could see Jacob's jaw tighten and contract, his fists opening and closing. "But I suppose being raised like a dog in the streets would do that to you."

"Where is my wife, Pachus?" Jacob growled, pulling his own sword out with a metallic rasp.

"Your wife?" Pachus chuckled. "It is too late. I have already given Lylith away to another man."

"Miriam," Jacob demanded. "Where is she?"

"That wretched daughter of a dog is your wife?" Pachus laughed out loud.

"Tell me where she is," Jacob shouted.

"I do not know," Pachus shot back, annoyed. "Ahiah is her keeper."

"No matter. I will find her anyway," Jacob snarled, his teeth clenched. "My orders now, though, are to take you prisoner."

Pachus sneered. "Not kill me?"

"I will take you alive, Pachus," he said.

Pachus scowled. "What does it matter to you if I die now, or at the hands of your judge?" Pachus backed away, but Jacob advanced on him, making up the ground as Pachus lost it.

"You are guilty of insurrection, Pachus. You have opened correspondence with the Lamanites, who fight to take away the freedom of your countrymen. Because of your greed, many innocent people have suffered and died. But it is not my place to punish you."

Pachus gave a wry smirk. "I will not be taken alive." With those words, Pachus raised his sword and brought it screaming toward Jacob's face where it struck with a clanging shower of sparks against the edge of Jacob's sword, lifted in time to deflect the blow. Puffing and cursing angrily, Pachus swung his sword in a wide arch, but the younger man stepped away, Pachus's sword grating as it struck stone.

Pachus's face was red, and he cursed bitterly, clumsily slicing his sword down on Jacob's shoulder, but Jacob darted nimbly out of the way, and his sword clanged dully against rock.

Falling back several paces from the Nephite who had not yet struck an offensive blow, he reached his left hand across to his right side, and pulled out his dagger, clutching it awkwardly. He glared suspiciously at the young man who waited, his feet apart, his chest heaving, determined to bring Pachus back to the city which was no longer his, where his followers were prisoners, and where Pahoran was again at the head.

"I told you, I won't be taken back. You cannot make me." Adrenaline surged in his veins as he watched Jacob's unwavering eyes for a misstep, or an unguarded spot. His heart pounded, and he could feel the sweat running down his face. Jacob stood as still as death. His eyes narrowed warily as Pachus opened his mouth and spoke in a tremulous voice.

"I will die a king." With those words, Pachus plunged the knife into his own belly, faintly aware that Jacob leapt forward to stop him. He felt himself fall to his knees, and then to his face against the cold stone. The knife twisted, causing a sensation of discomfort, and then his mind went black.

Ah, oblivion. He felt a wave of relief. Nonexistence seemed a wonderful escape, now that he knew he would not be held accountable for his crimes.

But suddenly he felt aware of himself again. He found himself standing, watching two men, one a Nephite warrior who knelt over another, checking for signs of life. The hilt of a knife stuck out of the belly of the man on the ground, his portly abdomen covered with blood. He realized with a wave of panic, that the dead man was his own body. His consciousness, his spirit, he realized with sick horror, was still alive, and he knew now, would never die.

He felt himself pulled from the scene, beyond the screen of mortality. He lifted his concentration to the sky that was rushing to meet him with incredible speed now, and he was filled with burning terror as he experienced a perfect awareness of all his guilt, and all that awaited him.

CB

Ahiah brushed a hand against his sweating forehead, and slowed to a stop beneath the sparse shade of a palm tree that arched out over the river. The girl behind him fell to her knees, gasping, almost in tears as the little boy patted her cheek, murmuring childish words of comfort.

"Ahiah," she cried a moment later when she had regained enough breath to speak, clutching at her stomach, "do you not understand how tired I am?"

"It isn't my fault that you can keep nothing in your stomach, foolish girl." He turned to her, his face twisted. "I will not slow down to be captured by the Nephites, because you are weak."

Gasping heavily, she looked steadily up at him. "Give us a moment's rest."

Forgetting his weariness, he seized her arm as if to jerk her to her feet. "We leave now."

"There is no need, Ahiah," a voice said behind Miriam.

Ahiah lifted his head, his face registering fright for a moment before he saw Nusair seated on a rock behind them. He smiled with relief. "Nusair, it is you."

"Yes, it is me." Nusair nodded, his eyes turning to Miriam.

His gaze moved over her, and Miriam clutched Zeram close, his little body trembling.

"Where are your weapons?" Ahiah hissed.

Nusair gave a half grin as he rose. "I need only this." He patted the dagger at his waist.

Ahiah gave a disbelieving snort. "What do you mean—." His voice cut short as he saw Nusair's half grin mutate into a snarl, the dagger drawn, clutched in his fist.

"It was unwise of you to keep her from me, Ahiah," he growled, as he lowered his stance, his eyes burning into Ahiah's. "You cannot enjoy a delicious piece of fruit and not expect me to want a taste as well."

"I have told you, boy, she is to be Ammoron's." Ahiah's jaw tightened.

"Liar," Nusair sneered. "I have seen the signs. Your woman is with child."

Clutching Zeram protectively, Miriam looked up at the two men who, for the moment, ignored her. She crouched on the ground, releasing the small boy from her arms.

"Zeram," she grated, pulling a leather band with a blue stone attached to it over her head, "run away from here. Find the Nephites. They will take care of you. Show them this necklace, and ask for Jacob, my husband. He is a lower captain."

Wordlessly, the little boy nodded, scrambled to his feet, and ran away and around a swell of rock, ignored by both men.

"You lie, Nusair," Ahiah seethed, but then his eyes widened as understanding came to him. Angrily, he turned on Miriam. "Unless . . ." He struck her face, and she fell beneath his blow to the unforgiving stone.

She pressed a hand against her burning cheek and tried to struggle away, but he reached her, and lifted her roughly to her feet. "Who was it? That whelp, Jacob, I should have killed years ago?"

She kept her mouth shut, her eyes turned from his, and he gripped her other arm with pinching pain and shook her roughly. "*Whose?*" he shrieked. His face, twisted demonically, was only inches from hers, his stale breath seething through his teeth.

"Nusair," she gasped, "is behind you."

Without an instant's hesitation, he dropped her again, spinning as the dagger descended. He caught Nusair's wrist, the blade halting inches from his face. The two men were instantly grappling desperately as they tumbled on the uneven ground, and rolled together across the rocks, the leash tugging Miriam after them. Desperately, she pulled at the knot at her throat, freeing the loop enough to pull it over her head. She turned from the scene, looking back over her shoulder at the two struggling men. She hurried faster when she saw the knife flash, and heard Ahiah cry out in pain.

With a cry of victory, Nusair raised his knife again above Ahiah's face. Before the knife could descend, however, Miriam heard a familiar hiss of air, and then a quivering thunk. She froze in place, gazing in wonder at the arrow that had flown from nowhere, and now protruded, quivering, from Nusair's chest. *Who could have possibly—*

"Ahiah? Where is my son? And Miriam?" Miriam gaped as Lylith stepped from between two leafy bushes. A bow was clutched in her trembling hand, but she quickly dropped it, her face blanching white when she saw Nusair, his eyes staring up at hers, disbelieving. Sickened, she turned away, her hands covering her face.

Ahiah threw the dying body of his foe off him, and limped to his feet, blood streaming from a wound in his arm. "Return to me, Daughter!"

At that, Miriam turned and began to run, fighting her weakness, and the nausea in her stomach. A wail of fear behind her stopped her, and she looked back.

"Daughter!" Ahiah's voice rose angrily in the air as he held Lylith around her neck like a great snake, ready to choke her, her small white hands grasping desperately at his arm. His knife was pointing at the wildly pulsating artery in her slender throat. "If you leave, I swear I will kill her."

Miriam stopped and turned. The tip of Ahiah's knife pressed against Lylith's throat as she contracted with sobs, pleading for her life.

She glanced back over her shoulder, across the rolling swells of the river valley. The walls of Zarahemla were visible in the distance.

"I will kill her if you go," Ahiah shouted.

Miriam hesitated only a moment longer. Then her head drooped as she started back toward Ahiah, trying to ignore the tightening around her heart.

"Hah!" Ahiah shouted, victoriously pushing Lylith to the ground. He reached down, and stripped the quiver from Lylith's back, then went to retrieve the bow she had dropped. "The two of you will accompany me to meet King Ammoron. He will be happy to have two new concubines." He turned with glaring eyes at Miriam, and addressed her, "Help up the queen. We have a long way to go."

Wordlessly, Miriam obeyed, and stooped over Lylith, putting a hand under her arm. She helped her to her feet, seeing the questioning look in her eyes.

"Why did you do this for me?"

"Because you are my sister," she said.

"Sister?" Lylith shook her head.

Miriam nodded. "The same God who is my Father is your Father as well."

"I know of no such god," Lylith snarled, bitterness heavy in her eyes.

"You have never been given the chance to know of Him."

"Will your ceaseless prattle never end, you foolish women?" Ahiah groaned, shoving them with the edge of the bow as he limped after them.

Miriam gazed into Lylith's sad eyes, and reached for her hand, gripping it in her own though it did not return her squeeze. Responding dumbly to Ahiah's orders, she turned southward, leading Lylith by the hand.

CHAPTER 25
31ST YEAR OF JUDGES

*T*here was no moon that night. A strong wind from the sea blew over the tents as Jacob moved to the edge of the camp. The walls of the city Moroni glimmered before him like an impossible mirage against the blackness. The torches set at intervals along the walls of the city illuminated each stone, the light whipping madly in the wind, and flickered with taunting jealousy off the spiked barricades that leaned out over the deep trenches.

He turned his eyes back to the distant walls, his fist tightening around a band of leather in his hand, a blue stone hanging from it. He dropped his eyes as he brought his hand up, letting the light of the fires behind him touch off the smooth surface of the stone.

He remembered vividly, the yellow haired little boy at the edge of the river Sidon, rumpled and dirty, who came tottering to him as if to his own father. In his little fist, he had held the necklace that Jacob had instantly recognized.

"My name is Zeram," he remembered the wearied little boy sobbing as Jacob reached down and gathered him up. "Miriam says to give this to you, and to find Jacob, her husband."

"I am Jacob," he had said, his heart leaping with hope. "Where is she?"

"Bad men have her," the little boy had sniffled.

"Do not worry, Zeram. We will find her." He had felt sure that he would, but other than the body of a kingman with an arrow in his chest, they had found no trace of Ahiah or Miriam.

With a groan of helplessness, Jacob fell heavily against a tree, his eyes on the mocking image in the distance. The bark was rough and solid against his back, and he drew in a deep breath.

"Where in all this land can she be?" Jacob finally groaned aloud. "We have taken back Nephihah and Lehi, and she was in neither of those cities."

A twig snapping behind him brought him back, and he turned to see Teancum.

The seasoned captain's presence comforted him, and he managed to offer a small twitch at the corners of his mouth.

"Perhaps she is here, in Moroni."

"Perhaps she is dead, sir," Jacob returned, his voice low.

"You will be at the front of the battle tomorrow, Jacob," he said quietly, laying a hand on his shoulder. "You must rest."

"Sir, I would prefer—,"

"It isn't a request, Jacob." Teancum cut his words off. His voice was gentle but strained.

The depths of his commander's eyes were strangely unreadable as he turned away, silently bidding Jacob to follow him.

As they passed from the wooded area into the open, he could hear the voices of men around him as they prepared to bed down for the night. He became aware of his own fatigue, yet Teancum, it seemed, brimmed with energy. Jacob was forced to a near run as they passed rows of tents making their way to the center of camp.

Even with their backs turned to him, Jacob recognized Moroni and Lehi, who sat staring into the fire. Lehi's broad shoulders were slumped in weariness, his silver hair was ruffled, and caked in dirt and sweat, and blood. Even Moroni's posture betrayed his fatigue. His chin rested in his hands, his elbows against his knees. The moment the men heard them coming, however, they rose to their feet and turned. Though he was the chief captain, Moroni's expression was almost apologetic.

"Teancum, you are back. We had begun to worry."

"Forgive me, sir. I have brought Jacob back. He will be at the head of my men tomorrow."

"And you?" Moroni asked, his brow furrowing.

"I—," Teancum paused painfully before he finished, "—will be at his side."

Moroni nodded, eyeing Teancum carefully, and traded a silent glance with Lehi whose lined face was drawn with exhaustion. "Very well, then. Good night."

Jacob saluted, and turned for his own tent, his muscles crying for rest, but as he lifted the flap, he turned back. Moroni and Lehi had disappeared, but Teancum had not moved. He stood stiffly, as if made of wood, his face taut and grim staring into the fire. "Sir?"

Teancum shook himself as if he was breaking a deep concentration. "Do not wait for me, Jacob."

Jacob nodded, too tired to argue, and bent his head through the door, crossing into partial darkness. He unrolled his stiff blanket against the powdery soil, and dropped heavily onto it, feeling himself slipping into unconsciousness. It seemed only to be a moment later when his eyes flickered open, unsure of what had awakened him. Blinking sleepily he lifted his head, and looked out the door at the firelight. Silhouetted against the dying coals, was Teancum's shadow, coiling a length of cord around his arm. As if he sensed himself being watched, he looked up to see Jacob's sleepy face.

"Forgive me, Jacob," he whispered. "It is only me. Go back to sleep."

"Yesir," Jacob mumbled as he closed his eyes again.

Teancum paused, looking down into the face of the sleeping young man whom he had looked on almost as a son for as long as he had known him. He shook his head to himself as he finished the last of the rope, and slung it about his shoulders. He had a task to perform tonight, one that allowed him no rest. His javelin stood planted in the ground, and he yanked it up, threading it through the belt at his back. He would travel lightly tonight, and would carry no other weapons. If all went as planned, Ammoron would die as his brother before him, with a javelin through his heart.[18]

Taking a long breath, Teancum turned away from the fire, and ran noiselessly into the darkness at the edge of camp. Nothing but silence, and the light of dying fires surrounded him.

у

Miriam could see the faint glow of fire beyond the walls of the city where the Nephite armies camped against the last stronghold of the Lamanites. It had been months since Ahiah had taken her from Zarahemla, but it seemed to her as if it had been years. The first faint movements within her had begun to grow stronger, and she smiled.

A hand went to her stomach, and she thought of her husband Jacob as she ran her fingers over her belly, swelling beneath the loose, roughly spun robe. Leaning her head back against the window frame, she closed her eyes. She breathed deeply of the calm night air, tasting the comforting smell of the sea, remembering Bountiful, and the sweet tang of the sea breezes that drifted through the city on cool nights.

Behind her, a muffled noise came from Lylith's pallet, and Miriam turned again, listening quietly. Lylith was crying. She lifted herself to her feet, and reached for a candle and the lighting instruments. She struck them together until a spark caught, and the room became bathed in a soft, yellow glow.

"Lylith, what is it?" she whispered as she stood over the other woman. Her pillow was wet with tears.

"I miss my little boy," Lylith sniveled, sitting up. "Zeram was the one good thing I had in all the world, and I do not know where he is, if he is alive or dead."

"I am sure he is safe," Miriam crooned, kneeling down beside her, and trying to put her hand over Lylith's. "Surely the Nephites found him."

"But what if they discover that he is the grandson of Pachus?" Lylith pulled her hand away.

"Lylith, Zeram is a child. They will not hurt him."

Lylith raised her eyes, brushing tears from her cheeks. "How can I know that?"

"Perhaps if we prayed together—," Miriam offered helplessly.

"I have never believed in what you seem so certain of." Lylith's voice was tart as she glanced away. "All I ever believed was that I was destined for great things, that I was not common, and could be nothing more than a queen. All your words do is convince me more and more of my own sins. I believed my father's words, not because they were true, but because they fed my vanity, and now I know that what I have believed all my life was a lie. Is anything not a lie?"

Miriam paused, wishing Lylith could understand. She had tried to help Lylith see a glimmer of truth in her words, but her heart had been wounded, and hardened.

"Lylith, you are as much God's daughter as I am. He wants to help you."

Lylith let out a short breath and shook her head, her eyes filling with tears as she turned away from Miriam. Her expression was tightened in pain. "We are nothing!" she moaned. "We are the concubines of Ammoron, and it is only a matter of time before he . . ." She stopped speaking, and shuddered.

"Lylith, do not fear."

Lylith shook her head. "Why shouldn't we?"

"The Spirit has told me that we will be kept safe," Miriam murmured, but Lylith sneered and glanced away.

At that moment, they heard a sound near the window, and their faces snapped in that direction, shocked to see the silhouette of a man dressed in the armor of a Nephite. Lylith gasped.

"Miriam?" Teancum's voice rasped in the darkness.

"Teancum! Why are you here?" Miriam hissed, fear mixed with joy. "If they find you, they will kill you!"

"I am searching for Ammoron—" The strength of his voice faded as he eyed the swell of her belly. His jaw knotted. "Who has done this to you? Tell me, and I will kill him as well."

"No one has touched us," Miriam said, rubbing her hand across her stomach. "The child is Jacob's." She glanced back at Lylith.

"It—it is true," Lylith agreed, her voice shaking. "They have left us alone."

Teancum's face relaxed. "Nevertheless, I will find this Ahiah who has brought you here and slay him, when I am finished with Ammoron. Then I will come back for the two of you, and bring you back to Jacob. He has been worried about you."

"Oh, please hurry then," Miriam pleaded.

"I will try not to be long," he promised. "Do you know where Ammoron is?"

"He is in the large tent not far from here," she whispered, pointing. "But be careful. His servants are with him, Ahiah among them."

He nodded his thanks, and with that, he disappeared, as silently as he had come.

"Who was that?" Lylith scowled. "How does he know Jacob?"

"He is Teancum, one of Moroni's captains. Jacob has known him since he enlisted. He is like a father to him. He baptized Jacob and confirmed him, and later conferred the priesthood upon him." Miriam drew a sigh. "He even performed the ceremony that made Jacob and me husband and wife."

Lylith sighed brokenly, her voice lost and forlorn in the darkness. "You love Jacob."

Miriam glanced at her. "More than my own life," she murmured.

"There was once a time when I thought I loved him." Lylith studied her hands, which were trembling. "And I cannot deny that I felt envy when I learned that he was your husband." She glanced up and met Miriam's gaze. "But I never loved him. Perhaps I am unable to feel love for any one." She gave a short, quiet laugh that sounded strange in the silence. "Nusair was a husband whose absence I longed for. He beat me, and also Zeram. And he had many harlots." In the dim light, tears sparkled on Lylith's cheeks. "And now, I have shed his blood, and my soul is lost."

"No," Miriam whispered, "you killed him to save me."

Lylith looked at Miriam sadly. "If ever there has been, or ever will be a worthy man for me, as there is for you, why would he ever have me? For no honorable man would want me now."

"No, Lylith. You are not who you were. Your heart is changing—." But Lylith turned away, and so Miriam grew silent, watching her with sadness in her large eyes.

The light from the stars was dim and hard to see by as Teancum parted the door of the tent, and glared over the group of Ammoron's captains. Strange enough, Teancum noticed with a humorless smirk, not one of them had dark skin. Each of the men here had been Nephite born.

In the silence, he scanned the room, waiting for his eyes to adjust, and then saw the one he was looking for. Like a deadly coral snake sprawled in sleep in the midst of his fellow serpents, Ammoron lay in the middle of the room, snoring softly. His long, unkempt beard was streaked now with gray.

Teancum's expression tightened. Thousands of Nephites had died because of this man and his brother and their greed to enslave those who were once their kin, to exercise power over those who were weaker. For a moment, his thoughts flashed to Jacob's young wife, her beautiful face touched with moonlight, lifted trustingly as she spoke to him, her belly swelling with the life of Jacob's child. And then, inadvertently, his thoughts traveled to his own wife, how her own long dark hair used to fall about her face when she left it unbound, how she used to smile in the days before the Lamanites had come through their village. He had been in the distant fields with the other men when the Lamanites had come and had fallen without mercy on the women and children, and though he had run with all his strength, he had not made it back in time.

He shook his head and let out a long breath, tightening his grip on the javelin. Carefully, he stepped over sleeping bodies as he made his way toward the center of the room, finally standing over Ammoron himself. He tightened his jaw, and with both hands, lifted the spear.

A scream reverberated through the silent city, tearing the night apart before it quieted into a low dying moan. Miriam jerked her head up. Lylith scrambled to her feet, and rushed to the window, watching what Miriam could only hear as the camp came awake at once. Then she gasped, and fell to her knees, turning away from the window.

"No," Lylith moaned, clenching her eyes shut as if trying to erase what she had seen from her mind. "That man who came . . ." She was unable to finish, and covered her face with her hands.

The pain of the arrow burying itself deep into his back was sudden and sharp, and he pitched forward, choking on the blood that poured into his throat and lungs. Hundreds of pairs of feet came thundering toward him, their weapons raised. But before the Lamanites could reach him, they faded away. Shouts of anger and the pounding of feet wavered, and finally disappeared.

"Teancum." The sound of her voice made his head jerk up. He started at whom he saw, and scrambled to his feet. He attempted to dust himself off, but there was no dust to brush away.

"Tirzah!" He smiled awkwardly, searching her face, as beautiful as he remembered. Her hair cascaded over her shoulders in the way that he loved, her frame clothed in a robe of white.

She smiled, and came toward him and caught his hand, smiling at his wonder. "Come with me," she laughed, taking him by the other hand. "Our children are waiting to see you."

"Lylith?" Miriam attempted quietly. "What—"

"Ahiah killed him," Lylith moaned, lifting her eyes as tears washed down her cheeks.

"That must have been Ammoron who screamed," Miriam realized, her heart growing heavy. "Teancum killed him, but before he died, he woke his servants."[19]

She dropped to her knees, and buried her face in her hands, and began to cry quietly, rocking back and forth in grief.

Lylith sat heavily on the corner of her pallet, and buried her forehead against her knees.

"You women! Why is your light burning? Go back to sleep." She lifted her tear-filled eyes to someone's barbed shout.

At that, Miriam rose to her feet, and blew out the candle. Shuddering with sobs, she lay down on her own pallet, though she knew that sleep would not come.

CHAPTER 26

*I*ts golden tendrils touched the sky with dazzling brilliance as the rim of the sun peeked over the edge of the world.

Jacob though, was barely aware of the brightening sky as he knelt at the edge of camp. The collar of his uniform was torn jaggedly as a sign of his grief, and bitter tears stung in his eyes. Guards of the middle watch had crept close to the walls of the city to inspect a huge commotion within, suspecting that the Lamanites were planning a night raid. The walls had stood unguarded when they arrived through the last of the trees and noticed Teancum's body as the Lamanites had flung it over the wall, and had safely retrieved it back to camp. It was as Teancum had said, Jacob would lead his men.

"Sir." He heard a quiet voice above him, and he looked up, blinking as he met the eyes of Moronihah. The young man's youthful face was sober and grim, like his father's before a battle. "My father says that it is time now."

Jacob nodded and rose to his feet. He raised a hand to signal his men to stand as well. He took up his weapons, girding them on, then fitted his helmet over his head, and fastened it under his chin. His movements were stiff, his face emotionless. In his mind, he was certain that he would not live to see the sun set, and his heart no longer cared.

He glanced soberly down at the heavy tree trunk they would use to batter against the gate. He and his men would be the first. No doubt, many of them would fall, himself among them. But it no longer mattered. He fastened a light, leather-bound shield to his left forearm. There was nothing left for him to live for any more. He secured the belt of his sword to his waist.

He signaled his group now to move forward. Between him and several of his men, they hefted the heavy trunk and tramped through the last of the underbrush out onto the edge of the trees. Lamanite archers stood on the wall over the portal watching as the line of Nephites broke through the jungle. He felt the first rush of adrenaline flow into his blood like a surge, and with a loud cry, signaled his men forward, and they began. Almost immediately, a shower of barb-tipped arrows began raining down. This shower of arrows was answered by an angry hiss from the bows of Nephite archers, and many Lamanites fell. The gate shuddered at the first blow, and again at the second, stinging his palms with the vibration. At the third, the gate bent inward, protesting with a muffled groan. But with the fourth blow, he heard a great crack, and the cross bar of the gate snapped inward, the gates swinging open before him.

The Lamanites on the other side waited, prepared to take their fresh vigorous anger out against the first Nephite they saw. But he no longer valued his own life, and seeing an opportunity to clear the way for those coming behind him, he took a breath and leaped through the battered gate, drawing his sword in the same motion. Immediately, he was met with fierce opposition as Lamanites eager to spill his blood pressed in around him. He pressed forward against his attackers with strength that amazed even himself, sending more than he wished to count to an eternal end.

Jacob could hear movement behind him. A lazy morning breeze, blowing with the smell of the sea, entered in through the shattered gate, tickling the hair against the back of his neck. He could also hear the rising cries of innumerable Nephites as they burst through the gate, causing the twisted faces of the Lamanites who still stood before him to drop into expressions of dismay. Horror etched their faces as they broke and ran, leaving him alone, his sword in his fist, his chest heaving.

He stood gasping for a moment, regaining his breath, fighting the sickness in the pit of his stomach, bewildered that he could be alive as he muttered a prayer beneath his breath for those who lay, unmoving, before him. After a moment, he shook himself, and rushed after his comrades. He was aware of the shrieks of fear being torn from the throats of the Lamanites as Nephite soldiers swarmed through the city, and he began to feel an inkling of pity. In an instant, however, the pity was crushed by a scream that was undoubtedly female. He looked beyond a mass of Lamanites who blocked one street, seeing a pale skinned man, fiery red hair covering his head and face, dragging a young woman away. The girl, he saw with his heart leaping into his throat, was a Nephite. She fought fiercely at the hold the man had on her, her golden hair falling about her face.

Jacob's fury renewed as he heard the man shout for the Lamanites to hold the line. "He cares nothing for you!" Jacob shouted back in their language as he started forward. His blood was on fire, his muscles working almost on their own. "He leaves you to die!" Jacob yelled, his voice already beginning to grow hoarse with the force of his shouting. "Look at him!" Several Lamanites did, and seeing their leader fleeing, broke and ran, leaving the way clear for Jacob.

"You!" he shouted, running with all his might after the dissenter. "Release her!"

The man took one look back at his disintegrating line of defense, and hefted the struggling girl on his shoulder. He fled with surprising swiftness for his size toward the city wall, the girl dangling from his shoulder, and mounted the steps of the scaffold.

Jacob followed him up, the sounds of battle raging behind him. Here, it was almost quiet, all but for the heavy, gasping breath of the dissenter, and the sobs of the terrified girl. The shining gold of her hair hid her face.

"Let her go," Jacob barked, advancing on the man.

"No!" the man shouted back, drawing his sword in his free hand.

"She is not yours to be bought and sold and owned like an animal!" Jacob shouted back.

Snarling, the man lunged forward, but Jacob stepped deftly aside. Heavy with the weight of the girl over his shoulder, the man lost his balance and tumbled, shrieking, over the wall. Jacob leaped forward and grabbed the girl's slender wrist before she fell as well.

"Hold on," he gasped. "I will pull you up."

She took a deep breath and did as he commanded, her hair

falling away from her face as she turned her eyes up toward his. Their eyes met, and they both gasped in the same instant.

"Lylith?!" Jacob cried in astonishment as he pulled her back up over the parapet.

"Jacob," she whispered in a voice that shook. Her face was ashen white and her whole body shook with aftershock. "I am surprised to see you."

"Why you are in Moroni?" he demanded.

"Ahiah brought me," she answered, her eyes not meeting his.

"Is it the same Ahiah that has Miriam?"

She sighed, "Yes. He kept us together, these many months until now."

He grasped her shoulders and almost shook her. "Where is she?"

"I—I do not know," she stammered. "Ahiah took her. He has surely escaped by now, and is on his way to the Land of Nephi."

Jacob turned and began to stride away as Lylith called after him, "If you follow him there, you will be killed."

Jacob turned, glaring. "I will die before I give up my search for her," he growled.

Angrily he turned away from her, but stopped and lifted his head when he heard a voice carried as if from far away. The voice rose above the din of war as the last bold Lamanites continued to fight, pressing closer and closer to the southern gate. It sounded like her voice. Again it came, and his eyes searched through the scarred city among the ruined buildings. And then he saw what made his heart stop. Struggling toward the gate not a hundred paces from where he stood, was Ahiah. A dark-haired woman struggled against his grip on her wrist, tears running down her cheeks as she cried Jacob's name. Her agonized face and ragged dress were smeared with mud, and her dark hair was hanging in a tangled disarray down her back. But at that moment, she was more beautiful than he ever remembered seeing her.

"Stay here," he ordered over his shoulder, then turned and rushed again down the scaffold steps. Ahiah was near the gate now, scrambling for the narrow pass that fell away into rough, hilly jungle.

"Ahiah!" Jacob shouted, the hoarseness in his voice gone as he gripped the hilt of his sword with renewed energy as he ran. "Let her go!"

Ahiah lifted his face, and froze with fear. "You! Why are you alive?"

"I have come for my wife," he answered, skidding to a stop paces from Ahiah. He glanced at Miriam's face for a moment. Her trembling lips formed his name as she tried to break from Ahiah's grip. All her effort rewarded her though, was an angry lunge as Ahiah viciously jerked her back, twisting her arm painfully behind her.

"My people!" Ahiah screamed as Miriam sobbed. "Here is a Nephite alone! Slay him!"

His words went unheeded. The Lamanites, intent on escape, ignored Ahiah.

"They have deserted you," Jacob growled, advancing on the Amlicite as he moved under the shadow of the open gate. "As you deserted your own people, Ahiah."

"I never had any people," Ahiah laughed, struggling to move away, yanking Miriam helplessly after him as he scrambled down the rocky canyon, closer to the jungle. "They were dead to me long ago."

"If that is so, why is Miriam not dead to you as well? Let her go. You cannot profit by taking her with you now," Jacob snapped as Ahiah backed away. Ahiah slipped into the jungle as Jacob followed after. The light dappled and speared as it pierced the canopy overhead.

Ahiah advanced down a shadowed trail, the noises growing muffled as he stepped backward. He kept his eyes on the younger man. Miriam stirred as if she meant to struggle free, and Ahiah pinched her wrist ever tighter in his painful grip. Her hand grew nearly white, and her eyes focused fearfully on Jacob while tears continued to stream down her face. She did not struggle against Ahiah's grip anymore.

"This creature is my seed," Ahiah spoke at last. "I will do with her what I will."

"She is the daughter of Aaron," Jacob snarled. "Miriam may not be of his blood, but she is of his spirit, and she has inherited his birthright. I love her, and if I must, I will kill you to take her back. Your army has fled from our lands,[20] but if you do as I say, you will leave alive."

Ahiah snarled. "Go ahead, then," he hissed, pulling Miriam with him, cruelly jerking a muffled sob from her as he stepped backward into a clearing where a huddle of small huts sat, their occupants having fled years ago, before the war. The houses were charred black, their skeleton walls collapsing. "Tell me what you have to say."

"Ahiah, give me an oath that you will never come again against the Nephites. Give me Miriam, and I will let you go."

"That is all?" he laughed. "You are a weak one, whelp. But very well. I covenant then, that I will never come again against the Nephites to make war. Is that sufficient?"

"It will do," Jacob said. He gripped his sword tightly. "Release her, and leave this place."

"Gladly." He released her wrist, and shoved her roughly to the ground. She stumbled forward, and collapsed heavily into a crumpled heap, but managed to push herself up, and lift her eyes to Jacob's.

"Miriam," Jacob murmured, and a glimmer sparkled in the sapphire of her eyes.

"You will not get her back alive!" Ahiah suddenly roared, and Jacob looked up. Ahiah held his knife by the tip, and raised it, his eyes hard, and full of hate.

"No!" Jacob cried, leaping forward, knowing as he did that he would be too late. In the instant that the blade flew from Ahiah's hand, he saw a white flash dash into his vision, and then the knife struck soft flesh with a sickening thunk.

Lylith cried out in pain as the force of the blow spun her around. She dropped roughly to the ground beside Miriam, clutching at the knife buried in her shoulder.

She and Miriam traded a wordless glance, Lylith's slight form shuddering in pain while Jacob stared in disbelief. Without a word, she scrambled up and dashed into the thickness of the forest.

"Lylith, come back! You are hurt!" Miriam cried, as the last hint of snarled golden hair disappeared in the green shadows. There was no response.

Jacob turned back to Ahiah, this time moving to place himself protectively between Miriam and the dissenter. "You broke your word."

Ahiah sneered and drew his sword.

Miriam could taste blood in her mouth as she crawled to the edge of the clearing. She struggled to her feet, pulling herself up against the blackened thatch wall of a burnt-out hut. She turned to watch the struggle as metal clashed against metal. Ahiah cursed between his teeth. And she flinched as Jacob recoiled from a blow against his battered shield, and came back, his sword and that of his opponent crossing again with a crash and a shower of sparks.

"You were raised to know the good from the bad, Ahiah," Jacob grated, his teeth clenched with exertion. Ahiah was a formidable opponent. He fought with both the strength of a young man, and the skill of a veteran. Jacob was hard pressed to match him. "Why did you fight against the truth?"

"There is no good or bad in this world, boy," Ahiah snarled, his eyes wide, showing the flaming depths of the Abyss behind them. "There are only the strong and the weak."

"You know the truth!" Jacob grunted, dodging a blow as Ahiah's sword slashed at him.

"And you sinned against it! How will you answer for yourself when you stand before God?"

"Do you not understand, Nephite? There is nothing more," he seethed. "Seize the day, for tomorrow we are dead. Destroy everything weaker than you. Only the strong survive."

Ahiah's face was red now, and he said nothing more. Silence permeated the air, rent each second as their swords crashed together. Miriam knew there was nothing she could do, but she could not leave Jacob. Clinging to the rough thatch, she backed away, her fearful round eyes focused on the fight, not watching what was at her feet until her foot caught something that rolled with the impact. Catching a gasp, she lowered her eyes to see the body of a Lamanite lying face down where he had crawled away to die. Her foot had touched his arm, extended above his head. In his fist, was a bow, and across his back, a quiver of arrows.

248 — THE BIRTHRIGHT

Her belly moved slightly with every breath. She lightly rubbed her stomach, feeling the little fire of life inside her, blinking so that tears would not block her vision. She reached down, and carefully pulled the bow from his hand, and drew an arrow from the quiver.

Ahiah's energy seemed limitless as he lashed out at Jacob, who, having been taxed by his earlier battles, was beginning to fall back. Ahiah sensed Jacob's waning strength, and a wicked glint shone in his wild eyes as he fought harder, relentlessly forcing the younger man back.

Finally, a stone connected with the back of Jacob's heel, and he went down. Scrambling desperately, he tried to rise again. But Ahiah, seeing his chance, kicked Jacob's wrist, sending his sword tumbling from his hand, and stood over him, his foot on his chest, his sword against Jacob's throat. Ahiah sneered.

A strange whistling sound rent the air, and stopped with a hollow sounding thump. Ahiah stiffened and wavered, and his sword dropped harmlessly from his hand. Jacob stared up at him, frozen. Then, comprehending that he was no longer in danger, scrambled safely away.

Ahiah crumpled to the ground. He focused his eyes on the young man who had risen, and stood on shaking legs, a look of sorrow on his young, chiseled face as he turned away and unfastened his bloody armor, letting it drop lifelessly to the ground. He wiped the blood from his sword against his kilt, returned it to its sheath, then fell, exhausted, to his knees.

Ahiah's eyes dimmed, and he trembled at what he saw. For all Ahiah had achieved in his life, he had nothing. This stark realization brought frustrated tears, and then his eyes closed.

Miriam dropped the bow and smiled weakly as Jacob lifted his head, focusing his eyes on her. She stumbled to him and fell to her knees, throwing her arms about his neck. A feeling of peace filled her heart as she felt his strong arms wrap around her, and pull her close. He started at the new shape of her growing belly, and sighed sadly, his shoulders sagging. "You are with child," he murmured into her hair, clutching her protectively.

"Yes, Jacob." She smiled, pressing her lips against his neck. "I am."

"I love you, Miriam," he moaned, pulling back. His hands cupped her face as tears filled his eyes, threatening to spill out. "And I will love the child as my own."

"Why, Jacob—," she began, surprised at the distress on his face. Then she smiled gently and shook her head. "Jacob, all these months, no one has harmed me. The child is yours."

His eyes widened, and he trembled as he struggled to absorb this sudden miraculous news that lifted the weighted fear that had hung heavily over him for months. And then he laughed with a relieved gasp and pulled her close. She was so soft in his arms, so precious to him, and especially more now because of the miracle she carried inside. He turned his lips to her brow, and felt her lift her head, bringing her own face toward his. He found her lips in need of warmth, and eagerly pressed his mouth against hers.

☃

The sky was filled with a profusion of gold and red, and the air was still as Jacob and Miriam stepped from the trees to look up at the stalwart walls of the city of Moroni. Already, the ramparts were lined with Nephite soldiers, and the Title of Liberty waved bravely from the battlements. The wind caught it, flashing the words upon it against the evening sunlight.

She read softly, "In memory of our God, our religion, and freedom, and our peace, our wives and our children."

"Each time I saw our banner and read the words upon it, I thought of you," he said. "I wanted to find you, more than I wanted to breathe. The thought of never being with you again . . ." He shuddered, and pulled her close. "Miriam, I would rather have died."

Miriam sighed, snuggling closer to his side. "I am grateful you did not."

Jacob dropped his eyes. "Many brave men died, so that we could keep our freedom."

"Teancum among them," Miriam murmured. "And Lylith too, I fear."

Jacob drew in a deep breath. "Perhaps not. When I left you and followed her trail, I found where she had collapsed from her blood loss, but she was not there. The tracks of a number of Lamanites passed through the clearing where her tracks ended. They must have found her, and carried her with them."

Miriam sighed softly, her eyes filling with worry.

"Lamanites of themselves are not without honor, Miriam." Jacob soothed. "We both know that. With as much blood as she was losing, she would have been dead before I found her. I believe they saw her wound, and took her with them to save her life."

"I pray you are right," Miriam sighed. "For I have yet to thank her for saving me. I will never forget her for her sacrifice."

He allowed a grin to spread across his face. "Nor has your family forgotten you."

"How will I let them know that all is well with me?" she asked, her eyes suddenly worried. "Esther and little Jacob do not know that I am safe—,"

He pressed his lips against her brow. "A letter won't take many days to reach Bountiful, and we can start back in a few days when you are better."

"I am better now," she insisted. She started forward, but stumbled. Jacob quickly caught her, and clutched her safely to his side. "Perhaps I am not as well as I thought," she murmured apologetically. Without protest, she allowed him to gather her up in his arms, and he lifted her easily. She could feel his breath against her cheek, and folded herself snugly into his embrace, draping her arms about his neck, and leaning her head against his shoulder.

"They will be overjoyed to see you," he said, starting up the slope toward the gate.

"No more than I am at this moment." She smiled.

EPILOGUE

*T*hree months later . . .

Miriam lay quietly now, her eyes closed to the orange light that filtered through the drawn curtains. She could feel Esther's cool hand against her cheek as she gently wiped away the sweat.

Across the room, she heard a resounding smack. In spite of her fatigue, she stirred and opened her eyes as the howling wail of a baby echoed through the room.

"My baby—," she whispered huskily as she gripped Esther's arm and tried to pull herself up.

"Shh, Miriam," she hushed her gently. "Lie still. You have a healthy son. Ishna is coming with him now."

Esther stood and released Miriam's hand to move away from the edge of the bed as the old Lamanite midwife came proudly to Miriam's side, holding a bundle that moved slightly beneath the thin blanket.

"My son—," Miriam repeated in the language of her birth, reaching her arms up weakly as her ancient friend placed the bundle gently in her arms. Her hands circled around her precious package as she lifted the blanket from the little red face, and looked on her first born. He had already discovered his own hand, and was sucking vigorously on his tiny fist.

"Oh, Grandmother, Esther, look at the tiny fingers," she murmured, tears filling her eyes.

The women moved together to stand over the tiny miracle, laying as exhausted and damp as his young mother, oblivious to the commotion he had caused. He seemed content to remain with his tiny fist in his mouth, his eyes screwed shut as his admirers looked on with awe.

Miriam smiled down on the little face, and then smiled up at the faces of the women. "Grandmother," she said as she reached a hand up to her ancient friend who took it in her old, gnarled hand, "I am grateful that you came to me. I could not have had a better midwife."

Ishna smiled. "When Thobor in Manti told me you were here, I knew I had to come."

Miriam's eyes then lowered to the young auburn-haired girl who stood at the foot of the bed looking at Miriam's calm face in wonder.

"Rachel," Ishna said, "go bring her husband in to see his son." The girl nodded, turning to go, and Miriam pulled the softness of the blanket over the baby's face to shield him from the rays of the reddening sun. Rachel opened the door, and the golden light brushed in. Along with it came Jacob, his face written with worry.

He dropped to one knee beside her bed and studied her drawn features, made more beautiful by the light that filled her and extended outward to him as she lay with the baby in her arms. He clasped her limp hand in his, and brushed her damp forehead. "Miriam, are you well?"

"I am tired, but I will recover." She smiled wearily. "Jacob, we have a son."

"A son?" His voice choked in his throat as he looked from her eyes to the struggling bundle in her arms. She lifted the blanket from the chubby little face, its eyes closed. Jacob gently released Miriam's hand, and slid his hand toward the baby. He froze in surprise as the baby pulled its fist from its mouth, yawned, and grabbed his smallest finger.

"Miriam, I—" His voice was choked and faltering. "He is holding my finger."

He turned to face her, and she smiled. The golden light that filtered through the window shone off his face, enhancing the depths of his eyes. His gentle hand continued to stroke her hair.

"I love you, Jacob." She smiled, raising a hand to brush against his lightly stubbled face.

"And I love you, Miriam," he murmured, leaning over her to kiss her gently.

"You may let the others in now, Rachel," Ishna said. Rachel opened the door, and ushered young Jacob, Thobor and Zeram inside. They moved cautiously into the room, their eyes wide, their footsteps soft as they looked on mother and son. Miriam raised her eyes and smiled at them.

"Bring Zeram here little Jacob, so he can see his new playmate." She smiled, beckoning with her hand.

Young Jacob hoisted the golden haired toddler up in his arms. Zeram's eyes were riveted on the tiny one swaddled in Miriam's arms. Thobor though, had lifted his eyes to Esther's and smiled a secret across the room as he moved to her side, and took her hand in his.

"What will you call him?" Young Jacob asked. He lifted his eyes and grinned at Rachel who stood at the foot of the bed. Her jade eyes were cast down, but when his eyes rested on her, she lifted her face and offered him a shy smile.

"We have decided that his name will be Aaron," Jacob declared as Miriam's grip on his hand tightened.

"Father never thought of himself as a great man, but he was," Miriam added, squeezing her little son closer to her, smiling into his sleeping face before she lifted her eyes to Jacob. "He did what he knew was right, and taught his children by his example. That was more important than anything else he could have done or been."

Jacob smiled down at her, and at the red-faced baby in her arms. Her sea-blue eyes silently adored him, and Jacob returned her soft smile, his love for her full within him. She was his life, he realized to himself. And as he lived righteously, she would be his forever, and he would be hers. Together, they would attain the greatest of birthrights promised to them, and though other blessings had bearing in his life, this one overshadowed them all.

SCRIPTURE REFERENCES

1. p. 18   *Alma 46-47* Amalickiah's dissension and conspiracy.

2. p. 25   *Alma 50:1-4* Description of Nephite fortifications.

3. p. 34   *Alma 50: 30-31* Morianton beats his maidservant who flees and tells Moroni of Morianton's plans.

4. p. 68   *Alma 51:13-16* kingmen refuse to take up arms. Pahoran agrees to allow Moroni to put a stop to the dissension.

5. p. 69   *Alma 51:5-6* Those who want a king are called "kingmen" while those who want Pahoran to remain as the chief judge, are called "free men."

6. p. 72   *Alma 51:23* Amalickiah takes city of Moroni because of insufficient numbers of Nephites.

7. p. 96   *Alma 51:26* Amalickiah takes possession of many fortified cities near the east sea.

8. p. 115   *Alma 51:28-32* Lamanites are repulsed and slain by Teancum and his army until dark.

9. p. 116   *Alma 51:33-37* Teancum with his servant goes into the Lamanites' camp, and slays Amalickiah.

10. p. 120 *Alma 52:1-3* Lamanites flee from Bountiful, Ammoron becomes king of Lamanites.
11. p. 132 *Alma 52:23-39* Moroni, Lehi, and Teancum retake Mulek, Moroni is wounded.

12. p. 133 *Alma 53:3* Lamanite prisoners compelled to dig trench along the wall of Bountiful.

13. p. 168   King James Bible, *Isaiah 40:29*

14. p. 169   *Alma 55:6-12* Laman and a small number of men take wine to the guards of the city of Gid.

15. p. 177   *Alma 55:16-24* The city of Gid is retaken.

16. p. 192   *Alma 61:4-5* Kingmen drive out Pahoran who flees to Gideon.

17. p. 217   *Alma 62:6-7*   Moroni and Pahoran come to Zarahemla, and go to battle against the king men.

18. p. 235   *Alma 62:35* Teancum is angry with Ammoron and plans to kill him.

19. p. 240   *Alma 62:36* Teancum slays Ammoron, and is slain by Ammoron's servants.

20. p. 246   *Alma 62:38*   Moroni and his armies drive the Lamanites out of the land.

ABOUT THE AUTHOR

Loralee Evans was born in Salt Lake City to Grant and Marilyn Woolston and grew up in South Jordan, Utah, as the fourth of nine children. She graduated from Bingham High in 1990, and then attended Southern Utah University in Cedar City with a scholarship in Track and Cross-Country. After completing an LDS mission to Sapporo, Japan, she married Steve Evans in the Bountiful Temple.

Loralee graduated from Southern Utah University with a teaching degree in Physical Education and English. She and Steve now live in Syracuse, Utah, and they have four children—Tyler, Rachel, Paul and Nichole.

She enjoys running, being with her family, reading, and her current calling as a Primary teacher in her ward.